Project XS

ARE WE READY TO BE ADVANCED?

A. Calans

authorHOUSE®

AuthorHouse™ UK
1663 Liberty Drive
Bloomington, IN 47403 USA
www.authorhouse.co.uk
Phone: 0800.197.4150

Published by AuthorHouse 12/03/2019

ISBN: 978-1-5462-9750-5 (sc)
ISBN: 978-1-5462-9749-9 (e)

Print information available on the last page.

This book is printed on acid-free paper.

Contents

Day 1

Shinjuku Station in Tokyo was busy during the early rush hour. Both SWAT members from New York absently looked around for something suspicious to appear from the crowd. Weirdly enough, their embedded sense made them cautious about any circumstance that involved vast numbers of people. And this was the world's megacity, Tokyo.

Matt Baker, about average height with a strong body structure, stared with great amazement at the Japanese people being diligently pushed into trains like livestock. The special uniformed staff pushed people into the already jam-packed cars as if it were the last train to a safe haven. People were commuting; they were like human-size ants. It was midsummer, and a slight, mild breeze mixed with the smell of food from the nearest vending machines on the ground level. Matt looked at his partner, Kayla Jenkins—nicknamed Crack—making her understand that they were not going to take public transport like this. Both of them felt dazzled by the busyness of Tokyo life. One train after another passed, yet the crowds didn't thin.

Matt rubbed his long, crooked nose and said, "Crack, let's take a taxi. I'm not ready to be pushed inside a train. Our backpacks are the size of a man. I suspect they might not understand us."

"Yeah, let's take it easy. This is our first time in Tokyo, and we just arrived yesterday. The city is so built up, and the culture is completely different." She tightened her backpack, which had gone slack on the side. "I feel like we are the only foreigners in this place," Jenkins whispered as Matt walked close behind her. "Can you see anyone who looks like us?"

"No, not a single one." He answered.

All around them, so many Japanese people rushed by. Matt walked downstairs, cautiously placing each step and making sure that he didn't accidentally bump into polite passersby. Commuters spared Matt and Jenkins occasional glances only to make sure that they didn't run into the two distracted Americans with huge backpacks who were trying to get downstairs.

Compared to Japanese women, Jenkins was of average height. She was African American with an athletic body and strong arms. She was wearing a black top without sleeves, and she held her backpack's straps with clenched fists, her bent arms showing well-toned muscles. Kayla Jenkins had a serious and transparent look that she'd acquired over her time in SWAT. Her eyes were big and glossy, and her facial features were sharp and well proportioned. Her skin was so tight that it reflected the faintest light landing on her face.

Making their way through the busy crowd, Matt and Jenkins descended to the vending machines, which offered a wide variety of food and drink.

What an awkward situation, Jenkins thought as she was unable to walk around a Japanese man in a suit. She raised her neat, sharp eyebrows in confusion. She and the Japanese man looked at each other, and each again took a step in the same direction, blocking each other's path.

"Just don't do anything," Matt said to her, watching their odd, unsuccessful exchange.

"Sorry," Jenkins apologized to the man, who quickly passed by. "I tried to be kind but failed," she admitted to Matt, who smiled and shook his head.

Matt combed his fingers through his light-brown hair. He was confused. "Hey, Crack! We have plenty of time before the boat departs from the coast. Aren't you hungry?"

"Damn, if you only knew how hungry I am" she responded as she glared at the colorfully painted vending machines that served almost everything. A sensation led her to one of the vending machines. "Neither of us can read these hieroglyphs." She placed her hand on the pictures. "You know what? I'll go by the pictures."

"Just watch the locals. Shouldn't be that hard," Matt said while looking for money. He pulled out a small leather wallet and separated yens from dollars.

Matt browsed through the pictures on the vending machines while occasionally glancing at a man who quickly handled a machine like it was nothing. Unexpectedly, the Japanese gentleman made a quick comment to Matt in Japanese. Based on his intonation, he'd made an offensive remark.

"I'm sorry. I don't speak Japanese," Matt responded in bewilderment.

The interaction seemed to leave both of them confused. Nonetheless, Matt went back to the pictures on the vending machine. He successfully chose noodle soup with chicken flavoring. Seconds later, he obtained a warm, steaming bowl of chicken-flavored soup. After carefully taking the bowl from the lower shelf, he strolled back to Jenkins.

She kept shifting her eyes up and down at the vending machines, which had made her frustrated. As Matt came close with his delicious-smelling bowl, she said, "How did you do that? Come on. Give me that bowl."

"Hold it for me please," he said calmly. "Watch and learn. I'll show you. It wasn't that hard."

"All right," she replied, already digging into his bowl.

"That's just mean," Matt said with scorn when he saw Jenkins eating his food.

Nevertheless, he repeated the same steps and got a new bowl with the same flavor.

They both enjoyed the food while standing and watching commuters. People burst forward in large numbers continuously; they never stopped. This was the busiest station in Tokyo.

Both Americans really stood out from the public. They stood watching, almost at anything which was new and unusual to them. As Jenkins quickly finished her bowl, she nudged Matt. "That was good. I want some more."

"Hey, take it easy," he said while trying to balance himself and prevent his food from spilling out. "Go do it yourself."

"Screw you. I will handle it," she said. She went to the vending machine where Matt had gotten the food. In a short time her frustration burst out again. "What the hell? I got something different. The machine is preparing something with shrimp or snail." Her facial expression turned to distaste.

A smile covered Matt's naturally sad-looking face. Despite getting something different from the previous time, Jenkins ate it anyway and gave Matt a look that said she didn't care about the mix-up.

Matt kept observing each passerby with curiosity and recalled something about this country. "You know, when I see these kind and orderly people, I remember something. This is part of *gaman*, the Japanese spirit of self-control and dedication to the greater good through self-discipline."

Jenkins stopped eating. "What do you mean?"

"This is how they've handled disasters like earthquakes and tsunamis through the years. Japan is located on active tectonic plates." Matt exhaled. "The *gaman* mindset is what keeps them mentally prepared and stronger than others."

"Well ..." Jenkins said. Then she paused while thinking. "We've been trained in a similar way. That's a good reminder about proper mindset, especially when that mindset is embedded in each individual. No wonder they've overcome such afflictions, which would destroy the West."

Matt lifted his head up to the sky. The weather was nice and mild but overcast. *It looks like there is no chance of getting any sun*, Matt thought. The huge Tokyo metropolis was alive with constant commuting and all kinds of sounds mixed together, making the city so distinctive. The streets were absolutely packed but clean. Occasional whistles almost startled him. It was hard to understand where the city started and ended. People were constantly running in and out, whether from buildings or public transport.

"Did you see that?" Jenkins pointed at the two men wearing Jersey of US team.

"Hey, yeah! Those buddies are Japanese," Matt said with light amazement.

"Perhaps they love baseball over here," she said.

"Actually, that might be true," Matt said, remembering some information he'd been told before coming to Tokyo.

They followed the baseball-uniformed Japanese men with curiosity. Suddenly, the two men blended into the huge moving mass of people.

Jenkins took off her heavy backpack and placed it on the ground vertically. They had finished their rushed breakfast from the unique vending machines. She stretched her arms in front of her, fingers interlocked and facing outward, then raised her arms up and stretched them a little backward. Her body was toned and well carved out with the waistline of a wasp.

Kayla Jenkins was only twenty-six. She'd been a sprinter in high school and had won lots of awards. After graduating, she'd immediately joined the police and quickly shown her serious dedication to service, which had drawn the attention of others. Something unsolved in her private life urged Jenkins to fight on justice's side. Later, she'd joined a SWAT team, where she'd met Matt Baker, who had been in the service longer than she had. They had conducted many missions together, which had led to them being marked as the best members of New York's SWAT. She'd acquired the nickname Crack because of her ruthless approach to criminals. Sometimes she handled them brutally. However, she never crossed the line, which would cause trouble and make lose her job.

Matt glanced at his watch and said, “We must go to the port.” They were going to meet the rest of the guys at the port, where a boat would take them to the Oshima island. He watched Jenkins stretching and continued, “Let’s get there in good time. Who knows how long it takes to commute from this hectic place to the port?”

He checked his pockets and then put his backpack on the ground and opened the zipper of the upper pocket. He pulled out a folded paper map of Tokyo. Diligently tracking his index finger over the map, he said, “We should take a taxi. This city is complex. Tokyo seems like an unnavigable maze.” He sighed. Then he picked the matchstick from his pocket and placed it between his lips. “I will show the map to a local cabdriver so he knows where we need to be. Hopefully, a taxi will be easier than the train, which is constantly overflowing.”

“All right, you take the lead,” Jenkins said as she picked up her backpack, ready to go into the streets. “Which way are we going?” She looked around with overconfidence while still relying on her partner to give directions.

“This way.” Matt pointed in the right direction while still intently examining the map. She took initiative and moved in front of him. As they got closer to the street, the crowd calmed down a little bit. However, new people appeared from nowhere, increasing the volume of the crowd. Jenkins’s eyes shifted to a shopping mall. It literally never ended. Colorful shops sat next to each other in an endless shopping area. *This is already overwhelming,* she thought.

As they reached the roadside, Matt walked to the nearest taxi, which he recognized by the labels. Jenkins lagged behind him, staring around with amazement at the Tokyo metropolis. He bent down by the window and said, automatically speaking in English, "Good morning, sir. Can you take us to the port?" The old and tired face of the taxi driver looked at him without any comprehension, and the man said something in Japanese that baffled Matt and Jenkins. Suddenly, Matt felt silly and realized the man didn't speak English. Quickly retrieving the creased map, he unfolded it and put his finger on the port, trying to make the driver understand that the port was their ultimate destination. The old man said something in Japanese, and a smile appeared on his bleak, tired face. He nodded, and so did Matt, the exchange indicating that Matt had successfully hired the taxi. "He will take us," Matt reassured Jenkins with a warm smile that highlighted his crow's-feet.

After some time driving very slowly through the busy Tokyo traffic, Jenkins said, "It's gonna take ages to get to the port." She stared out the window and rhythmically tapped on her knee to make herself busy. She was getting impatient.

"I know. At least we're moving," Mat replied, carefully studying the map. Seconds later he folded the map and put it back into his pocket. After a long, deep sigh, he asked, "Why did you agree to this mission—Project XS?"

"You know the answer," she said, looking at buildings covered with countless anime ads, which they passed slowly in traffic.

"You just can't stop challenging yourself. You're crazy, Crack," Matt said with a chuckle. He knew Jenkins the best of all the other SWAT members. "I can't let you go on your own," he said.

"Shut up! I can be completely fine on my own," she snapped with a short smile before resuming her serious, badass look as if she didn't feel mercy. "What I don't get about you, Matt, is why you didn't stay in the Bronx with your wife and five-year-old daughter. You're crazier than me." She looked at Matt, who calmly listened and kept looking out the car's window. "Project XS, this mission we've both been assigned to, could lead to great danger. Neither of us knows what's going to unfold when we get to that island." She got heated up, then suddenly calmed down, realizing that the cabdriver, who could hear everything, might be recording their conversation. Jenkins got overly suspicious of any civilian who was around, almost obsessively so.

"Perhaps I am crazy!" Matt said. "It sounds strange, but it feels like this is my life's turning point. My gut is trying to say something." Matt turned his eyes to the cabdriver and carefully chose his words. "I love my wife and my daughter, even though we've recently had a lot of arguments about my service. I'm sure my absence will create even more tension. I can sense that my wife is willing to split up with me because I'm so rarely at home. They mean everything to me, though. It's just so complicated…you know." His face was overwhelmed with sudden incomprehension. "However, there's something bigger that must be overcome. Sometimes, I can't sleep at night. Sounds mad, but I just want to stop all the crime. Is it the call of my destiny?"

"You are screwed!" Jenkins said, raising her voice.

"Shut up, Crack. I can't let you have all the fun of this project. I must make sure that you are looked after. I was in the service for years before you joined," Matt teased, causing an awkward moment of silence. "You know, you have become like my foster child or more like the sister I never had," Matt said, teasing her some more. She nudged him firmly and turned back to the view outside the car.

"You're just eight years older than me," Jenkins said. "Don't you dare call me your foster child."

After a long crawl through the busy city traffic, they finally arrived at the port. The taxi took them close to the port. Matt recognized and pointed at the military boat, and the driver pulled over. The ride had resulted in a surprisingly huge bill. *That seems a lot to me,* Matt thought while looking for notes to pay. Meanwhile, Jenkins quickly jumped out of the car and enjoyed a full-body stretch. After paying the taxi driver and pulling their backpacks from the trunk, Matt joined her.

"How much was it?" she asked.

"I think … hang on." He did some math in his head to convert the currency. As he came up with the result, he exclaimed, "What the heck! It was about a hundred bucks." He was truly shocked by the fare.

Jenkins's eyebrows raised in surprise. "Are you serious? We should have walked and gotten some physical training instead. That's just a rip-off."

"Forget about that," he said and looked at the boat, where some uniformed military guys were standing and chatting. "Let's go over there. Apparently some of them have arrived earlier than us." Matt and Jenkins put on their backpacks and headed to meet the others.

The port was busy. So much was happening. City never slows down; it doesn't take a break. The wind had built up, and it felt cooler here than in the inner city. Everywhere forklift trucks and other vehicles moved at a quick yet extremely organized pace. Matt and Jenkins felt an instant chaotic energy around the place where a lot of fishermen were gathering. They were near a fish market. The smell of fish was everywhere, and trolley carts of fish raced past in a hectic manner.

"Watch out!" Jenkins exclaimed as Matt had a near miss with a trolley cart.

"I didn't see it coming," Matt said, feeling surprised. *This place is essentially a city within the city,* he thought. "Why are they shouting like preparing for battle?" Matt asked, his eyes drawn to the huge hangar where the shouts were coming from. "I suppose a tuna auction is taking place inside," he said, answering his own question.

Walking closer to the boat, they got the attention of two young, athletic guys who looked identical. They were energized and constantly doing something rather than sitting down and waiting for someone to go over the objectives of the mission. Matt and Jenkins glanced at each other simultaneously and proceeded to walk closer. The two men, who had shaved heads and youthful skin like that of teenagers, turned their attention to the SWAT members from New York. Both were dark skinned and about the same height. It was quite obvious that they were twin brothers of Mexican descent.

"Project XS?" one of the twin brothers asked them.

"Yeah," Matt replied.

"My name is Alejandro Javier, and this is my twin brother, Antonio. We both are from the military."

"I'm Matt Baker, and this is my partner, Kayla Jenkins. We're from New York's SWAT." They shook hands with each other. "Do you know the approximate time we'll be departing this port?" Matt immediately inquired.

Alejandro thought while rubbing his shaved head and replied, "We're still waiting for the last man to arrive. As soon as all the squad members are assembled together, we will move. That was the latest update from the captain."

"Understood," Matt said. His attention was drawn to another man who looked like a military person but who was dressed all in black with broad shoulders. He was sitting on the cargo pile and smoking a thin cigarette that he'd evidently rolled himself. The man looked serious and stone faced. "Is that guy with us?" Matt asked Alejandro while pointing at the smoking man.

"Yeah, he is. Well … he doesn't speak that much."

"C'mon, Crack, let's go to see him," Matt urged.

Jenkins felt neutral but agreed. As they walked closer, Jenkins kept looking around the busy port. She felt indifferent to the man who was sitting apart from the rest, a half-burned cigarette squeezed between his thumb and index finger. With a quick flip of his fingers, he tossed the cigarette with a great curve into the water. His arm displays a big tattoo of a skull wrapped with barbed wire and a date—06.06.2016. Matt and Jenkins had come close enough for the man to detect their presence, but he apparently didn't care to maintain eye contact and kept staring at water.

"Hey, Project XS! My name is Matt Baker, and this is my partner, Kayla Jenkins," Matt said, raising his voice in order to draw the ignorant man's attention.

"Sean Price," the man replied in a calm and low tone. His facial expression remained unchanged, but he looked over at the SWAT members from New York for a couple of seconds. Sean Price had dark hair, masculine facial features, and bushy eyebrows that almost covered his eyes. There was long and awkward pause between them. Matt was confused and a bit annoyed by Price's short answer that didn't give any further information about his occupation.

Jenkins looked at Price, who kept his poker face, and asked, "Where you from? Are you from military or another enforcement body?" There was a moment of strange silence again. She didn't get an instant answer, which made her look at Price with spurn. Seconds later Jenkins turned around and walked back to the twins, who at least talked more, leaving Matt with the mystery man named Sean Price. It was an awkward moment that created an odd atmosphere before the mission even began. Eventually, Matt gave up and didn't inquire any further. Instead, he went back to the others, leaving Price on his own.

Alejandro, seeing that Matt was obviously disappointed, said, "I told you! He isn't gifted with social skills."

"I'm just wondering ... We're supposed to conduct this mission together, and he doesn't feel like a part of the squad. Anyway, let's wait for the last man to arrive," Matt said.

Jenkins and the twins were getting along well. They exchanged stories about their service. Sometimes one of the twin brothers would get up and act out the movements as he recalled a memory. Obviously, the twins had a long and rich experience in the military, which drew Jenkins's interest. She had never been in the military. Occasionally, both brothers imitated moves and tactics so energetically, making an improvised show for her. They were fueled by a lot of energy and were keen to show off complicated martial arts moves that involved flips and throws.

Matt turned his attention to the military boat, which wasn't big. It had an angular shape with a sharp front. It was a stealth military craft designed to go out in any conditions. The boat joggled continuously in the water by the embankment as waves gradually lapped against shore.

Matt Baker lingered, and as he stared at the boat, he thought about something. *There is no sign of the captain nor any other crew.* "This will never end! Why have I agreed to this mission?" Matt whispered to himself, low enough that no one else could hear. He grew thoughtful and looked around. He adored Tokyo, but he had mixed feelings. "I have my family, at the other end of the world, but I can't stop doing this," he said to himself. "I must find answers for why something inside me keeps dragging me into new and greater challenges that put my life at risk and cause my family to suffer occasionally because of my job." Matt glanced at Sean Price, who was killing his time by sharpening a military knife, it was really big. "Maybe I will soon understand that eccentric with rock-hard face," he concluded, keeping his eyes on Price, who hadn't move an inch since their arrival.

In the far distance a taxi car appeared behind the running forklift trucks. It got closer and then stopped. Even from a distance, it was clear that some kind of heated dispute was happening between the passenger and driver. Suddenly the back door wildly bust outward with fury. A casually dressed man with blond hair was shouting and yelling at the cabdriver. He bent down by the driver's window, threw some money inside, and stood back up. Before the taxi drove off, the passenger thanked the driver loudly in a sarcastic tone, as if ridiculing the driver, and said, "Sayonara!" Matt remembered his and Jenkins's huge taxi bill. Apparently the same thing had happened with this newly arrived and extremely angry man. As the man, presumably the last squad member, walked toward them, Matt chuckled.

"Can you believe that? He charged me something that requires a calculator with long display!" the handsome blond man with broad cheekbones said before greeting anyone. As he got close to the group, he cursed more. "That was a fucking rip-off, to say the least." He didn't stop expressing his great frustration to the others. "This place is jam-packed with people and nonstop hustle. How do they even manage to share the place among themselves?" He inhaled deeply while dropping his head backward and said in a suddenly relaxed tone, "Now it feels better, yeah … The smell of the ocean, the fish kingdom, and a lot of testosterone." Of course he meant the people who were waiting for him to arrive.

"Project XS?" he asked with an overly self-confident look with a little arrogance.

"Yeah. We've been waiting for you. What's your name?" Matt took the initiative to begin introductions while the others kept observing the last squad member with mistrust.

"I'm Jack Kelly from Boston SWAT," the man said. As he reached out his hand to shake, he positioned his wrist on top, as if to show his importance.

"Matt Baker, New York SWAT." They held the handshake for a brief time while maintaining strong eye contact. It created a strange ambience among the group.

"So you look after bankers' asses on Wall Street?" Kelly didn't hesitate to make the sarcastic remark and continued, "Who else is from SWAT?" He looked around arrogantly and waited for a response.

Matt responded, "I see … you like to be noticed." He sighed and turned his head toward Jenkins, who looked at Kelly with disgust. "My partner, Kayla Jenkins, is also from SWAT," he said.

Jack Kelly was intrigued and slowly walked closer to her. Keeping his confident smile, he extended his hand as if inviting her to dance. "Hey, how are you?" Kelly said in a flirtatious tone. Jenkins kept looking at him with disdain but extended her hand to welcome him. He tried to kiss her hand, but a sudden sharp slap to his face from Jenkins prevented that.

"Hey! Keep your old-fashioned flirting tricks away from me!" she warned.

"Wow, easy, girl! I'm just showing a warm welcome. We are going to be together for this mission." He was rubbing his face in a theatrical way to soothe it from the slap, but he kept looking at her with his winning attitude. Slowly turning his head to the twin brothers, he couldn't stop another sarcastic remark. "Fuck me! Are you clones? Since I'm in Tokyo, I've seen millions of look-alikes. Have you been cloned in one of the city's basements or somewhere?"

"You're a funny guy," Alejandro said and responded in a similar manner. "We will do everything to prevent your own cloning from happen, as it would only create more global mess."

"Ha," Kelly chuckled. "You know, it would shake things up. The world needs more men like me. I'm the hope to all mankind. I'm an eye-opener." He glanced at Jenkins and winked as he added, "And, of course, I have an irresistible charm that ladies can't resist."

Despite exchanging insults, Kelly and Alejandro shook hands. Kelly shook hands with the other twin as well and then looked around, spotting the man sitting on the cargo pile with something busy in his hands. "Who is that guy? Is he with us?" He extended his neck in curiosity to see more.

Matt jumped in with a suggestion. "I would recommend that you not make rash insults to him. For your knowledge, he is Sean Price."

"Chill, man. If he is with us, then I must meet him too." He raised his palms up to Matt Baker, showing that he would do what he wanted anyway. Kelly began to walk toward the sitting man with that same arrogant smile.

Suddenly, captain Berks, who was about middle age and dressed in military uniform, stepped outside the boat and announced in a loud voice, "All the squad on board immediately." He climbed outside onto the embankment, waiting for the group to assemble. Kelly stopped and walked back to the rest of the group while keeping his eyes on Sean Price. Kelly's face flinched, seeing captain's ugly burnt scars on the neck; then he pulled his own collar to check his scars on the upper chest which were smaller. Everyone picked up their backpacks and moved closer to the boat in front of the captain. Sean Price slid his knife inside a holder on his leg before picking up his backpack and walking to the others. His face remained the same—motionless. Kelly stared at him with curiosity, eager to know more. As Price joined the rest of the squad, the captain declared loudly, "All right, squad, we are departing now to Oshima Island. Follow me." The captain was the first to jump on the military boat, which was capable of carrying a twenty-person crew. Waves constantly shifted the ship lightly from side to side.

Before Jenkins boarded, Kelly didn't hesitate to say, "After you, sweetheart." She looked at him with half-closed eyes and an unpleasant facial expression but proceeded inside without responding to the grinning, handsome douchebag. Everyone in the squad, one by one, went inside the cabin, which had a carbon fiber interior. The hard steel roof was camouflage colored. The boat slowly retreated from the coast and turned its sharp front toward the island.

Some time later, as the boat headed for the island, the waves increased in height and power. The sturdy boat plowed straight through the seemingly rock-solid waves, the front lifting up after crashing into each wave. Sometimes the boat dropped like a stone as it tackled the restless water.

Huge explosions of water constantly hit the bulletproof glass of the cabin. The captain remained calm despite the raging waves. Inside the boat's cabin, the squad members were sitting against each other on hard plastic chairs on both sides of the small room. The light inside was vaguely dim, and the cabin smelled stale. There was silence among all of them except for Jack Kelly. "Wow! That was something!" he exclaimed loudly when the boat hit another wave. Soon the waves calmed down, and things got less shaky inside the cabin. "I think I'm going to show what I ate hours ago," Kelly said while slowly inhaling. The rest of the group cringed, especially Jenkins, who felt more disgusted than the others.

"We don't want to see anything that your egocentric cakehole has swallowed before," Jenkins said, making a face like she'd smelled something repulsive.

Kelly grinned, looked at her, and said, "It was just sushi. You know … raw fish. If I throw up, they will swim away." He laughed loudly.

"You are one repulsive man," she said.

"Yeah …" Kelly calmly said and groped into his pockets for something. He pulled out a small transparent-orange pill container. He swiftly swallowed two white pills and drank some water from a bottle. As he swallowed, Kelly sighed in relief. "What you looking at?" he asked the men who sat opposite him.

"Prescription pills?" Matt asked.

"Painkillers," Kelly said. He explained in a low, controlled voice, "These pills are opium based. Once you start taking them, you soon have them in your breakfast cereal bowl." Kelly laughed again and couldn't stop, his body shaking.

"What's your problem?" Matt asked.

As his laughs eased, Kelly answered, "Headaches and some past injuries in my shoulder. I can handle them without pills, but now it's too late." He reached his hand in his other pocket and found some chewing gum. He offered some to all, who refused.

About ten minutes later Kelly was chewing his gum energetically and staring at Sean Price. The almost palpable tension between the two men was on the rise. Kelly's head was dropped backward, his eyes angled at Price, who kept his rock-solid face expressionless and didn't look back directly.

"Hey, don't you think it's rude? Why don't you introduce yourself to us?" Kelly kept chewing and continued, "We are on the same boat. We are assigned to the same mission." There was no response from Price, and Kelly raised his voice unexpectedly. "Hey, Price, have you cut your tongue while sharpening your knife?"

Matt intervened angrily, "Shut up, Kelly! Save your poison for mission."

Kelly turned his head to Matt and said coarsely, "Who the fuck is this moron? I bet he is one of the government's watchdogs. He's been sent to sabotage the mission or whatever." He turned back to watch Price's face with a sharp, eagle-eyed look. Despite the insults, Sean Price remained extremely calm, showing no sign of reaction, as if he were on the boat alone.

The boat shook slightly from the waves, drawing Kelly's attention. As the boat evened out, he resumed his irritating tone with the squad members. Some brief silence remained among them, but tensions had raised invisibly. The twin brothers sat on the same side of the cabin as Kelly; two SWAT agents form New York and a strange man sat opposite them.

"Hey, New Yorkers," Kelly said, switching his attention away from Price, "we're from the same playground. We have so much in common. The only difference is that I'm from Boston, but we know the game. Don't we?" Both Matt and Jenkins looked at him, expecting insults to follow. They didn't say anything back but kept their attention on him, waiting for some more. Kelly continued, "We are the chosen ones—the best of the best. I can smell excessive testosterone and feel your crave for some blood. The government knows that well. That's why they are making moves, but we ..." He paused briefly and stared at them with a grin on his overly confident face. He resumed, "We are just pawns, disposable ones, you know."

"Shut the hell up, Kelly!" Jenkins yelled furiously while leaning a little bit forward. "I can guarantee that you've been mistaken for someone else and should have been sent to cuckoo land instead of this island." Her eyes showed certainty.

Matt abruptly turned to her and said in a calming tone, "Hey, Crack, don't respond to him. This is what he wants." But her blood was boiling.

"Crack?" It was the first time Kelly had heard her nickname, and he was intrigued. He chuckled, his face showing curiosity. "Hey, Crack, what's the story of your bizarre nickname?"

Jenkins got even more worked up, and her tone escalated, showing her wrath. "Listen, pretty face! I've been working as a SWAT agent for a while. During my service, I've come across all sizes of criminals, who happened to be men predominantly. Pretty soon I realized that you men have a weak spot between your legs. In order to stop them, I practice hard the old self-defense method—the nutcracker. You know what? It works perfectly. So if you don't shut up for one fucking minute, I won't hesitate to make your nuts pop out through your throat like a champagne cork." Jenkins leaned back when she was finished.

"I like you," Kelly said with great interest, clapping his hands together a couple of times. Apparently, he didn't take her warnings seriously, as he kept teasing her, "You're turning me on. Crack, we will have so much fun on that island."

She was infuriated but kept silent, glaring angrily at him. It looked like Jenkins was about to kick his ass at any moment when Matt put his arm on her shoulder and said, "Just chill. Don't waste your energy with that douche." She leaned back and turned her head sideways, looking away from Kelly. Somehow, Matt managed to calm her down. However, it wasn't over yet.

Jack Kelly just couldn't get enough and continued, "Why don't you cut off the strings attached to your shoulders? You know … set yourself loose. Take some time for yourself and ponder why you're on this mission."

"Jack Kelly," Matt said seriously. Is it your goal to push us all until someone loses their temper and strangles you? I bet if it wasn't for our mutual mission, Sean would have put you underwater a long time ago."

"How about you?" Kelly stared at both from New Yorkers if feeling nothing. "Don't you both hate me already? Or do I need to try harder?" It looked like he would pick up the fight inside the boat with Matt.

Matt stayed calm and collected. Then he concluded, "You're not a volunteer, Kelly."

Kelly clapped his hands again. "Bingo! You got that right." Kelly felt impressed and, as if reading Matt's mind, added, "Yeah, I didn't volunteer. I had no choice. You know …"

He was about to say something else when the captain made an announcement over the speaker, interrupting him. "Ready, squad, to get off at the coast. Over," the captain announced, the intercom giving a vague sizzling sound. The boat suddenly dropped its speed several knots, slowing down to a float in the shallow waters. The ocean seemed very calm by this island. The captain was the first to step outside on the deck. He observed the water and the off-road amphibious-type truck that had already arrived and was waiting for them by the coast. He focused his view down at the cabin, waiting for the squad to peek out. One by one the squad members got outside on the deck. Jack Kelly lagged behind and was the last one. Once all of them had assembled, the captain pointed to where the American military base was set up, in the middle of the nearby hill. Where the boat had docked, they had a good view of the base and surrounding island. The island was mostly green with some gray parts and a carbon-black sand beach. The sky was still overcast with a fresh breeze. The military base was quite impressive with a lot of buildings and huge tents covered with camouflage elements. The island itself was small, and its terrain wasn't flat but hilly.

"All right, ladies! Leave the boat!" the captain announced in a loud and dry voice.

The twin brothers were the first who jumped into the shallow waters, making a huge splash; they were on their way to the truck. Without any hesitation, the rest of the squad jumped off the boat. Standing on deck, the captain observed them, his hands behind his back. He made sure that all reached the coast and then went back inside the cabin.

Jack Kelly turned around to see the boat. He crossed his forearms in front of him, whacking against each other. His voice was mockingly loud & humming. Saying: "Project Extreeeeme Sabotaaaaage begins now."

The driver of the truck, a military soldier, stepped out of the truck with a list in his hands. As soon as the squad was near the truck, the driver said, "Project XS! I will call your names to confirm everyone is present. Okay! Baker, Jenkins, Price, Alejandro Javier, Antonio Javier, and Kelly! Has anyone been missed?" The driver glanced over to see their response. Apparently, everyone had arrived. "Great. Get inside the truck. I will take you to the base," the driver said and waited for everyone to get inside.

The truck's V8 engine roared loudly, and they were off to the American military base. The terrain was rough, which made the drive bumpy. *The roller coaster just goes on,* Kelly thought and felt worn out already. Luckily for the squad, the base wasn't far away. As they drove, Kelly noticed somebody dressed in light-colored clothes. His curiosity made him ask the driver, "Hey, do you know how many locals live on this island?"

The driver leaned his head toward them and said loudly, "I think less than ten thousand. You won't see them that much, because the base is halfway up the mountain, which is inhabitable." To the others' surprise, Kelly didn't inquire any further. Oshima Island had drawn his attention. It excited him more than having pointless arguments with the rest of the squad. The journey from Tokyo had taken a toll on them, both mentally and physically. The boat had been constantly shaking because of its small size and the strong waves. But this truck was even worse. It took the tiniest holes and bumps and magnified their impact ten times. "We're almost there!" the driver called loudly.

The truck arrived at the gates, which were guarded by two men. The fence was high, about ten feet, and set up with bulky, razor-sharp barbed wire all around the perimeter, which stretched into the woods. One of the armored guards approached the new arrivals. He confirmed their clearance with the driver and directed them where to go next while sticking his nose inside to see the squad. The guards manually opened the gates, and the high-clearance truck moved inside the military camp. There were a couple of barracks, massive tents, other facilities, and garages for vehicles. *This place is quite impressive,* Matt thought, looking around.

"Attention!" the driver said to the squad. "You will now go to the barracks, which are located on the east side." He pointed. "There you will meet your instructor, Sergeant Bakerman. He is also in charge of Project XS."

As soon as the driver mentioned Bakerman, Kelly got amused and instantly looked at Matt. "Is that your father?" he asked, grinning. Nobody was amused except for him.

There was a short pause from the driver, who looked at Kelly with remorse. Then he continued, "You are the best of the best. Huh, anyway … you will handle him." The driver relaxed, turned back toward the steering wheel, and sighed. Everyone was baffled by his remark except Sean Price. Despite the driver's strange attitude, the squad stepped outside and walked to the barracks as they'd been told.

"What's that supposed to mean?" Matt asked, looking at Jenkins and rubbing his nose.

"Honestly, I've got no idea. Let's find out," she said, putting her backpack on and proceeding to walk to the barracks.

Inside, the barracks were completely empty and dead silent, except for the wind, which nipped inside through the open main doors. It felt as if all living presence had left these premises forever. *It's a no-good atmosphere,* Matt thought. At the other end of the hall was a dark corridor that apparently led to the sergeant's office. The main hall and the corridor were not separated by any doors. Jenkins was getting curious and, after taking off her backpack, walked closer to the dark corridor. Meanwhile the rest of the squad looked around for beds to put their stuff on.

"Line up!" A loud and hollow voice echoed out of the dark, narrow corridor. It was so powerful and daunting, like a hit. All the squad members immediately dropped their bags and got into position. The sound of boots against the wooden floor made its way to the hall where everyone was lined up. The steps grew louder and louder. However, the figure wasn't revealed yet. There he was, standing in the arch of the corridor. He was six feet and five inches tall and had an incredibly strong physique, which made his appearance more daunting. His sleeves were rolled up, revealing masculine, hairy arms and hands with some ugly scars. The shadow from his hat's brim hid his eyes and much of his face. It looked like his frowning muscles were frozen. The sergeant's strong jaw was energetically moving, chewing something. He slowly turned his head around to see the squad. His first appearance was surprisingly daunting for everyone. There was an awkward moment of silence, which created more tension.

"I'm your instructor, Sergeant Bakerman. I'm in charge of Project XS," he said loudly. "And I hate you," he slowly reported with a tone of contempt.

Everyone was baffled by what was going on. Just before introductions, the instructor had declared hate for the squad. *What a bizarre and unpredictable move,* Jenkins thought while keeping one eye on the large man.

"What's Project XS about?" Kelly asked, which was a really stupid thing to do. Jenkins looked at him with awe and worry. *This is not going to end well,* she thought, sensing dread.

Suddenly the sergeant walked quickly to Kelly. His rage was instant. He grabbed Kelly's face with his hand, which was so enormous it covered most of Kelly's face. The sergeant leaned toward Kelly's ear and said quietly while strongly pressing his face, "Listen carefully. I will not repeat myself again." Nobody else could hear what he was saying, because he was whispering, but his strength and rage were obvious and beyond description. "There are two phases: first phase, I hate you; second phase, I get rid of the things I hate and replace them with new ones. Do you want to get to the second phase? Do you?" the sergeant shouted while holding Kelly's head so hard it seemed he would crush it like a boiled potato. Kelly was trying so hard to say something, but he couldn't. It had almost come to the point where he would be suffocated. Suddenly, his face was free from the sergeant's strong grip. He said nothing, catching his breath and recovering from the lack of air. He hadn't been expecting that to happen, especially at their very first meeting.

Sergeant Bakerman stepped back from Kelly and moved to the center of the line. He looked intently at Jenkins. Shivers ran down her spine. He walked closer to her and asked, "Name?"

"Sir, Kayla Jenkins, sir!" she loudly responded.

"I don't believe in women for this kind of shit. If you are here, that means you've got balls. Well, do you have them?"

Jenkins was confused about how to respond to his awkward statement. The sergeant's daunting appearance and unpredictable moves made the situation more complicated. He was very close to her, sniffing her like a predator sniffing prey.

"Sir, yes, sir!" she shouted, though she felt stupid saying it.

"Well, why don't you take off your pants and prove it? If that turns me on, does it make me a gay?" the sergeant asked, raising his tone at the end of his question. It was now a really awkward situation.

Jenkins kept silent. She didn't want to say anything that would make it worse. She remained still and prepared herself for the possible hit. The sergeant stood in front of her constantly chewing and making random sounds while inhaling air. His imitating presence was so overwhelming that he could probably scare even the toughest man in the world. Unexpectedly, he walked away from her without any further outrageous commands. Placing his impressing presence at the center of the line, he turned his eyes to the twin brothers. He walked over to them while shifting his head from one brother to the other. There was a moment of silence. It was apparent how the twins had grown tense, preparing themselves for any mad actions from the sergeant. Sweat dripped down the head of one of the brothers. Alejandro winked as the salty drop rolled into his eye. The sergeant observed them, looking down at them from above, and suddenly exclaimed in a sharp voice, "Names?"

"Sir, Alejandro Javier, sir!" the first twin brother responded loudly and energetically. Then the sergeant slowly turned his head to the other brother, waiting for him to say his name.

"Sir, Antonio Javier, sir!" he responded in the same manner as his brother.

Sergeant Bakerman looked at them with a little confusion. He inhaled and exhaled. "Brothers, right? Damn, you look so identical." Seeing their ethnic appearance, he didn't hesitate to make an offensive remark. "One of you amigos should have stayed back home and started a cactus-juice business rather than challenging death in this damn shithole." Both twins remained still, listening to his insults. "Because you are so identical, I will refer to you with numbers. Alejandro will be number one and Antonio number two."

He walked away from the twins in order to meet the extremely calm and measured Price, who didn't show any reaction to the sergeant's behavior. Bakerman walked around Price, checking his body from the bottom to the top. Price remained the same: sedate and emotionless. The sergeant noticed something and kneeled down. Taking out Price's huge military knife, the sergeant asked, "What's your name?"

"Sir, Sean Price, sir!" he responded loudly.

Sergeant Bakerman twisted the knife around and assessed the reflective blade. He placed the knife between his fingers, holding it by the blade. Then he pulled his arm backward and swiftly threw the knife against the wooden board behind Price. Almost half of the blade's length pierced into the board. The throw had been very strong and accurate and would have been lethal if aimed at a man. The sergeant got heated up. "No such tool is allowed to be carried under my watch unless I have given my permission. You are my tools here! I will make you sharper than the best samurai sword found in Japan. Is that clear, Price?" he shouted very close to Price's face with spit flying out.

"Yes, sir!" Price responded loudly again.

"Good," the sergeant said, calming down his voice. He turned around. "What else do we have here?" He walked to Matt, who didn't show any excitation and tried to remain as cool as Price. "Your name?" the sergeant asked.

"Sir, Matt Baker, sir!" he responded, as loudly as everyone else had.

"What's your occupation?"

"Sir, I'm from New York SWAT, sir!" Matt replied loudly.

"Any military experience?"

"Sir, no! I've been in enforcement service since nineteen."

"I didn't ask your history, Baker!" the sergeant replied.

Sergeant Bakerman turned toward the rest of the squad. His mood had evidently shifted from extremely mad and unpredictable to calm. His voice lowered, he said, "You were sent to me because you're the best of the best. In my view you are just beginners. I will make the most of you. I will push you to your limits. This is how I've successfully completed numerous missions for Uncle Sam." As he talked, the sergeant walked slowly down the line and then returned to his original place in the center. He shouted, "Ready! Down! Give me ninety push-ups since you are supposedly the best!" All the squad members dropped to the ground and began doing their push-ups. The sergeant reached into his pocket and pulled out a counter with a clicking sound. He began clicking, marking each push-up.

Walking and counting, he informed the squad, "You have been assigned to Project XS. This is the most advanced mission I have come across. And I am in charge! Tomorrow you will be introduced to your new weapons. I've been involved with this project since the first weapon was made. The mission objective is to prevent the development of new nuclear bombs in Far Eastern countries. Project XS is the government's most secret weapon and is, of course, very expensive. I will make sure that you don't mess it up. We are here to prepare you for the first mission in human history that involves this unique weapon." Sergeant Bakerman kept walking back and forth while clicking his counter. Then he paused by Price, who was doing the push-ups with little effort. He knelt down and resumed his speech. "You are machines! You will think like machines. This is how my men have succeeded in the past."

A little later, he got up and checked the counter: ninety-one. "All right, squad, get up." Sergeant Bakerman was pleased with them but didn't show it with any facial expression. All the squad members had completed the task without stopping. Kelly was breathing heavily from the effort, but he'd done all the push-ups, even through the pain. His shoulder reminded him of a past injury, and he rubbed it.

At the other end of the hall, the black cat that lived inside the barracks walked inside, entering through the main doors, which had been left ajar. The cat stopped dead in his tracks by the entrance as if he were suddenly reevaluating his entire mortal existence. Abruptly the sergeant said, "Everyone, dismissed." He cooled down upon seeing the cat walking on his own and majestically waving his tail. The squad members picked up their backpacks and moved to their beds.

Meanwhile, the sergeant walked slowly toward the black cat, which was randomly strolling around. As he got close, the cat rose his head, meowed, and rubbed his head against the sergeant's leg. "Mr. Charcoal, where you been? I told you to stay at home." The sergeant gently picked up the cat with his big hands. Stroking the cat's black fur, he looked kindly into the cat's eyes. The cat was fluffing him up like a pillow. Everyone who saw it was confused, almost shocked.

How come that monster, who acts so ferociously toward other people, becomes so soft with an ordinary cat? Matt thought, watching with surprise.

"Squad, you are free now. The schedule is attached above your beds. We will meet tomorrow," Sergeant Bakerman declared loudly while carefully holding the black cat in his arms. He walked back to the dark corridor and disappeared from the main hall, still softly talking to the animal.

Matt prepared his stuff and checked out his bed and the rest of the nearby bunks. Then he studied the schedule and the other information on the laminated white paper above his bed. He tracked his fingers down the sheet of paper until he came to the information about the food court. Feeling his hunger, Matt called, "Hey, Crack! Aren't you hungry? We can use our free time to have some food. What do you think?"

Jenkins was lying on her bed playing with her braid. She was obviously thinking about something else besides having a dish. Then she turned to Matt and said, "All right, let's do this." She got up, walked to Matt, and looked at where his index finger pointed, showing the location of the food court. "It's not that far," she said, sounding relaxed.

"Okay! Let's go figure it out," Matt urged while turning his head around to see if anyone else was interested in doing something.

Meanwhile, Jenkins stood nearby and looked at the twins. Then she shifted her eyes toward Price because he was up to something, fiddling with something in his hands. Once again, his intentions remained inexplicable to her. Unexpectedly, he got up by his bed and grabbed his knife, which was strongly pierced into the wall. *Well, that's interesting,* she thought. Price, using his right leg against the wall and all his strength, tried to pull out the knife. He succeeded, but it took a lot of effort to get it out. He sighed deeply after retrieving the blade. Price nimbly twirled the knife in his hand and put it back in its holder with style. *That sergeant must be some kind of alien,* Jenkins concluded to herself. Then she turned her attention to Kelly, who was lying on his bed with his head tilted backward carelessly. Somehow he realized that Jenkins was looking at him. Using the opportunity, he put on his winning smile and sent a flying kiss to her with a wink. "Fuck off, Kelly," she said while showing him the middle finger.

Matt and Jenkins left to go to the food court, leaving the doors of the barracks open behind them. Once they'd walked some distance away, Jenkins stopped and began to express her frustration and inability to comprehend the situation. "What the hell is happening? This is the most unhinged instructor I've ever come across in my life. He is mentally unstable." Her eyes were shaky, looking back at the barracks. "You know … at one moment when he was facing me and forcing those awful questions on me, I was scared that he was going to shag me in front of everyone. His whole presence is so oppressive. I bet that battery acid runs through his veins." Amused by her colorful remark, Matt chuckled but then suddenly stopped, realizing that Jenkins was being serious. Her nostrils flared.

"Sorry, Crack," he said once he'd wiped the smile from his face. "I agree with you. It's nuts that he is in charge of this so-called advanced mission. Well … no wonder the driver who brought us here was so bleak when he mentioned Sergeant Bakerman. I guess we should brace ourselves for more crazy stuff to come up in the following days."

"I'm just thinking back to volunteering for this mission. Was it a smart thing to do?" Jenkins questioned herself. She almost felt trapped by this situation.

"You know why our superiors came to us with this opportunity? Because we are the best," he said, though he felt like he shouldn't be here either. "Crack, you had a choice to stay in New York. You could've stayed! It was my own deliberate choice to participate in this mission." He paused.

Suddenly Jenkins raised her voice. "What is this nonsense? Screw you. I'm with you because we are an inseparable unit. You know that very well. All those dirty missions and lost lives are part of us. Without you I would be dead and vice versa. If I had stayed in the Big Apple without you, it would have been the beginning of the end." She almost had come to the point of an emotional outburst, but she collected herself and stayed calm.

Matt felt stupid and didn't know what to say next. His deep eyes glazed over as he tried to say something else. He hesitated. His thoughts about the service were already wrecking his mind.

Kayla Jenkins had saved Matt's life two times, once during a dangerous and immensely stressful mission to eliminate an organized crime lair and another time on a mission to prevent counterfeiting in New York's basements. In the first instance, a mob member had jumped at Matt out of nowhere and stabbed him. Jenkins had reacted quickly, shooting down the attacker, who had almost killed Matt. The other time, Matt had taken the initiative and swapped positions with Jenkins during the mission. When they'd kicked down the door, a gun had been pointed directly at Matt's head. Because of the sudden chaos, he'd failed to notice the gunman. In the matter of half a second, Jenkins had shot the gunman, who had pulled his trigger too late. If Jenkins had gone first, as initially planned, she could have been shot by that gunman. Extremely stressful situations had become a norm for them. This was what bound them so close—covering each other's backs. Whether it was lucky coincidence that they'd survived these missions or the influence of something higher, the experiences had taken a toll on their mental state. Sleepless nights, mood shifting, and lots of private visits to specialists were common to them. Their friendship kept them on track, but recently Matt and Jenkins had been arguing a lot. The reason was they both wanted to quit the service but couldn't. They just simply couldn't cope with doing something other than conducting extremely dangerous missions. Nevertheless, their occasional arguments always cooled down quickly, and they resumed their high level of professionalism.

Inside the food court were lots of wooden tables. The air was filled with the smell of freshly cooked meat. The smell of all kinds of cooked fish was especially dominating. There was a long bar with a tall pile of nicely stacked plates at the beginning. It was a self-service bar. Jenkins walked to the bar first, sniffing at the trays of various food. Behind the bar, the chef came out with a huge pot of steaming food and topped up the half-empty trays using long tongs to fish out the pieces. There were other military personnel in the food court; about a dozen of them were chatting and eating at the other end of the hall. Jenkins chose her food carefully, taking only things that looked familiar to her—nothing unusual or strange looking. She filled her plate with rice, chicken breast, and a lot of salad. Matt looked at her plate and chose the same for himself. As a side for his chicken he added a fried fish that looked familiar to him.

"Where do we get the drinks?" she asked while holding her white tray and wandering around.

"There, at the end of bar." Matt pointed to a soft drink machine with a lot of nozzles.

Once they'd gotten their drinks, they sat opposite each other at a table in the middle of the room, where no one else was around. Time after time one of the military personnel glanced at them out of curiosity.

"Tastes good!" Jenkins said while energetically chewing the chicken breast and imagining that it tasted better than it actually did.

"Yeah," Matt agreed. He started with his fish first and carefully flipped it over with his chopsticks.

A few minutes later the twin brothers showed up. One of the brothers noticed them, smiled, and waved. They quickly got food trays and hustled through the bar like they knew everything. After filling their plates with gigantic portions, they headed to Matt and Jenkins's table. "Do you guys mind if we join you?" Alejandro asked, holding his tray filled with gigantic portions.

Matt moved aside and responded, "Not at all."

"What do you guys think about our new instructor?" Jenkins instantly asked.

"Honestly, I'm not really surprised by his attitude toward us. What concerns me the most is that he is in charge of this project that we have no clue about yet," Alejandro said, shifting his attention to her.

Jenkins felt the same. Fidgeting with her fork, she leaned closer, saying in a low tone, "That's what bothers me too—this advanced, secret mission trusted to an unbalanced giant who wouldn't hesitate to kill us with his bare hands. That's how I foresee the future."

Matt interrupted, "By the way, guys, where you from? I forgot to ask when we met at the port."

"We're both from Texas," Alejandro replied.

"How long you been in the service?" Jenkins asked.

Alejandro looked at Antonio as if trying to guess the years they'd already spent in the military. "Somewhere around ten years," he said, sounding unsure of the answer.

Matt turned his attention to Antonio, who hadn't said anything so far. "Why are you here? Did you volunteer, or was it an order from above?"

"It was more like an order than a volunteer request," Alejandro said. "But we spent most of our service years in the Middle East, and we'd both had enough of that place. It is hot as hell. It makes Texas look like a winter resort. In addition, lately it's been so boring there. So we had plans to move somewhere else. Unexpectedly, about a month ago, we were told about this mission on a Japanese island, and we signed up straightaway. Here we are." Alejandro demonstrated surprise by opening his arms and widening his eyes.

"Are you Navy SEALs?" Matt asked, holding his chopsticks in midair.

"Yes, we are. My brother and I are referred to as reckless ones. I guess that's why we got assigned to this mission in the first place."

"Looks like you really enjoy being in the service."

"Well … sort of. We both can't imagine ourselves doing something else. You know, this is like living on the fast train. Things are always happening with new challenges, and, weirdly, we want to be a part of that," Alejandro said, remembering the service with bitter nostalgia.

"Yeah, I get you. We have similar feelings." Matt sympathized and maintained eye contact with Jenkins. He then looked at Antonio, who still hadn't said a word. The twin had a small notepad at his right side and occasionally made some marks inside.

"You don't seem that talkative, Antonio. What are you up to?" Matt asked, his curiosity piqued as Antonio scribbled something down in his notebook.

Antonio looked at him briefly and replied in a low tone, "My mind is occupied with writing." It was apparent that Antonio felt uncomfortable discussing the matter. He had fallen into himself, his shoulders almost above his head.

"Umm ..." Matt paused, his eyes stuck on the notepad. "What do you write?"

"Nothing." Antonio froze after giving the short answer. He swiftly put the pen back in his pocket. Before picking up his fork from the table, he said, "Poems." It seemed to make him feel abashed.

Jenkins got excited and said with admiration, "Wow, that's really cool. Why don't you read us something?" She leaned closer and waited for him to reveal his artwork.

Antonio said reluctantly, "I don't think so. It's just a rough draft. It requires some work to clean it up."

"C'mon, give us something at least. I want to hear," she persisted and waited eagerly.

Antonio sighed and browsed through his notebook, looking for some poems. He stopped on a page and read a poem aloud.

I go where everyone else goes.
Crowds know what's right.
"What do I know?"
I stopped and asked myself.
Some say, "You will miss out—get along!"
They took my time away,
or was it me giving time for them?

I go where everyone else goes.
Crowds know where it's better.
"What is good for me?"
I stopped, wondered, and analyzed.
Another says, "You will miss out—get along."
They took my own good from me,
or was it me giving my good for them?

I go where everyone else goes.
Crowds know where happiness is.
"Do I feel happy?"
I stopped and tried to feel.
Nobody says anything
but proceeds without feelings.
They tried to take my happiness,
and I stopped again to feel.

"That was so beautiful, Antonio," Jenkins exclaimed with delight, her face glowing with joy.

"Yeah, man! I really like your message," Matt said. "How many poems have you written?"

"Thanks. Somewhere around fifty or more. I haven't counted yet. I'm just killing my time with this writing," he said modestly. Antonio closed his notebook, put it back in his pocket, and resumed his meal.

"You should publish your poems," Jenkins said seriously. "That's your passion. You can't waste your true feelings at this military hot spot. That's what your poem is trying to say."

"That's my problem, perhaps—I contradict myself often." He stopped eating and stared at a certain point, as if feeling a little remorse. "I don't think anyone is going to read my poems." He resumed eating again.

Suddenly, the food court doors opened wide with a loud noise. Jack Kelly, now dressed in a military uniform, had decided to have some food too. He immediately found the squad chatting at the table and gave them a thumbs-up. He walked slowly by the bar with a casual manner. Constantly sniffing the aromas of hot food, he winced sometimes, as if he'd smelled something disgusting. Obviously, Kelly was very particular, sometimes picking up food and then immediately putting it back because something dissatisfied him. *How can he be so choosy?* Jenkins thought, watching him with scorn. It took a long time for him to finish filling the dish on his plate. Finally, he was done, and he turned around and made his way toward the squad.

"Hey, brothers and New Yorkers! Do you mind?" Kelly stood a few steps away and waited for them to make a place for him. He looked at them with a confident and calm grin, patiently waiting for the space to be freed. Nobody said nothing and reluctantly moved aside. "Thank you!" he said and flipped his blond hair with his fingers. Before digging into his food, Kelly said, "I can't stand that Price. He's up to something. He keeps staring silently at his knife."

"At least he knows how to keep his mouth shut, unlike you," Jenkins said. Lowering her eyebrows, she leaned forward. "You will learn how to keep your tongue behind your teeth. It really worked out when Sergeant Bakerman was about to crush your pretty face." She smiled.

"Jenkins ... hey, Jenkins, you are so beautiful when you smile. You see, I'm here to keep you happy. For goodness' sake, isn't that more important than this outrageous mission, which nobody really has a clue about?" Kelly said in a relaxed tone while gazing at Jenkins, who grew serious, once more looking at Kelly like he was despicable. However, she didn't challenge him to any more arguments. As he picked up a piece of chicken with his fork, he said, "Do you think I was willing to come to this shithole? I had no choice. Even though I'm the best of Boston's SWAT, it doesn't guarantee any special treatmentfor me. Right, my SWAT mates?" He watched Matt with a transparent look.

"What are you talking about?" Matt asked with a little confusion.

Kelly briefly shifted his eyes between Matt and Jenkins and asked, "Have you ever counted how many people you've killed, being the best agents?" He looked at them with interest.

"Screw you, Kelly! We've killed only bad guys—that's the ultimate order," Jenkins said vigorously.

"Oh, really?" Kelly leaned a bit backward, preparing himself for further discussion. "What's your definition of bad guys then? Life is like a chess game. Both sides have good and bad people. First they get rid of pawns, then horses, then towers, and finally queens and kings. You should know your employers are from Wall Street. They pick and choose where you go next."

"We had a choice whether to come or not to come. That nonsense about Wall Street is bullshit," Matt said as he finished his plate and put his chopsticks neatly to the side.

"Same with me. As soon as I refused, though, my superiors came back to me with a huge pile of files proving that I killed innocent people during my missions. *What the fuck*, I thought. I was doing my job, for goodness' sake." Kelly got serious. The rest of them vaguely paid attention to him, listening to his concerns. "That's why they're choosing the best. The best means who has the most experience and who has survived the most missions. Whether you like it or not, many have been killed because of me pulling my trigger. Many of my partners—good people—have lost their lives or been seriously injured. I myself have come close to being shot dead. Somehow I got lucky. To be honest, I wouldn't mind retiring from SWAT and banging my pretty girlfriend who lives in Boston. But here I am, with the same doomed souls!" He resumed eating his meal. "Argh," he abruptly groaned while holding his head. Then he quickly groped in his pockets for his painkillers. After swallowing two pills without water, Kelly continued to eat.

"You're addicted. Aren't you?" Matt raised his eyebrows in distaste while looking at Kelly.

"Sometimes the stuff that goes in your body—painkillers, steroids, drugs, etcetera—can dramatically influence what goes on in your brain," Jenkins said, demonstrating her knowledge. "It just triggers your already despicable nature even more."

Kelly stopped eating. "You know what? You're right," he agreed, this time without adding any insults. He sucked in his lips and looked over at the end of the food court. He explained in a low tone, "It sometimes causes wild fluctuations of my blood sugar levels. That's why I don't eat junk food or other shit. On top of that comes stress in large amounts from my job. It all adds up, you know. This is how I can control myself, keeping me from premature self-destruction—pills and drugs."

It looked like Jenkins almost sympathized with him. She said slowly, "For the very first time, I don't want to punch your Hollywood face." She shook her head and leaned back in her chair. "You're like a bomb with a fuse, walking through a dry valley with a high risk of fire."

Kelly sighed and chuckled, feeling euphoric.

Both brothers stood up from the table and walked away, nodding their heads in acknowledgment. Seconds later, Matt and Jenkins stood up as well. Before making his way out, Matt turned to Kelly and said, "I think you're judging this mission too soon. We haven't even seen those weapons yet." They stared at each other briefly, and Kelly recoiled, smiling sarcastically, as if he believed his foreboding predictions would come true.

A strong stream of water poured over Sean Price's masculine shoulders. He was taking a cold shower in the barracks while the rest of the squad was at the food court. With his hands propped against the white tiles, he enjoyed the refreshing, strong water stream. Occasionally, the showerhead twitched and the stream disappeared, but it soon returned to normal. The pipes were rusted and sometimes made increasing sounds because of low pressure. Price exhaled slowly and looked at his tattoo of a skull and barbed wire with the date of 06.06.2016.

"Sean," a voice called suddenly from behind him. It was an unusual man's voice, like a spooky juvenile.

Price remained in the shower, motionless except for his eyes, which he slowly moved to the side. Shutting off the shower knobs, he turned around, but nobody was there. All he saw was some open lockers with his stuff hanging outside. He reached for his towel, wrapped it around his waist, and walked into the changing room. Making some quick observations around the lockers, he found nobody and nothing but dead silence. His mind far from calm, Price peeked into the main hall. The Javier twins were chatting by their beds. He knew the voice hadn't been one of theirs. Price returned to the changing room. Before dressing, he stared at his tattoo again and recalled the memories. His face flinched, as if he were experiencing physical pain. "Shit," he cursed and hurried to dress.

Day 2

The next day, everyone woke early in the morning. The sky was sunny and cloudless, and it looked like it would stay that way all day long. About ten minutes before eight o'clock, Sean Price stood by the schedule above his bed and checked the daily routine while scratching his jutting chin. Nearby was a window that had a view of the perimeter grid fence, which didn't obscure the island's landscape. Price calmly looked out the window, enjoying the view of bright sun reflecting on rough green terrain. He was ready for the physical drill, which was the first item on the list, titled "Teamwork." Meanwhile, Kelly lay relaxing on his bed and observed Price with a puzzled face. Price didn't bother giving Kelly any attention and kept to himself as usual—determined, ignorant of those around him, and overly focused on the mission.

Deep in the corridor, a door shut wildly and loudly, echoing all the way down to the main hall. Then loud steps made their way to the hall. Everyone jumped into a line, already recognizing the dread sound. Their first experience with the instructor yesterday had put them on edge. Sergeant

Bakerman walked into the hall, chewing something again. He closely observed everyone. Walking along the line, he examined each person from top to bottom, making sure everyone was ready for today's drill. As he came to Kelly, the sergeant stopped. There was a tense moment of silence. The others stayed in their places, eyes focused straight ahead. Something unpredictable was going to happen. Kelly kept calm on the outside, but inside his guts were raving. "What's your name, Face?" Sergeant Bakerman asked, raising his voice.

"Sir, Jack Kelly, sir!" he responded loudly.

The sergeant's chest increased in size as he inhaled a large amount of air. A loud order followed his exhale. "All right, squad, today we will start with a drill. First, a three-mile run up the hill. Then we will return back to base, where you will be introduced to your new weapons." He turned his back on Kelly and walked to the middle of the line, making each step strident. "Follow me!" he loudly announced as he walked to the exit.

Outside the barracks the heat was picking up already despite the early hour. The squad followed closely behind their instructor, who led them to the front gates. Some military trucks that had arrived from the coast passed by. Almost every military person recognized Bakerman and greeted him as they passed by. By the entrance, he turned to the squad and pointed up the hill. "That gray rock is our destination. I will lead you."

The area appeared to have no roads—just tough green terrain all the way uphill—but as the sergeant started to run, he took them to a narrow, rocky path. His pace was slow but gradually increased until he was striding with amazing speed for a man so heavy. Running on the path was really hard for everyone because they weren't familiar with this difficult terrain. Occasional stumbles and awkward bumps into each other were common in the beginning. Sergeant Bakerman didn't look back and kept running like a tank. The squad was gradually left behind, except for Price, who broke to the front and made a gap between him and the other squad members. The path was uneven with lots of ups and downs. Sometimes there were huge holes in the ground, and the squad had to stop to avoid them. Soon they realized that they needed to push themselves harder, or they would lose their instructor, whom they could already barely see.

"C'mon, follow my pattern!" Alejandro urged everyone. He'd navigated a similar environment in his past. His brother was close to him, copying his steps. Antonio turned around to the rest and pointed to his feet to make them understand what Alejandro meant.

"Do as the brothers do!" Matt said while looking at Jenkins and Kelly. Already he was gasping for air. "Matt quickly began copying each step the brothers made. It really helped, allowing him to run faster. The sergeant had already disappeared from their sight, but Price was still visible, and he must be able to see the sergeant. It was just the first mile when they realized how hard the run was. Sometimes the inclines were so steep and long that the group walked instead of running, and some of the descents were so steep that they were dangerous to run down. Despite the unexpected challenges, the squad managed to keep up with their instructor. The teamwork strategy really helped the squad to keep up, though Price was on his own.

"Shit!" Kelly shouted while stumbling over a gigantic rock that had been hidden by the long grass. Jenkins noticed immediately, turned around, and helped him get up.

"C'mon!" she urged him and resumed the wacky switchbacks. Strangely, she gave Kelly a look of compassion.

After a long and torturous run they successfully reached their destination. If they hadn't been able to see Price ahead of them, they would have gotten lost. The sergeant was waiting for them to arrive. He held a stopwatch and was sweating buckets. As soon as Kelly, who was the last arrive, showed up, the sergeant stopped the watch. To the squad's surprise, he nodded his head and said, "Well done!"

The place where they'd stopped was flat with a lot of smaller rocks and clusters of grass. It looked like a place where people used to camp. "We will do some exercises here. Then we will run down!" the sergeant said and walked to a rusted metal frame that looked like part of an old crane. It was partially covered with bushes and tree branches. The place was mostly shaded from the nearby trees, but it was getting hotter. Sergeant Bakerman pulled his counter from his pocket. "All right, squad! Get up and grab the bar!" he commanded. Without hesitation, all of them jumped up and hung from the bar. "One," he counted aloud as he strolled along the bar. Everybody executed the first pull-up. "Today you will be introduced to some new technology. It is highly advanced and has great potential. You'll be the first to use this technology. The authorities have sent me the best of you." He stopped counting aloud but kept clicking the counter. All understood and kept doing pull-ups. "This will also be my first time conducting a mission with these new weapons. So far I've been using the weapons for training and testing purposes only. I can say, this technology is unique and possibly game-changing for our army."

Suddenly, Kelly released the bar and dropped to the ground, shortly followed by Jenkins. The sergeant looked at his counter: twenty-six. He resumed clicking and continued, "No army has a weapon like what we have now. In this game we are ahead again, like we were in the past." The sergeant got thoughtful and paused a moment. He added in a lower voice, "When some ugly bombs were dropped just nearby and wiped out a lot of innocent lives, causing collateral damage."

Matt released the bar. After some more clicks, the twin brothers simultaneously joined him. The sergeant again glanced at his counter: thirty-two. Price didn't show any sign of getting exhausted. Every click was translated into a perfectly executed pull-up by Price. Sergeant Bakerman stopped talking and turned his attention to Price. He kept clicking until Price began to slow down. The sound of the counter continued—click, click, and final click. Price's body had finally reached its limit. Price released the bar and landed on the ground. The sergeant checked his counter again: forty-three. "That's impressive," he said. Walking closer to the frame, he said, "Price, you are physically ahead of your peers. But you have *failed*!" He looked down at Price from above and, pointing at the others, said, "Look at them. What do you see?"

Price looked at them, a bit confused. "Sir, I see a squad, sir," he answered.

"Wrong answer! This is your team! They haven't failed, because they were acting like a team." Sergeant walked around Price, watching him. "You were the first to get here, arriving on your own. You left your squad behind. They kept together as a team. That's your failure, and you should know it."

"Yes, sir!" Price obediently agreed.

"I sense that you've been through some serious shit in your career. I recognized that almost immediately. What's your experience, Price?" he asked.

"More than ten years in special forces."

"Well, what the hell has happened to your memory? Teamwork is essential! This is your creed. On this island it's no different. If you forge ahead on your own, you will go fast. If you forge ahead together, you will go far."

"Yes, sir!"

"Okay, we need to relearn things from the beginning." The sergeant looked at everyone, hands folded behind him. "Starting now, Price will be given time to organize the return to base. Task objectives." The sergeant's loud voice ceased suddenly. He rocked back and forth on his heavy heels, his face wise with profundity. He resumed laying out the task. "Price will figure out how to get us back to the base without me walking." The sergeant looked up at the bright sky; the sun cast light on his strong facial features. "Because it is warm already, he will also figure out how to cool me down and, of course, make it comfortable." He added, took out his stopwatch. "Let's go, Price! This is about teamwork."

Price had an instant idea. Surprisingly, he wasn't knocked off the rails but instead took action rapidly. Looking around, he noticed a lot of material that would help to build a stretcher. He walked closer to the rest of the squad and gave instructions. "We will make a stretcher. We'll use the trunks of two smaller trees for the wooden poles and will use thinner branches to form the bed of the stretcher." Price looked at the metallic frame and noticed an old tarpaulin rug. "That old tarpaulin will be great to complete the bed."

"How about cooling down the sergeant?" Jenkins reminded.

Price thought and responded quickly, "Yes, of course. You will create the fan from the plants around." She nodded. "Okay, guys! Javier twins, you go find two wooden poles." The twins nodded. "Baker and Kelly, you gather tree branches for the bed. Meanwhile, I will get that old tarpaulin." Once everyone was clear about their tasks, they immediately set to work as instructed by Price.

From a short distance away, Sergeant Bakerman watched them hustling around. The twins quickly chose the nearest trees that looked thin enough to break with their body strength. Alejandro pointed at a cluster of rocks. "Let's do it this way. You bring that huge rock over and put it near the tree about one meter away. Then I'll jump on the tree, and using my body weight, I'll break it over the rock's sharp edge."

"Got it," Antonio replied, already headed over to the nearest rock that was big enough to break the tree. The twins did their job quickly, and one tree was down. Repeating the same actions again, they retrieved another one.

Meanwhile, Matt and Kelly plucked a lot of branches of the same size. They pulled off the leaves with their bare hands, making the branches clear. At the same time, Price energetically pulled out the tarpaulin from under the frame. He grabbed it by a week spot and, using his strength, ripped off a chunk easily. The twin brothers had already brought over the foundational material for the stretcher—two tree trunks of almost the same size. Soon Matt and Kelly joined them with a lot of thin, flexible tree branches for the bed. Eventually, Price came over with the retrieved tarpaulin.

"Okay, guys, let's build it," Price said, his voice breaking with hope and tension. Looking at all the material, he urged them to build the stretcher together. Jenkins soon joined them with a large fern to use as a fan. Now, all of them were involved in binding together the two wooden poles with smaller tree branches. Price had organized them very well. A couple of minutes later, he took the tarpaulin and wrapped it around the stretcher to make it more stable. The stretcher complete, he said in a loud voice, "Listen up. Our strategy is to have a safe descent back to base. We'll have three of us on both sides of the stretcher. Each of us will fan the sergeant for one hundred steps and then will pass the fan to the next person until we reach the base. Is that clear?" Obviously everyone agreed.

"Sir, we are ready to go!" Price announced to the sergeant.

"All right! Bring it over to me," Sergeant Bakerman said, stopping his stopwatch. It had taken the squad only a little over ten minutes to build the stretcher. He didn't show the slightest movement in his face but simply waited for them to reach him. As the squad came close to him, the sergeant instructed, "Now is the time about trust. Stand behind me." He turned his head backward, showing where they should stand. "I will do a free fall into the stretcher. You will make my landing as soft as possible. Don't screw my landing, or you will experience Godzilla waking up from a deep sleep," he warned.

Everybody took their positions behind the sergeant, who was already starting his fall backward. They caught him and made it soft. That was a tense moment for everyone. None of them wanted to make a hard landing for the furious sergeant. He lay back in the stretcher, feeling relaxed. He pulled his hat's brim over his eyes, thus avoiding being dazzled by the bright sun. "Back to base!" he said. "For goodness' sake, it is hot. Cool me down!" He turned his head toward Jenkins, who was holding the fan. She quickly started to fan him with her free arm, feeling a bit anxious. "That's better," he sighed.

The squad was on their way back to base, carrying the sergeant in the stretcher. Everyone was sweating buckets. So far it had been a tense physical effort. Jenkins counted each step while fanning the sergeant. She was located at the end of the stretcher, so she couldn't see the difficult path in front of them, just the back of one of the twin brothers. *Fuck, will we make it?* Jenkins thought, endeavoring to keep up. After the first hundred steps, she passed the fan to the next person. Oddly, the sergeant hadn't said anything so far, even though the stretcher shook considerably sometimes.

"The importance of teamwork," the sergeant said. "A team is like a clockwork mechanism. If one of the gears decides to do its own thing, soon the whole clockwork will be defective. How to fix the problem?" The sergeant paused as the stretcher shook suddenly. Soon he resumed the lecture. "Easy—we take out the faulty gear and check whether it's possible to fix or not. If it's not fixable, then we replace it with a new one. Replacing it is much cheaper than keeping the clockwork running with a faulty gear."

The squad kept walking, carefully placing their steps until they reached some thick bushes with berries. The bushes drew the sergeant's attention, and he commanded loudly, "Stop here! Squad, lower me down!" The exhausted squad members lowered the stretcher. The sergeant reached out to pick some juicy berries. He tossed some in his mouth. "These are so good." Having a full hand of freshly picked berries, he said, "Resume the walk." All the squad members groaned simultaneously while extending their bodies.

The squad had carried the sergeant more than halfway down. From time to time they passed the fan, taking turns cooling down their instructor. Their pace had significantly slowed; exhaustion was apparent on their faces. *How much longer?* Kelly thought, looking at Jenkins, who was across the stretcher from him on the end. He felt even more exhausted than the others. However, he pushed himself to his limits because he knew the sergeant wouldn't tolerate failure. He was able to keep going partly thanks to Jenkins, who occasionally mouthed to him, "C'mon". She supported him in that way. Everyone was so thirsty because of sweating so much from the intense physical activities on this hot morning.

"How much longer?" the sergeant asked, his hat over his face. None of them gave an answer but kept walking with great effort down the difficult path. Matt raised his head and saw that they were about to reach the base. "What on earth! Are you blind? Are you even taking me back to base?" the sergeant exclaimed, still relaxing in the stretcher.

"We are nearly there, sir!" Matt replied.

"That's good," the sergeant said.

Finally, the squad reached the gates of the base, having endured much toil and strain. They held the stretcher and waited for the sergeant to say something. Suddenly, Matt said in a loud voice, "Sir, we have reached the base."

The sergeant commanded, "Bring me down to a standing position like you picked me up!" The squad members tapped each other on the shoulder—the signal to lower the stretcher. Matt and Price squatted down first because they were in the front, shortly followed by the others. The descent was smooth enough for Sergeant Bakerman to get out. He said, "Nice work!" He looked at the overly exhausted squad in the heat. "This was a teamwork exercise. I hope we will not have to relearn the basics about that again. If we do, I'll make it as difficult as possible. Is everyone clear?" he said, shouting the last sentence.

"Sir, yes, sir!" everyone responded, gathering their breath.

"Good! You have a two-hour break starting now." The sergeant checked his watch and added, "Meet in the barracks in two hours' time. Dismissed."

As soon as the sergeant walked off, the squad stared with great thirst at the water tank outside the food court. Suddenly they all took off running toward the water. "That was a fucking torment!" Kelly said. They looked at the water tap like hungry wolves. Kelly turned on the water and kneeled down by the stream. He felt an instant euphoria, and life returned to his worn-out body. Meanwhile, the rest of the group grabbed the nearby bottles and tried to fill them up while bumping into Kelly, who was selfishly drinking straight from the tap, gulping noisily.

"Get off!" Matt angrily said. "You're not the only one dying of thirst." He held his bottle under the strong, refreshing water stream. Once it was full, he passed it to one of the squad members and started filling up a second bottle. He kept filling until everyone had a bottle.

As everyone satisfied their thirst, they sat on the ground in the shade and took a deep rest. They watched the sergeant go inside the barracks. Sean Price briefly left the group and went inside the food court without saying anything.

"Thanks, Price!" Kelly said sarcastically, watching him leaving. "This was a valuable lesson in teamwork. You son of a bitch!" He rolled his orange pill container in his hands. He tossed a couple of pills in his mouth, swallowed, and leaned his head against the wall.

"Nevertheless, he coped with his task quickly, and it worked out perfectly. I must give him credit for that," Matt said while holding his half-empty bottle.

Kelly rolled his head to the side, looking indifferently at Matt. "I don't give a ..." Kelly trailed off out of exhaustion. He sighed and added, "Anyway, I hate that mute."

"What's this?" Alejandro stood up, noticing some action at the fence near the armory. Some men were running around among artificial obstacles with toy guns. His brother looked over too. "They're playing paintball!" Alejandro exclaimed in surprise.

Kelly sat against the wall and began chuckling ceaselessly. His body shook from his laughter, which grew louder. As he calmed down, Kelly said, "These are the weapons of Project XS. I love this place." Again he laughed as if he'd heard a very good joke.

Jenkins, who was sitting nearby, shook her head like she was listening to some dumb individual, which happened to be Kelly. Whacking dust off her army trousers, she stood up and turned to Matt. "Let's go get something to eat." She glided over and patted him on the arm.

"Hey …" Kelly said seductively, extending his hand toward Jenkins. "Help me get up, Cracky girl. Teamwork is essential."

She leaned toward him with extended arm. Her eyes were hiding something. Before giving Kelly support, Jenkins clenched her fist and blinked. Suddenly she tapped firmly on his smiley cheek, saying, "First, learn how to say thank you, Face." She was referring to their recent teamwork exercise.

"Thank you," Kelly said quietly, almost whispering. He got up by himself and followed them to the food court.

Inside the barracks, the sergeant walked through the hall looking for Mr. Charcoal. The cat was not there. He headed to his office in the corridor. Slowly opening the door, he saw his cat. Mr. Charcoal was relaxing on the windowsill with eyes half-open. The window had been left ajar.

"Hello, buddy. Are you hungry?" the sergeant asked, walking closer to stroke the cat's black fur. Then he checked the cat's tray, which still had food inside. Opening the fridge, he took out some mineral water and ready-made sandwiches for himself. Meanwhile, the cat stared at him carelessly, slowly blinking his eyes as if falling asleep. Sergeant Bakerman inserted a cartridge into the espresso machine and poured in the mineral water. The machine brewed the coffee, the aroma of which was already filling his office.

The sergeant sat at his massive office desk, which had neatly ordered and well-organized stationery on top. Opening the mahogany drawer, he took out his cigar box and cutter. Carefully cutting off the end of cigar, he said to the cat, "It's getting hot today, buddy." Sergeant Bakerman looked at the cat, who was stretched out and licking his belly fur. After lighting the cigar with a nice silver lighter, the sergeant stood up and walked to the window. He then gently picked up the cat and brought him to the sofa, making sure that Mr. Charcoal didn't have to breathe the smoke. Sergeant Bakerman stood by the window and smoked in a repetitive, fast motion. The espresso machine beeped to indicate the coffee was ready. Putting down the cigar on an ashtray, he took his arabica and walked back to the desk. He bit into his sandwich and sat in his swivel chair. Suddenly the cat rose up, slowly walked over, and jumped on the sergeant's lap, making himself comfortable. The sergeant stroked the cat's fur. "How long will I be able to do this? It's just one way for me: go ahead and jump into a new conflict, which, oddly, keeps me sane." He lingered on memories of the past that made his facial expression shift from calm to bitter remorse. "Why am I still alive? Why was I fortunate enough to survive all my past missions?"

The sergeant had fought in a couple of warzones years ago and had lost a lot of his fellow soldiers. Some of his missions in the Middle East had been ugly. In some cases he'd accidently blown up local citizens. He'd had to wait for orders from above for the permission to detonate the bombs. It had been total chaos and a volatile atmosphere, real hell on earth. The order had been delayed, which had created extreme tension. If the circumstances had been different, his action would have saved his fellow soldiers. The bombs had been meant for terrorists, but they'd gotten the location wrong. When he received his orders, Bakerman had detonated the bombs and blown up the civilian house with innocent people inside, including children. Later he'd discovered the error, which had caused immeasurable devastation to Bakerman. His heart had shattered into pieces like a broken crystal vase. He'd killed innocent people by following orders from above. That had been the beginning of the end. Situations had only gotten worse later on. After that horrible incident, he'd decided to leave the service. Unfortunately, his superiors had forced him to stay and conduct the mission till the end; if he'd refused, they would have brought him to a war tribunal. In that time, the only thought in Bakerman's mind had been *I want to see my wife and daughter.* Unfortunately, due to a bad coincidence of circumstances, things had only gotten worse.

"I can't even cry anymore. My tear glands have become dysfunctional." The sergeant stroked his cat while remembering the past trauma. "Sometimes, it feels like I'm dead. My whole existence is like being a corpse with consciousness. I tried so hard ... Why did life play against me?" Recalling the painful memories made him angry, and his jaw trembled.

When he'd eventually completed the mission, he'd been given leave, as his superiors had promised. The day he was to head back home to the US to see his beloved family, whom he hadn't seen for months, he received a phone call from his wife's parents. An instant feeling that something was wrong overwhelmed his entire body. As he picked up the phone, he heard his wife's mother sobbing and crying. She hesitated.

Bakerman had tears in his eyes and a frightened feeling. It was like his internal organs became numb and ceased working. "What's wrong? Tell me," he said anxiously.

His mother-in-law said in a grieving tone, "Your wife and your daughter died in a car accident. A drunk truck driver crashed into them. They died instantly."

Upon hearing that devastating news, Bakerman abruptly collapsed. His eyes tightened, and his face crumpled. Then he screamed, yelling, "*Why?*"

He went back to the US in order to bury his family. Soon after the funeral, he called the army head office and asked to apply for missions as soon as possible. It was hard. He couldn't live with the pain at home. Bakerman soon realized that if he stayed home, he would either commit suicide or go mental.

When he returned to the warzone, he took all available missions, which pleased his commanding officers. Bakerman became so determined and highly trained that he drew everyone's attention. He completed every following mission more successfully and quickly than the previous one. Soon his superiors trusted him to train new recruits for warfare because of his quickly growing experience and effective approach. Bakerman had become a ruthless killing machine—highly tactical and strong. Quick decision-making was another of his strengths. Soon he'd reached the point where he craved new conflicts, but much of the time there had been nothing to do but wait as they acquired new information on terrorists' locations. During his missions Bakerman had killed many enemies. He was surprised by how he had managed to survive.

"Mr. Charcoal, I can't stop. I won't," the sergeant said and frowned, feeling a rampant desire to do something incongruous. He sucked in his breath noisily, his attention on the framed poster of Uncle Sam on the wall. Suddenly, he managed to reduce his stress level and stabilize his breath. He put his cat on the sofa and poured some more coffee. Mr. Charcoal seemed very drowsy. He briefly looked at the poster again and thought remorsefully, *You got me. I'm yours.* Putting down his coffee mug, he checked his watch. Two hours had almost passed.

He left his office and walked to the main hall. The squad was waiting for him, already lined up. A state of suspense was present as the sergeant's eyes glazed over, this time with more abhorrence. Even though he said nothing, the long silence created an odd feeling. With heavy steps, he made his way to the center of the hall. "Squad, follow me," he commanded. Bakerman walked outside, the group following.

Within the base there was a well-hidden underground facility that the squad hadn't been shown yet. As the squad walked through the base, they passed military personnel hustling, clamoring, and doing their own thing. It looked like the staff was mainly doing vehicle maintenance. Eventually they reached a slope that led down to the underground facility. So far the squad had no clue what the Project XS weapon looked like. Sergeant Bakerman went down the slope to the wide, impressive armored steel doors. They were black with camouflage elements of green and brown. He pulled out his key card and swiped it through the device. A short and sharp beep echoed. The heavy doors rolled up into the ground above, revealing the man-made basement, which was chilly, dim, and almost empty.

"Come in," the sergeant said. The main room was spacious but oppressing with dark tones everywhere. However, it wasn't the only room. Regular doors led to some kind of office. There were people inside, and the artificial lights of the office made the room much brighter than the much-bigger hall where they were. Sergeant Bakerman walked inside the smaller room, where five people were working on computers. Shortly the rest of the squad joined him and curiously observed the room, which was crammed with computers and technologies. The air inside was ventilated by fans built into the ceiling that made an annoying sound.

"Mr. Sevchenko!" Sergeant Bakerman called.

A man at a computer stood up. He was tall and skinny and dressed casually. He had a long beard and hair that reached his shoulders. "Sir," he said, shifting his deep-brown eyes to the squad members.

Sergeant Bakerman turned to his squad and said, "This is software engineer Michael Sevchenko. He is the one who started this project on the most important improvements to Project XS. I've been with him since the project was launched," he explained.

Sevchenko walked to each squad member, vigorously shook each person's hand, and asked for his or her name. He was intrigued and smiled while getting to know each of them. The sergeant then headed back to the main room and asked the others to follow.

"Show them what Project XS is about," he said to Sevchenko.

"Oh, yeah. Sure." Sevchenko rushed to pull out a small remote and pressed the button.

Suddenly a sharp hissing sound, almost irritable to the ears, came from both sides of the room. The squad still had no idea what they were going to see soon. Hollow and mechanical sounds followed, growing increasingly louder. A sound of metals getting push and pulled then followed by a hiss of cool water vapor. The impressively large wall extensions split on each side, revealing nine-foot-tall robot suits. Each suit looked like it could carry a person inside, with the person controlling the suit. On each side, the robot suits had many enormous guns that weren't directly attached. There were about twenty robot suits total. All the squad members got excited and thrilled by the robot suits.

Sevchenko coughed and said, "These are exoskeleton machines that can be guided by humans, in this case you. They are highly capable and built out of the best materials available, a mixture of carbon fiber and titanium, making them light and durable. They are packed with the latest technology, which makes them extremely expensive. Each exoskeleton costs twenty million US dollars. In this basement we have eighteen of them, and to my knowledge, these eighteen are the only ones in existence. Since you are the best, you have the privilege of using them first. So be careful with these expensive toys." Sevchenko walked closer to the machines. "The power source is a battery that uses the latest material: graphene. It has way better properties than conventional battery materials. For example, charging is five times faster, and the battery life is longer than normal. Moreover, the exoskeleton can charge itself at any power source available, no matter how high or low voltage, as soon as it can gain access."

Sergeant Bakerman had his arms crossed in front of him and patiently waited for Sevchenko to finish the overall briefing about the machines. The engineer turned to the sergeant and continued, "Your instructor will teach you the basics of handling these machines, which is quite simple. My team and I are constantly working on new updates that will improve the exoskeletons' capabilities. What else?" He thought a moment. "Oh, yeah. These suits are equipped with two grappling hooks, mounted on the back. The shooting range of the grappling hooks is one hundred and sixty yards, very accurate." Sevchenko rubbed his hands together and pointed at guns. "As you can see, there are massive guns next to the suits, and these guns can be mounted on the exoskeletons' arms. Needless to say, these guns are versatile and lethal." Sevchenko stopped and thought about what else he had forgotten to mention, grinding his teeth. Suddenly, he remembered and called out to one of his crew members to bring over the overall instructions about the machines. His colleague, Rob, briskly brought over six manuals from the computer room and passed one out to each squad member. The manual wasn't big; it was more like a small pamphlet, and it seemed to have been printed recently. The squad members were intrigued and keen to get the machines in action.

"Engineer," the sergeant said, "explain about emergency exits from the suits and the connection with the body."

"Oh, yeah!" Sevchenko said. "Please study the entire manual, especially the bit about emergency exits." He grabbed the nearest squad member's book, opened it to the last section on emergencies, and handed it back. All the squad members flipped to the same section almost simultaneously. "My team is constantly working on new system upgrades that will improve the exoskeletons' ability to come back to base in case of host death."

Jenkins got worried hearing that and turned her attention to the nearby suit, which made her feel a bit suspicious. A sour expression, almost righteous in the degree of its displeasure, appeared on her face.

Sevchenko paused and looked at everyone. Slowly, stressing each word like a warning, he said, "If it happens that you are seriously hit or unconscious, the exoskeleton will immediately detect your critical life status and give you a boost. In this case, a built-in defibrillator will give you a shock to get you back to life. So don't worry. This won't happen during your training, but it might happen during your assigned missions. Thanks to my latest update, the exoskeletons could help to bring back the host even if he or she is dead. It will be possible once the systems are updated."

The engineer was about to say something else when the sergeant interrupted. "All right, that's enough, engineer." He then declared loudly, "Squad, this is over. Study your manuals, and tomorrow you will have your first training day with me and these machines." He watched them with a coldhearted face, loudly adding, "Dismissed!"

All the squad members lingered a moment and watched how the exoskeletons were pulled back into the wall. The built-in sections of the wall had been smartly made; it was hard to notice that something like this was being hidden in the basement. *Security is at its highest*, Matt thought while appreciating the place. Massive amounts of cold water vapor reappeared again before the sections were completely shut. The squad members walked outside, feeling astonished and rubbing their bodies because of the cold. Finally they had seen what Project XS was about.

As soon as the squad left the basement, the sergeant urged Sevchenko to go inside the computer room. His facial expression indicated fury and trouble. Inside the computer room, the crew turned their attention to the frustrated sergeant and surprised Sevchenko. *Something is not good,* one man thought, fidgeting with his pen in fear.

"What the hell were you talking about back there?" Sergeant Bakerman yelled, the veins of his neck bulging as he moved closer to the engineer.

"What do you mean, sir?" Sevchenko was confused.

"Updates to the exoskeletons that can make them walk back to base!"

"Well … I haven't set up those updates yet," Sevchenko stammered.

The sergeant grew louder. "And you won't! I have the final say on this damn island about any updates installed on Project XS. Unless the general calls me and says otherwise, you will not upgrade them. Do you understand, Sevchenko?"

The engineer was physically pushed a little backward by him and dared to say, "My team and I were part of this project long before you got proxy command, sir. These updates are essential to save these expensive machines. Whether you like it or not, I will urge our general to approve the update." He looked at the sergeant, afraid he was about to get an unpredictable and unpleasant response.

"Don't you dare challenge my position!" the sergeant said angrily. "I can suspend you anytime and send you back to Tokyo, where you will eat flying fish soup and remember the importance of rules. I can do it, even without a call to the general. Is that clear?"

"Yes, sir," Sevchenko reluctantly responded and sat down at his computer sluggishly.

Seconds later the sergeant slammed the doors loudly as he left the tiny computer room with the upset crew. The atmosphere inside was oppressive due to the recent argument.

Sevchenko sat staring at his computer screen and thinking. He slowly closed his eyes as if remembering a pain. He placed his elbows on the table and grabbed his head with his hands. Meanwhile, the other crew members gradually resumed their work. Then Sevchenko dropped back in his chair, reaching for his cigarettes. "Who wants to have a smoke break?" He looked around at the crew. Some were too busy working, but one man agreed and stood up to take the cigarette Sevchenko held out in offering. "Let's go outside."

Both men left the room while the rest continued working, vigorously tapping on keyboards. Coming aboveground, they walked to the smoking area. Sevchenko lit his cigarette and sat down. He took a few drags with his head pointed downward. Silence lasted among them for a minute as they contemplated the recent argument. The weather was still hot, almost unbearable. The sun was bright, although it was late afternoon.

"What do you think, Michael?" the engineer's colleague asked.

"I don't know. It's my greatest lifework. You know …" He blew out a thick billow of smoke.

"I can't believe that nut Bakerman has been given control over the system updates. He should focus on training his people rather than sticking his nose in our software."

"This is just unfair." Sevchenko angrily dropped his half-burnt cigarette in the nearby bucket. "I really fear for my ass if I violate his rules about upgrades. Bakerman will kick me to Tokyo without blinking an eye. That's for sure."

"Yeah, I don't doubt that."

"Last time when I explained these upgrades to the general, he agreed in some ways." Sevchenko spat in the bucket and said with contempt, "But Bakerman has the fucking final say."

"I can't imagine what would happen if you urged the general to install the ultimate upgrade."

Sevchenko's face turned thoughtful. "Well ... I wouldn't do that. Whether we like it or not, we must do these updates step by step. The ultimate upgrade would be too risky to install while skipping the existing updates." He pulled his hands over his tired face and said, "Let's wrap it up. Soon the basement must be closed."

With a grave look, his colleague held him by the arm. He said in a subdued voice while looking around, "Michael, you should stop contacting that Chinese girl. You could put this project under serious scrutiny."

"She doesn't know anything about this project. I worked on different things with her a long time ago, before the exoskeletons were even conceived." Something had shifted in Michael's mind. He added, "I like her, and we're planning to meet soon."

"Just keep it off of the computers in the basement." The colleague seemed worried. "Michael, this is the last thing you need. Project XS's main objective is to intervene in the nuclear weapon development in China. And you keep in touch with this Chinese girl?" The colleague shook his head, sensing difficulties. "You are walking on thin ice, Michael."

Michael straightened up in confidence and said, "I haven't sent her any messages recently. So it should be fine. Nevertheless, I didn't mention any details about this project in my emails whatsoever." Michael tried to reassure his anxious friend, who seemed skeptical. After gazing at the afternoon sun for a moment, both engineers walked back to the basement.

Meanwhile in the barracks, the air conditioner was on full speed. The sun had heated up the whole building; now it was like a greenhouse inside, despite the chilling air-conditioning. Matt, Jenkins, and Kelly were studying their newly received manuals in their beds. The twins and Sean Price were outside, either in the food court or hanging around somewhere. Jenkins put her manual on the cupboard next to her bed and stood up. She felt uncomfortable inside and made her way outside for a walk. Immediately, Kelly's attention was drawn by that; he held his book in front of him and turned a curious eye toward her. He felt an instant urge to follow her. Energetically passing his fingers through his blond hair, he got up. He noticed then that Matt had put away the manual and switched to a new book. He seemed to be meditating while reading. Kelly frowned, curiously peeking over in order to see the book. It was the Bible. Passing Matt's bed, he said, "Reading tales?"

"Sorry, what?" Matt said.

"That book you're holding—the fairy-tale collection." Kelly sarcastically pointed at the Bible. "Read the manual—that's your savior."

"Get lost, Kelly!" Matt snapped and lay down, resting his feet on the edge of the bed.

"All right, all right," Kelly said and proceeded toward the exit. As he got outside, he looked for Jenkins. *Where's she gone?* he eagerly wondered. Surveying all over, he suddenly noticed her leaving through the gates. He picked up his pace and hurried after her.

Jenkins walked along the uneven path outside the base. A multitude of green plants swayed in the mild breeze on either side of the trail, and the lava rocks cracked under her feet, creating quirky sounds. The bushes lining the path were shorter than the average human. Jenkins plucked some flowers and smelled them. She suddenly froze because she heard someone running behind her.

"Hey, Jenkins!" Kelly called.

She recognized Kelly's voice, and her face shifted from calm to annoyance. "What the hell do you want? Why do you follow me?" she asked. Jenkins wanted some time for herself; instead she'd have to put up with this douchebag.

As he got close, he said, "Do you mind? You know, it's kinda boring in the barracks." He kept a safe distance; it looked like she was going to punch him. However, she cooled down.

"Try not to piss me off in the first ten seconds," she said with a warning look, one eyebrow raised.

"Chill. I'm not going to get on your nerves."

"Good start then." She resumed her walk and continued enjoying the sunny afternoon. Kelly started walking as well, slowly reducing the gap between them without her noticing.

"Have you thought about how we're going to be on this island for some time? We should hang out together more to get to know each other better," Kelly calmly said, smiling.

"What if I don't want to know you?" Jenkins turned her head to look at him. Kelly's eyes were half-shut because of the bright sun reflecting off his face.

"I like you. You're like an unpolished diamond with sharp edges. That is so cool. And it's like your body is made of pure steel while keeping and highlighting your woman's sophisticated form." Kelly was flirting and smiled wider. "That time when you smiled, my heart pumped such excessive amounts of blood it was like a small power station."

Both stopped and looked at each other as if something strange had just happened. Jenkins felt dazed for a moment, and her face relaxed a little. She said, "Face, you have a girl in Boston, as you mentioned earlier in the food court. Don't you think you should have saved those compliments for her?" She started walking again.

"C'mon, give me a break, Jenkins. She is probably spending some stormy nights with other men." He felt disappointed. "I picked her up in a nightclub, which is her second home, if not the first. And yeah," he sighed, "she looks like a birthday cake, and everyone wants a piece of her."

"That's your problem, then."

"Hey, Jenkins, or should I say Kayla? Do you have anyone?" he asked with interest.

"No, I don't have anyone."

"You are awesome. What's your preference?"

"Both," she replied shortly.

"Both?" He was confused. "What do you mean by that?" Kelly was intrigued and was excited that he had established some conversation with her.

"Both men and women," she answered and turned to him. She held his eyes a moment, then slowly shifted her gaze to his shoulders. She gave his arm a quick, sharp nudge. Eventually she relaxed and smiled.

"Ouch!" Kelly rubbed his arm. "So you're bisexual. Sounds exciting. I like that." He showed his delight.

Jenkins came close to Kelly and said in a confident manner, "When it comes to women, I dominate. I apply the same principle to men."

She was so close that Kelly could feel the sexual energy flowing over her, yet he tried to be careful. "You are turning me on, Kayla." He was feeling horny and couldn't stop himself from flirting with her, despite her unpredictable reactions, which could happen anytime. Nevertheless, he dared to say, "I want you to dominate me."

She regarded him with bright-eyed perspicacity but made no sound.

They had come to a place where the trees were taller with bushy leaves and more grass. The trees cast shadows on the ground, which was even with long grass. The base was about one mile away. There was nobody around except them. She looked around, checking to make sure nobody was present. "C'mon, Face. If you get me down, we will play the game." Jenkins took a battle stance, as if preparing for a close-contact fight. She dropped her braid behind her back with a swift shake of her head. Kelly immediately got excited and walked around slowly, assessing her body language from the bottom to the top.

"I must say, I don't hit women," he said, "but I see you're going to hit me anyway."

"Don't be soft." She smiled with a mixture of thrill and wariness.

"I accept your challenge!"

"Show me, tiger. What you got."

Both took attacking poses and circled each other carefully, waiting for a good moment to attack. Kelly combed his hair backward with his fingers and prepared to attack. He suddenly ran toward her, trying to grab her by her slim waist. Before making a counterattack, Jenkins jumped aside. Then she grabbed Kelly's arm, twisted it around, and kicked him away. "Save your charm, Face! You won't win that easy." She chuckled confidently.

A little dazed and surprised by her self-defense skills, Kelly stood up and changed his approach. "All right, I'll get you down." He gave her a crooked smile. Then he eagerly stepped toward her again. *I've underestimated that girl,* Kelly thought.

Holding his hands close to his upper body, he jumped on her. In a matter of seconds, Jenkins punched at him, trying to reach his solar plexus, which was a weak spot. Kelly quickly reacted, grabbed her punching arm, twisted it behind her, and placed himself close behind her back. For the moment she couldn't move. However, with some quick techniques, she managed to knock him off his balance. She almost freed herself, but Kelly grabbed her tighter. Both fell to the ground, with Kelly on top with a winning grin. Suddenly, he screamed as she twisted his loose wrist, briskly shifting their body positions. Now she was on top of him.

"You lost the game, Jack Kelly," she said calmly while intently watching his surprised light-blue eyes.

"Give me another try," he said, looking at her with lust.

There was a moment of silence. Their bodies pulsed at the same rhythm. Jenkins slowly pulled her hand from Kelly's shoulder to his face while bringing her lips closer to his. At the same time, Kelly slid his free hand over her round butt and slowly sneaked it underneath her tight black top. Unexpectedly, Kelly moaned because of pain. She had grabbed his groin hard and clenched it even harder.

"I told you that I dominate regardless," she said confidently, feeling her absolute dominance.

"Ugh, I just remembered your nickname, Crack," he responded hoarsely, trying to withstand the pain. However, he enjoyed that she was dominating him. He enjoyed the unusual sexual tension.

Suddenly, something stopped them from enjoying each other. "Someone is coming!" Jenkins exclaimed and got up. Behind the trees a human shadow was cast on the ground, slowly growing closer. Kelly immediately got frustrated and remained lying on the ground.

"Who's there?" he asked with bitterness.

She kept tracking the approaching figure until it was revealed to be Sean Price. He was on his own as always. It just so happened that he was strolling along the quiet place where they had been wrestling. Price didn't feel bothered even though he noticed them. He just kept walking with his regular indifferent grimace.

"That's Price," Jenkins said and put her appearance in order. Obviously, she wasn't in the mood to play around with Kelly anymore, which infuriated him.

"That fucking moron!" he said loudly with great contempt. Shortly his headache returned with a sharp pain. "Argh!" He grabbed his head.

"I'm going back to the barracks to study the exoskeleton manual," she said to him while arranging her black top.

Kelly was outraged and got up to see where Price had gone. He was not going to settle down until he had dealt with Price. He noticed Price walking on the dusty path and quickly chased after him. Soon Kelly was close enough to draw Price's attention. "Hey, Price!" he shouted.

Price said nothing but did turn his head around to see who was calling. As soon he recognized Kelly, he ignored him and kept walking.

"Hey, Price! What's your problem? Answer me," Kelly demanded angrily, coming very close. Abruptly he grabbed Price's wide shoulder from behind and tried to turn him around by force. Price reacted rapidly. He twisted Kelly's wrist and gave him a strong punch to the chest, pushing him a couple of steps backward. Kelly inhaled deeply at the sudden impact and scolded, "You fucking mute!"

Price looked at him calmly with his regular emotionless expression. The tension was rising. Kelly prepared himself for a fight, clenching his fists, guarding his face, and taking a battle stance. Suddenly, he attacked Price, throwing fists vigorously. None of the punches reached Price. During the hustle, dust from the ground had been whacked up in the air. Price masterfully and fluidly avoided each executed punch. Again he grabbed Kelly's wrist. He broke to the side, twisted, and hit Kelly's upper body with his elbow. This time the impact was harder and dropped Kelly to the ground.

Despite the counterattack, Kelly persistently continued the fight. His anger was growing. When Price wasn't looking, Kelly scraped a handful of dirt from the ground. He would fight ugly now. Getting up on his feet again, he carefully hid his fist with dirt in it. Finding an advantageous moment, Kelly threw the dirt in Price's eyes. His move was successful and blinded Price, who grabbed his face with both hands. Kelly, without hesitation, executed a spinning side kick to Price's chest. The blow dropped the blinded Price to the ground. He was temporarily abashed and quickly got up to a squatting stance. Covering his face with both arms, he spit and coughed.

"Argh," Price groaned, breathing heavily. He sensed that the fight was not over and reached for his knife, which was wrapped around his leg. Holding the knife strongly, he placed it in front of him and circled defensively, still blind. The blade was sharp, and the sun reflected off its edge.

"C'mon, Price! You're craving some blood. I can sense that. C'mon!" Kelly challenged, fixedly watching Price's slow circling with the knife. It had come to a point where they were both about to fight nasty.

In the near distance a loud voice shouted, "Cut it out!" It was Jenkins, who was enraged to see them both fighting like dogs. She ran to them and immediately jumped in front of Kelly with a wrathful face. Pushing him hard in the chest, she yelled, "Have you lost your mind?" Then she turned to Price, who was blindly waiting for a possible attack, still in a ducked position, knife held at an angle. "Hey, Price! It's over," she said, trying to calm him down.

Price stayed in his defensive position for a while longer, for protection's sake. Feeling that nobody was going to attack him, he swiftly spun his knife around and neatly put it back into its holder. He was still rubbing dirt out of his face and spitting a lot. Kelly had managed to throw the dirt right into his eyes, causing such torture.

"Price, do you need help?" Jenkins showed her concern.

"I'll be good," he answered, twitching.

"Are you sure?"

"Just leave me alone, and we'll all benefit," he said calmly and loudly. He stretched his body and opened his red eyes, still blinking a lot with tears.

Kelly stared at him, not feeling any pity. He walked off to the barracks while whacking the dust from his clothes and twisting his shoulder around to ease the discomfort.

Jenkins stood nearby Price for some time, just in case he needed something. As he was able to see better, he gave her a look that said, *Get lost. I'm fine.* Jenkins felt confused about what to do. She slowly walked backward a few steps and then turned around and ran off after the bully who had caused this trouble.

"Why the fuck did you have to challenge him?" Jenkins asked, pulling Kelly by his hand to make him confront her.

"Actually, he started it. He punched me first," Kelly said carelessly. "You know, whatever."

"Stop being an asshole! That could be a good start for you." Jenkins was still heated. "We are a squad, not high school bullies who crave attention."

He didn't care to listen and continued to walk. He felt that he'd done the right thing.

In a short moment, Kelly changed his approach. "It was my headache," he explained. "I forgot to take my painkillers, and doing that can cause sudden outbursts of anger."

"But Price was doing nothing to you."

"I know…but he did trigger the anger, though."

"You are barely holding it together," Jenkins said.

"I'm addicted to this shit." Kelly looked at her like he felt sick and continued, "It all started with steroids, and then later I got mixed up with these strong painkillers. I wish I hadn't put so much into my body." His voice took on a tone of repentance.

She watched him incredulously for a while before noticing his occasional physical contractions, which indicated his body's dependence on the drugs. However, she decided to keep silent. She stopped and looked backward. Price had stayed in the spot of the fight, but he seemed to be doing better. The sun shone on the horizon, but dusk was still a long way off. Nonetheless, she walked back to the barracks with Kelly, who had caused this incident. They both kept a short distance from each other and said nothing.

Day 3

On the third day heavy morning rain awakened everyone. Waterdrops hit hard against the roof, making tremendous noise. It was early, just before seven. Today was going to be their first time training with the exoskeleton machines. It was more than one hour when Jenkins lied in the bed with her eyes open; she couldn't sleep anymore. She was awakened by the rain showers, she felt grumpy. Tossing in her bed from one side to another, she looked to see if anyone else was awake. "This is not cool," she said, pulling herself up to a seated position. She rubbed her face and stood up by her bed. Before going to the bathroom, she glanced at the schedule for the daily routine. After that, Jenkins walked to the bathroom in her underwear.

"Nice ass," a husky voice said. Of course that was Kelly, who kept his eyes on her.

"Stop jerking off to me," she said without looking at him and went inside the bathroom.

One hour later, everyone was up and ready to meet Sergeant Bakerman. The black cat peeked his curious whiskers out from the dark corridor to the sergeant's office.

Shortly after, the sound of boots echoed in the corridor, which meant one thing—the sergeant was on his way. Sergeant Bakerman lifted the cat up with his strong hands and numerous scars.

"Morning, Mr. Charcoal," the sergeant said softly while looking out a window. "Today it's raining. You must stay home until the rain stops. Can you promise me that?" He looked at the cat's indifferent face and then walked back to his office. The squad had already lined up, even though they hadn't been ordered to yet.

Just a moment later, the sergeant returned to the main hall with his typical look of contempt, his coat folded in his hands. He was chewing something as usual. Glancing over each squad member, he said, "Ready, squad! Suit up in wet suits; otherwise you will get soaked like a sponge in the fast food kitchen." The sergeant pointed at their beds, where elastic one-piece suits were hung. "Let's go to the basement," he commanded and put his raincoat on.

Inside the basement seven exoskeleton machines had already been pulled out of the walls. A misty cloud enveloped the machines, half obscuring them. It was cold inside, and Sevchenko and the engineer crew were already busy working. Laptops were connected by cable to the exoskeleton machines. As soon as the squad came down, the engineers unplugged their laptops from the machines.

Sergeant Bakerman walked to Sevchenko with his arms crossed behind his back and asked, "Are they ready?"

"Yes, they are. I have checked everything. Batteries are full, software works perfectly, and ... yeah, you can use them." Sevchenko was talking fast, sometimes anxiously fast, as if he was worried he had missed something. He constantly was checking the data operations on his laptop.

"Perfect," the sergeant declared and turned to the squad. "I will show you how to get in," he said while turning his back to the enormous machines. "It's quite simple. Just do as I show you." Then he put his foot on an exoskeleton's knee, climbed up, and dropped himself inside, filling the void. Sergeant Bakerman and machine became as one unit. Slowly the straps and light material molded, adjusting to his legs. Then he put his big arms inside the mechanical arms. Nobody could see what was happening inside the arms.

The sergeant explained, "You don't see what's happening, but you feel it. There are built-in rings inside the machines' arms. Don't be afraid. They will gently adjust to your arms and fingers. These are nerve indicators, which will copy your moves." Once the arm adjustments were complete, the shoulder pads lowered down from behind and neatly adjusted to his body. Sergeant Bakerman was silent briefly, paying attention to how the machine felt. "Feels good," he said and raised his mechanical arms. Then he extended one arm and demonstrated the fingers' immaculate movement. The fingers swiftly ran back and forth in perfect harmony. The sound was strange, like a thousand bees had gone mad inside their hive.

The squad observed the machine with great awe and couldn't wait to get inside their own machines. The sergeant's head wasn't completely guarded. However, the machine had pads on each side of his head that covered his face partially. On both shoulders two bulging cameras activated. They looked like octopus eyes. *This is a bit daunting,* Matt thought. Then a transparent face shield slid into place, covering the top half of the sergeant's face. It was the main instrument panel and also showed important data.

"Squad, back off," the sergeant said loudly. He took a few steps forward in demonstration. The machine's movement was impressive. The machine was like a giant copy of a human being that remained graceful and accurate. Sergeant Bakerman stood in the middle of the room and browsed through the machine's menu. Using finger movements, he chose "Eject" on the screen. Suddenly the machine gradually released all the body guards and molds. It bent down, and the sergeant stepped outside the suit. "Now you will do the same," he commanded the squad. The machine stayed frozen but kept buzzing softly.

All the squad members were excited but nervous, all at once. Each machine, open in the front, looked like it could eat a person. Everyone stood in front of a machine, ready to repeat the steps the sergeant had shown them. Without any hesitation, the twin brothers were the first ones to get inside their machines, shortly followed by the others.

Sevchenko walked to one of the Javier brothers and questioned him numerous times about options found in the manual. Then he repeated the process with each squad member. As soon as Sevchenko finished with them, he stepped back and said, shivering a little, "Please look after these exoskeletons. They are precious things."

It was obvious that these machines meant everything to the engineer. He kept a close eye on the machines the squad was using. Of course, Sevchenko and his crew had contributed the most to these machines, constantly making improvements and fixing software glitches. No matter how bizarre it was, though, Sergeant Bakerman was more in charge than the engineers. That was Sevchenko's greatest concern. The latest upgrade he'd developed included a return-to-base command that would save the machines in case of host death and would also allow the machines to bring back injured hosts. Nevertheless, soon the general would give final consent and override the sergeant, allowing Sevchenko to set up his most wanted upgrade.

For some time, the engineer anxiously ran to each machine, making sure that everyone was looked after. The machines impressively stood tall like ancient Greek god statues.

"All right, squad! We are taking a walk," the sergeant said, jumping inside his exoskeleton. "At my command, follow me." The squad members were cautiously adapting to the new machines. They were making good progress.

Matt caught Jenkins's eye and encouraged her to take a few steps. He demonstrated how easy it was to walk. However, she hesitated and played with the arms first, just to feel out the machine. Meanwhile, the rest of the squad was already standing behind the sergeant and waiting for his command. It was still raining heavily with huge waterdrops, almost like hail. The wide entrance to the basement was opened.

"Let's go!" Sergeant Bakerman ordered loudly. Before going outside, Kelly noticed that the machines had more cameras on the back. The bulging domes looked alive, constantly scanning and spinning vigorously. Kelly felt strange, like someone was staring at him through these small, daunting eyes. "Drop the shield in front of your face!" the sergeant commanded. He made his way aboveground into the heavy rain. Everyone followed shortly. Sevchenko watched them leave, feeling impressed but also concerned.

While the sergeant diligently explained the objectives, Matt wondered about the instrument panel, which was displayed in front of his face. It was doing calculations of distance, showing the temperature, monitoring his heartbeat, and so much more. He was blown away by this unique machine. It gave him an instant feeling of great power and excitement.

"We will run up that mountain. That's our goal." The sergeant pointed at the island's only mountain, which could hardly be seen because of the rain. The guards at the entrance, standing in the rain, opened the main gates. "Don't be afraid to fall. The machines are programmed to recognize imbalance and will keep you up and running even if you stumble accidentally." The sergeant stood at the main gates and turned around. Without any further instructions he picked up the pace and was off to the mountain. Not worrying long, the Javier twins followed after him with amazement. They made the movements look easy, and the rest of squad joined them.

Matt's first impressions of running were striking. It felt like he was softly floating despite the uneven uphill trek. The machine worked extremely quickly, calculating each step. A couple of times, he deliberately provoked a fall to the side. The system recognized the loss of balance instantly and put the machine back on track. "Oh my goodness! This is so cool!" Matt exclaimed in excitement. He turned his attention to the others and saw them feeling the same. Some squad members were making impressive leaps, which encouraged him to do the same. As he executed the first leaps, he was blown away again. "This is just getting better." He was amazed. Even though the rain was not losing any of its power, it was no obstacle to the machines, which adapted to the circumstances. In just a short time they had gone halfway up the mountain with little effort, despite the weather and tough uphill terrain. *These machines are a remarkable invention,* Matt thought.

Soon they reached the crater at the top of the rocky mountain. Sergeant Bakerman stood on the edge of the crater in front of the squad. He gave further instructions. "We are going to descend down into the crater. As soon as we reach the bottom, we will practice using the grappling hooks. Is everyone clear?" The squad responded in the affirmative simultaneously. The sergeant confidently approached the edge. Without any hesitation, he slid off and disappeared from the squad's sight, leaving with squeaking sounds.

The Javier brothers were the first to approach the edge. They stood and looked at each other, silently understanding that they would go down at the same time, even though they didn't know how. As they slid off the edge, their machines automatically pushed a small curved spike out of the back of each foot. The spikes penetrated into the ground, slowing the steep descent. At the same time, the machines maintained a good angle for balance. The squeaking sound echoed in the crater as they slid down.

"This is so cool, Brother!" Alejandro exclaimed with amazement. They both successfully reached the bottom.

Now it was the others' turn. Sergeant Bakerman stood waiting for everyone to descend. Soon the remaining squad members who had hesitated at the top started their wacky slides into the crater, their spikes leaving long streaks in the rock. As all of them came down, the sergeant ordered them to line up for the next task.

"Look at that edge." He pointed up to the lip of the crater. "We are going to get up there without climbing or walking." He stepped in front of the others and looked at the twin brothers. "Javier number one, come over," he ordered. Antonio obeyed. The sergeant made him turn around and pointed at two long shafts on the exoskeleton's back. "These are the grappling hooks. Each machine has two of them. It is not hard to use them." He stopped for a moment like he had forgotten something. Then he observed the crater's edge. After a few seconds' silence, he continued, "Remember one thing: one hook is for getting you to the place you want, and the other hook is for returning back." He tapped Antonio on the shoulder, signaling for him to go back to the squad. "Soon, the time will come for us to conduct a real mission with these machines. The exact location of the mission is unknown currently, but it is in China somewhere. Our main objective is to dismantle their nuclear weapon facilities, preventing further development. As far as I'm aware, the facilities are hidden in a tough environment that includes hills, rifts, and similar types of obstacles. The exact position is not clear yet, but our army drones are constantly surveying the place. Soon we will receive an exact location. So we must be ready, which means mastering these machines to the fullest."

The sergeant continued, "To shoot a grappling hook, choose the appropriate mode on your face shield. Then bend down on one knee. The machine will provide stabilization against the recoil. Make sure that nobody is behind you." The sergeant demonstrated the steps as he explained. "Extend one arm toward the place you want to shoot the hook. The machine will lock the arm with the upper body, stabilizing the precise shot. You will see the distance and crosshairs on your face shield. Take aim at a solid surface, and the target will lock as soon as the system approves the chosen location. Then you can shoot anytime." As he'd explained how to use the grappling hooks, the rain had eased. Now he stood up and looked at the group for someone to demonstrate. "Javier number two, come over."

"Yes, sir!" Alejandro said, moving over by the sergeant.

"Repeat the process I just told you."

"Yes, sir!" Alejandro obediently took the shooting stance as instructed. He was on one knee with his arm extended and locked with the machine's upper body.

"Good," the sergeant said firmly. "Do you see the target?"

Alejandro aimed the crosshairs on the upper edge of the crater. "Yes, sir!" he replied.

"Shoot when the target is locked," the sergeant said and stepped back, making a safe spot. Alejandro hesitated to shoot because it was his first time. On his face display, the digital crosshairs turned green, indicating the target had been locked. There was a loud noise and a little recoil as he executed the shot. A sharp gad pierced rapidly in the ground behind him for support. At the same time the grappling hook with wire flew all the way to the crater's edge. It attached firmly into the wall, splitting smaller rock particles away. The exoskeleton's mechanism tightened the wire automatically. Nothing else happened for the moment.

Alejandro stayed in position and asked, "Sir, what should I do now?"

"You should see 'Activate trail' on your display. To complete this task you must confirm that option. When you reach the top of the crater, confirm 'Complete trail.'"

"Yes, sir." Using his index finger, Alejandro confirmed the message. Suddenly the mounted mechanism on his back pulled the wire between small rollers, and he was rapidly pulled up the wire with a loud buzzing noise. Alejandro felt scared as he was quickly carried toward the crater's solid wall. The distance number on his shield dropped rapidly as he approached the end. The machine automatically slowed to a complete stop right at the edge, leaving him hanging. He was confused. Alejandro looked down and gasped. He was so high up from the ground. "Complete trail," the machine alerted with a voice reminder, as Alejandro had missed the initial message on the screen. "Complete trail," it repeated.

"What's taking so long?" the sergeant asked in frustration, observing Alejandro from down below.

"Ooh, yes. I suppose I will do the same as I did with trailing here." Alejandro confirmed the message, and the wire abruptly released from the rollers. He instantly began to free-fall. Thanks to his instincts, he quickly grabbed the edge of the crater and pulled himself up. If he had hesitated, he would have fallen all the way down.

Sergeant Bakerman browsed his menu and found the radio communication option. He activated it. Everyone wearing the exoskeletons received a message on their face shields prompting them to accept the radio communication request. "Squad, accept the radio request!" the sergeant said loudly. Everyone now heard his angry voice from their speakers. "All right, Javier number one, you're next!" the sergeant commanded.

Antonio did the same thing and launched his grappling hook perfectly. He felt more confident and helped to encourage the rest to complete the task. One by one they executed the task. Matt Baker was the last to complete the task. The rain had just stopped completely; the air quality was so pure and refreshing up on the mountain. Matt inhaled and was ready to make his attempt. Before he bent down in preparation, a sharp twitching movement in the machine's arm disturbed him.

"Baker, what you waiting for?" the sergeant asked in irritation.

Matt looked at him with a puzzled face and tried to bend down on one knee. Before he could get down, a sharper twitch in the right arm tossed him backward. Suddenly, he got a warning message on his face shield: "Off grid … System malfunction. Off grid … System malfunction."

"Baker, what's going on?" the sergeant shouted, losing his patience.

"I don't know," Matt said anxiously while frantically browsing through the menu. An icy shiver ran down his neck. The warning message persisted. The right arm continued to twitch harder and more frequently. He began panicking and tried to walk. Unfortunately, the machine had seized up, and taking steps was getting very hard. He felt instantly claustrophobic and threatened, like he was experiencing a real-life nightmare where he couldn't run away from a predator.

Sergeant Bakerman realized that something serious had gone wrong. He urged Matt loudly, "C'mon, eject yourself!" He wanted to grab Matt and help him. However, the sergeant struggled while watching the machine's irregular arm movements.

"What a hell is going on down there?" Kelly wondered looking at Jenkins

"I don't know. It looks creepy."

"Why that brain damaged sarge isn't doing anything?"

"That brain damaged sarge can hear everything what you say, Kelly." Sergeant's voice interrupted through radio. Jenkins saw how sudden uneasiness covered Kelly's face. He lost his language, watching down in the crater where the sergeant turned around to see them on the top.

Suddenly, a beam of light flickered across Matt's eyelids from the shield. Countless messages chaotically appeared in front of him. The arm was twitching so hard that at any moment it could break Matt's arm. In the heat of stress, Matt desperately tried to get to the eject option. These circumstances scared the living daylights out of him. He managed to get the eject option on the screen a few different times, but warning messages kept covering it, making it difficult to actually select it. Luckily, Matt caught it at the right moment and confirmed ejection. Immediately, the machine stopped its daunting arm twitching, and the error messages disappeared. It very slowly released the trapped Matt from trouble. He desperately squeezed outside like he was fighting for his life. Once he got out of the suit, Matt was breathing heavily. Stepping away, he looked at the machine like it was a car press that destroyed humans instead of old junkers.

What an unexpected incident, the sergeant thought. He walked cautiously toward Matt's exoskeleton.

Meanwhile, the rest of the squad members were extremely bothered watching Matt's torture in the machine. They were baffled. What was going on down there? Suddenly, they heard the sergeant's voice through the radio: "Squad, come down immediately. Descend where it's the least steep. Over!"

This was the first time they'd heard the sergeant sound suspicious and uncertain.

Matt was still recovering from shock, which he was experiencing for the first time. Sergeant Bakerman browsed through his menu and ejected himself from his machine. Out of the exoskeleton, he took his own radio and called base immediately. There was a squeaking sound mixed with occasional unclear hissing, and then a man's voice said, "Yes, base listening. How can I help you? Over."

"This is Sergeant Bakerman. I need a recovery helicopter in the crater of the mountain. We've got a problem over here. Over."

"Roger that. The pilot has been informed. Over."

Sergeant Bakerman put his radio back in its holder and stared at the exoskeleton that had almost broken Mat's arm. His face was a mixture of puzzlement and suspicion. Then he turned his eyes to the squad, who were quickly sliding down the slope faster than before. Obviously, they were afraid that something similar could happen with them. "Are you all right, Baker?" the sergeant asked.

"Sir, yes. I'll be fine," Matt responded, now calm but still a little alarmed.

"We are going back to base. A helicopter will arrive soon." With his firm and dull response, the sergeant wasn't showing any empathy to Matt. However, he was getting mindful and became reluctant to figure out Matt's exoskeleton, leaving it like a standing ghost on the wet and muddy ground.

Soon the rest of the squad had made it downhill, covered with mud. As they got closer, they watched Matt to see how he was coping. Jenkins dared to ask, "Sir, can we free ourselves from these machines?" She was truly worried after seeing Matt struggle with his exoskeleton.

This time, the sergeant was reasonable. "Yes, you can do that," he answered.

The entire squad ejected themselves from the machines without hesitation. It felt like everybody was expecting the same thing that happened to Matt to happen to them when they least expected it. Sergeant Bakerman paced, thinking. He crossed his arms behind his back and stared at the overcast sky. It was apparent to the others that even their tough sergeant had grown cautious with the machines. His usual chewing slowed down as he tried to analyze the machine's malfunction.

Jenkins quickly moved over by Matt. "Hey, you're okay?" she asked, giving him a comforting nudge, breathing heavily.

"Yeah, thanks, Crack," he replied while staring at the machine with a dreadful feeling.

"What happened?"

"System malfunction. The machine ceased copying my moves. Instead, it was tossing my right arm backward. I couldn't even move," he explained quietly. "I was truly scared." His eyes were big and serious as he looked at her.

"So was I," Jenkins said softly, so the sergeant didn't hear. "I can see that he is bothered as much as we are." She observed the sergeant walking around holding the radio. Then she rubbed Matt's shoulders to cheer him up.

After some time, a whirring, hollow sound echoed in the distance as the approaching rescue helicopter made its way to the crater. The sergeant observed it intently. As the helicopter got close, it created a massive air blast. The sergeant ordered everyone to make the space clear. Once the helicopter had landed, the sergeant walked to the flying crew while holding his hat. The rotor noise was loud and oppressive. Sergeant Bakerman shouted, "We need to bring one defective exoskeleton back to base along with one squad member!" The pilot and another military person nodded. Sergeant Bakerman turned to the squad and pointed out the defective machine, which was too big to be carried inside the cabin.

"Hey, Sarge!" the pilot shouted, drawing his attention. "We'll have to use the winch. The exoskeleton won't fit inside."

"That's fine!" he responded. "C'mon, let's bring it back to base." Sergeant Bakerman attached the heavy winch hook to the defective machine and gestured to the pilot that it was secure.

"C'mon, Baker, go to the helicopter!" Sergeant Bakerman commanded.

Meanwhile, the rest of the squad looked at each other without any clue what was going to happen next. The helicopter's engine speed increased, creating a powerful air force. Jenkins turned her face away and half closed her eyes to prevent loose chips flying in. The helicopter rose about fifteen feet. Then the winch tightened and lifted the defective exoskeleton, which swung in the air. Inside the helicopter, Matt dropped into the seat, exhausted. He looked down at Jenkins, who stayed inside the crater with the rest of the men. The sergeant observed the leaving helicopter for some time until it disappeared beyond the crater's edge.

There was an awkward moment inside the crater as Sergeant Bakerman stood with the rest of the squad. All the functioning machines had been left open nearby. Everyone patiently waited for their next orders but secretly hoped for different maneuvers. The squad was worried. None of them wanted to get inside the machines again, but they sensed that they would have to help get the machines back to base, because the sergeant hadn't given any commands for the pilot to come back. The sergeant stared at them individually and pulled out his radio.

"Base, connect with the engineer Sevchenko. Over!" he said.

An answer quickly came back over the radio. "Sir, give me a minute. Over."

The sergeant inhaled, exhaled, and spat out his chewing tobacco. He wanted to check with the engineers what the malfunction possibility was for the remaining machines. Suddenly the radio buzzed.

"This is Michael Sevchenko. How can I help you?" the engineer asked hoarsely over the radio.

Firmly holding the radio, the sergeant said, "One of the exoskeletons experienced a system error. It ceased working properly and almost injured one of my men." He then turned his eyes to the remaining machines. "The rest of the exoskeletons appear to be fine. I need your assistance. The squad and I will bring them back to base like we came over here." The squad's worries were clearly visible on their faces. The sergeant continued, "Can you and your crew connect to the machines remotely?"

"Yes, that's possible," Sevchenko said.

"That's good," the sergeant said. He added more gravely, "I need you to make sure to do one thing. If any machine detects a malfunction or error, can you disable all functions remotely?"

Sevchenko hesitated. After a few seconds he said, "I can disable all factory settings, which will cause a complete system shutdown. I'm reluctant to do that, though, because my team will have to start from scratch to restore the whole system."

The sergeant raised his voice. "You must be ready to do that because our lives depend on it. Is that clear?" He stressed his last words.

"Yes, sir," Sevchenko answered grudgingly.

The conversation was over. The squad had heard everything. Evidently they had no choice but to obey.

"Squad! Get back inside the machines now! We are going back to base," Sergeant Bakerman commanded and watched them. He himself was placed to be last to get back in an exoskeleton. The squad hesitated. The sergeant repeated furiously, "Get inside! What are you staring at?"

Suddenly, Price calmly walked to his machine and stepped inside. The others got encouraged and followed, except Jenkins. She was scared and stood waiting like facing a death sentence. It was a tense moment. The sergeant was pissed at her complete disregard of his command. Jenkins had turned her back to Bakerman, who made his way to her. She prepared herself for a beating while biting her lower lip. Strong hands gripped her shoulder and rapidly shifted her body around. Glaring down at her, the sergeant yelled, "This is your last chance, Jenkins! Don't make me put you inside with force."

She felt paralyzed for a few seconds, but somehow she collected herself and went back to her machine. *What's the difference whether the sergeant kills me or this creature?* she thought. With a careless facial expression, she got inside the machine. "Good," the sergeant said. It was a cheeky move on his part. Apparently, he wanted to see if something would happen with his squad before getting in his own machine. After waiting a short moment, the sergeant got inside his exoskeleton. "Squad, back to base!" he ordered through the radio.

They used the grappling hooks again to get back up on the crater's edge. This time they moved faster and more confidently despite the recent incident. Unsurprisingly, everyone ran faster than before, fearing an unexpected system malfunction. Even the sergeant seemed nervous and advanced far ahead of them. Although the machines were running smoothly, they kept increasing their speed, as if they were running away from a rolling boulder. Jenkins felt so uncomfortable and frightened in the machine that she even managed to overtake the sergeant.

In less than ten minutes, the sergeant and Jenkins arrived at the base. Jenkins's heart was pounding; her face shield showed a high heart rate, almost critical. The guards opened the gates wide and greeted Jenkins and the sergeant with a hand gesture.

Meanwhile, inside the base, the helicopter's engine slowed, its rotor blades still spinning. It had arrived quite some time before the squad reached the base. A special platform on wheels carried the defective exoskeleton back to the basement. Matt patiently waited nearby with some other military personnel. He had calmed himself down by this point.

The rest of the squad gathered at the main gates. "Let's go to the basement," the sergeant said, his voice echoing through each machine's speakers. He led them down to the cold underground facility where Sevchenko and his crew were waiting. The engineers were wearing warm jackets made of water-resistant material and looking surprised. Some of them had gathered around the defective exoskeleton, which sat in the middle of the room on the portable platform.

"Squad, return your exoskeletons to their designated areas," the sergeant commanded. He moved over to his exoskeleton's storage section and ejected himself. The others did the same, feeling anxious. It was apparent how relieved they all felt to get out of the machines, except for Sean Price, who felt quite comfortable using the exoskeleton and calmly stepped out of it.

"Squad, dismissed!" the sergeant commanded. He waited for the squad to leave the basement. Then he turned to Sevchenko, who looked rather upset, his long hair disheveled. His edgy face looked as if someone had killed his beloved dog. "What do you think? What might be the problem?" the sergeant asked while looking at the defective machine.

"I suppose it could be related to an old upgrade that has a glitch," Sevchenko explained, scratching his head. "But I'm not entirely sure. I must connect to the machine with a computer and run some diagnostics."

"Okay, Sevchenko. Do your job and report to me when you have fixed the problem," the sergeant said. He put his foot on the platform, leaning closer to the machine. As he gazed at the exoskeleton with a skeptical eye, he added, "And one more thing ... we're gonna carry on training tomorrow. Make sure that failure won't occur again."

"Yes, sir."

The sergeant lingered inside the basement for a while, walking around to check each exoskeleton by the wall sections. In the meantime, one of the engineers brought over laptops and wires from the small room. The engineers connected to the defective machine and got busy tackling the issue. Just a moment later, the sergeant left. The crew watched him leave.

"Hey, let's take a smoke break," Sevchenko said to his colleague Rob.

"Okay." The colleague stood up from the platform and joined him.

Outside in the smoking area, Sevchenko checked to make sure nobody was around and lit a cigarette. He'd brought his hot coffee mug with him and set it down next to him. Then he looked at his colleague with a facial expression of discovery.

"What's on your mind, Michael?"

As he blew out some smoke, Sevchenko said, "The system needs the next upgrade. That malfunction probably happened because of obsolete software. We simply haven't paid any attention to improving glitches of old software." He took a sip of his coffee and continued, "Sooner or later, a malfunction might happen with the rest of the exoskeletons. It just doesn't make sense to improve old software. It's a waste of time, especially knowing that the new upgrade will help to increase the machines' capacity forty percent if not more."

His colleague grew thoughtful and reluctant. "I don't know, Michael. It's just a huge risk. You know that the general hasn't given consent completely."

"We can hide it." Sevchenko nodded, knowing the solution.

"How?"

"I can remotely deactivate some settings on the system without the others knowing and set up the new upgrade." Michael shook the ashes off his cigarette and turned closer to his fellow engineer. "Don't you remember Bakerman asking me to disable the factory settings because he was worried about possible malfunction?" He looked his colleague in the eye and waited.

"And this is the good loophole ..." the colleague said, as if reading Sevchenko's mind.

"Exactly!" Michael extinguished the last half of his cigarette, dropped it in the bucket, and added with burning determination, "Holy sprockets! This is my project, probably the greatest project of my life. None of those deranged war dogs have contributed anything to these machines. These are our toys. I would rather die trying to get the machines to their full potential than let them restrict my greatest development."

"Well, you are right! But you're playing with fire, you know." The colleague still had doubts, but now he was leaning more on Sevchenko's side. He looked around and felt encouraged to participate. "Whatever, let's use this loophole!" he eventually agreed.

Both Javier brothers lingered around the base feeling bored. They had taken off their wet suits, which were partially covered with mud.

"Hey, Antonio," Alejandro called while watching some guys playing paintball. "Let's have some fun and play paintball."

"I don't know."

"C'mon, we have missed most of the excitement because of the exoskeleton breakdown." Alejandro was intrigued and urged his brother, pointing his head at the pitch where the guys were playing.

Antonio sighed and gave a little grin, saying, "Let's kick their asses, then."

"Yeah!" Alejandro cheered up and put his hand around his brother's neck. As they went closer to the pitch, he called to a nearby man, "Hey, we want to join the game!"

"We're in the middle of the game," the man said in frustration, taking off his mask. Assessing the situation, he said, "All right, follow me." He jumped over the fence and took the twin brothers to the armory, where the paintball equipment was kept.

As soon as the brothers joined, they spent the paintball game showing off with extreme moves, like intense jumps and flips. They didn't care to join a team but had fun shooting at everyone. It was obvious that the other players were confused and a bit annoyed by their excessive energy and rebellious approach. The twins totally ruined the game, which made the others leave the playing pitch soon after the twins joined. Now the brothers were left on their own shooting at each other like crazy. As soon as all the colored bullets ran out, they took off their masks and went by some stacked pallets. They laughed at each other, seeing how each of them was colored from the bottom to the top.

"We spoiled the game," Alejandro said, looking at the men who had gone to the armory.

"At least we kicked their asses," Antonio chuckled and sat down by the pallets, tossing his gun by his side.

"This is our game on this island, right, Brother?" Alejandro said while aiming his gun at the armory.

"Yeah, like it is everywhere we go."

"Remember Jessica, who we fooled around with?" Alejandro's eyes glowed with nostalgia.

"That was my girl!" Antonio specified. "Well … she could have become my girl if you hadn't screwed everything up. You slept with her first before I even managed to kiss her." Antonio turned to him with judgmental eyes. "You took advantage of our identical appearance."

"Still angry about that? It was ages ago." Alejandro chuckled.

"Ahh, not really," Antonio said. "Anyway, she was a bitch and gold digger. I know my weakness—I fall in love quickly with any girl who smiles at me."

"And you forgot to mention that she was dumb too. At that time I had a mustache, and you didn't." Alejandro burst out in laughter. "So I did you a favor."

"Sort of," Antonio sighed, scratching his knee. "This can't last forever, Brother. We should learn how to split up and live our lives independently. We've been together since you first dropped naked on the tiles."

Alejandro laughed, his body shaking. As he calmed down, he said, "I guess you're right, Brother. I don't know what else to do apart from the military, but you …" Alejandro looked gravely into his brother's eyes. "You have a vivid imagination; you should pursue your creative side to its fullest, not do this military thing. This is not you, Antonio."

"Do you think I'm that good at poems?" Antonio looked at the ground, feeling unsure.

"Give me a break! You at least have something—passion," Alejandro said. "Me? I don't know. Perhaps I will breed longhorns for sale."

"Don't forget to start a cactus-juice business like our nuts instructor suggested on the first day." Antonio began to grin and added, "Who knows? Maybe it would turn out to be lucrative."

Alejandro laughed and got up, saying, "All right, let's go get a bite, Brother."

Later, in the food court, Matt and Jenkins looked for a bite to eat. This time the food court was busy. A lot of military personnel were chatting and hassling each other. The queue had built up, and Matt and Jenkins were forced to wait to get to the trays. Meanwhile, Jenkins surveyed around, looking for someone. To her surprise, she noticed some more women in military uniforms. Apparently, she was not the only one, as she'd initially thought. Matt kept silent; he was not in his usual mood. Evidently, the incident in the crater had made him ponder the project. "Are you all right?" Jenkins asked in a subdued voice while looking around.

"Well … yeah." It wasn't a convincing answer. Matt was clearly rather upset.

Leaning her head backward, Jenkins whispered, "Let's talk about it at the table."

After the long queue and hassle by the bar, they found a table where they could discuss more without anyone hearing. Jenkins sat opposite him and quickly glanced around. Slowly forking his food, Matt began, "Today, I felt really bizarre and feared for my life. You know, Crack, we had a lot of tough and ugly missions in New York, but I've never felt how I felt up there in the crater." He stopped and hesitated to eat. "This is no good. We're gambling with our freedom and lives with these machines."

Jenkins looked at him. She almost felt the same, even though she hadn't experienced what Matt had. She hadn't heard him talk like this before.

Matt continued, "It might be the small malfunction, but in that moment I had the strongest desire to escape that creature. I felt like it had become conscious and was trying to eat me alive. I had no power over the system."

"Yeah, I completely get you, Matt," she sympathized. "I think the entire squad was worried that the same would happen with them. It was so hard for me to get back inside the machine, but I had to. Otherwise that nut Bakerman would have brutally forced me to." She forked her food around.

Matt obviously had lost his appetite; his mind was still busy mulling over recent happenings. *Why did I come here?* he questioned himself again. Then he looked at Jenkins, who at least was enjoying her meal with occasional looks at him. They were so close as partners. He couldn't imagine himself without Jenkins on this island. Remembering his wife and daughter, he said bleakly, "Maybe I am screwed like you said before, Crack." He tried to eat something.

"We both are screwed," she said gravely, feeling doomed. "Otherwise we wouldn't be here."

The Javier brothers found Matt and Jenkins among the crowd and walked over to them. "Do you mind?" Alejandro asked, already leaning toward the table, a massive tray of food in his hands.

"Not at all. Come join us," Jenkins said while making more space on her side. The twins sat opposite each other.

"You all right?" Alejandro asked, looking closely at Matt.

"Thanks, I'll be okay."

"I must say we all were scared about you. I got concerned that the same shit would happen with us. As we returned back to base, we literally launched from the crater in order to get out of those machines as fast as possible. Even Sergeant Bakerman was suspicious, and he ordered us to get in the machines first while watching," Alejandro said, turning his attention to Jenkins.

She nodded and turned to his brother, Antonio, who was quiet as usual. He simply listened as he ate his gigantic portion. "Hey, have you written anything new?" she asked. Antonio was hard to understand. None of them, except his brother, were really sure what he was thinking.

"No, I have not," he said. "Sometimes the words just don't come out." He felt frustrated saying that and continued to eat. Apparently, he didn't want to be bothered anymore about his poems.

"Hey, by the way," Jenkins said, remembering something she'd been wanting to ask the twins, "you're both in the military, right? If you've spent most of your time in the Middle East, haven't you heard anything about our instructor? I bet he's been there too."

Alejandro tried to remember. Then he said, "Actually, I've heard some stories about one big soldier in the Middle East who became so determined and ruthless he'd jump at any mission. It was almost like he wanted to die on the battlefield. Folks said that he'd even killed a goat with his bare arms in order to survive." Putting the pieces of his memories together, he added, "I'm not entirely sure that guy is Bakerman, but based on Bakerman's behavior and appearance, he could be."

"That sounds like him," Jenkins said. Then she glanced at Matt, who was eating his food slowly. None of them, apart from Jenkins, were willing to talk. Inside the food court the noise slowly subsided. Many of the military personnel had gradually left, leaving the crowds thinner.

Meanwhile, in the basement, Sevchenko was diligently working with the defective exoskeleton. He had almost finished setting up the new upgrade, which hadn't been approved by the authorities. Stepping away from the machine, he activated it. The machine began moving as it did when preparing to take a host inside. It lowered itself down, and all the body guards opened. "Perfect," Sevchenko said with a delighted expression.

Curious, his colleague came to him and asked in a whisper, "Did you set up the next upgrade?"

"Yes, I did, like we talked about before." Sevchenko grabbed his computer and browsed through the settings. "I will disable some factory settings, which will prevent the machine from activating self-return in case of the host's death." He frantically looked inside his pocket for his flash drive. He found it and plugged it into the computer. "The new software will be backed up and stored. Our machine will have the latest upgrade and will work better."

His colleague felt uneasy and checked his wristwatch. "Michael, we've checked the rest of the machines. They didn't show any sign of possible error." He looked at his watch again and urged Sevchenko, "We must leave the premises now. It is already eight o'clock. You know that if we stay longer, it will be a breach of the rules."

Sevchenko didn't bother to check the time. He said while browsing through the data, "I must set up this update on the rest of the machines. It won't be long." He unplugged the computer and said, "I have acquired the update quickly. Don't worry; I'll do it myself. You can go."

"Michael, c'mon. We'll get in trouble if someone checks the basement now." His colleague tried to convince him to stop working but soon realized it was futile. "Okay, I'm leaving," he said, dropping his arms to his side. As his colleague left, Sevchenko ran back to the small computer room, ignoring his colleague's endeavors to stop him.

Inside Sergeant Bakerman's office, a lit cigar fumed by the half-open window, a thick billow of smoke slowly drifting outside like a lame creature. The sergeant was on the couch reviewing the latest maps he'd received from the general. Drones had recently attained the exact location of the nuclear weapon facilities. Twisting his head around, he stood up, walked over to the cigar, and took a couple of drags. Holding the map in his hand, he studied the location closer. "There it is," he said. Then he put the map on his massive table desk to see the overall area better. Something made him wonder. The sergeant looked at the silver bowl with the inscription "Mr. Charcoal." He walked to the window and stared outside for the cat. Mr. Charcoal wasn't outside, nor was he inside the office. "Charcoal, where are you? Come back home!" he called through the window. The grass outside was wet, and the sky was still miserably overcast. Abruptly, the sergeant's attention turned to finding the cat instead of studying the map.

He rushed into the barracks, where the squad was resting. "Has anyone seen the cat?" he asked loudly, looking at everyone, his nostrils flared. Almost all the squad members shook their heads in confusion. The sergeant's face had shifted because of the missing cat. He seemed greatly concerned and was dying to know where Mr. Charcoal had gone. The squad had never seen the sergeant like this before. He was usually apathetic, angry, and emotionless.

Sergeant Bakerman quickly rushed outside to look for the cat, going around to the back of the building where his office window was open. The cat was not there. "Mr. Charcoal!" he called again, worried. The sergeant got nervous and didn't know where to seek the missing cat. Usually, the cat was back home by this time, inside the office asking for his late dinner. Unexpectedly, a sad meow echoed nearby. "Where are you, my friend?" The sergeant looked around anxiously to obtain the cat's exact location. Then he found him. Charcoal had climbed up a tree and now struggled to get down. The tree had very solid and slippery bark, which made it hard for the cat to get his claws into it. The cat looked sad and helpless. "Ooh, you little silly one." The sergeant approached the tree, looking up. Then he quickly looked around, searching for something to use to climb the tree. He found some unfinished scaffolding, and using that, he reached for his anxious cat. "Mr. Charcoal, how come a cat like you can't climb down this tree?" he said while lifting the cat off the branch.

After helping the cat out of the tree, the sergeant moved to his open office window and let the cat inside. Charcoal quickly ran to his half-finished tray. He was hungry. The sergeant started to walk around the other side of the building to get back to his office. He had a view of the underground facility from this side of the building, and he paused. "What the …?" he questioned while checking his watch. It was half past eight, but the basement's massive doors were still open. According to the rules, the basement must be shut before eight. "What on earth is happening?" He picked up his pace toward the basement.

Sergeant Bakerman went down to the basement; the lights were on. He looked around, but nobody was there. His eyes stopped at the small computer room. There was some commotion inside. He aggressively opened the door to the room, creating a loud noise that startled Sevchenko, who was busy working on the computers on his own. "What the hell are you doing here?" the sergeant asked.

"I'm finishing up," Sevchenko stammered. He was confused, shooting his eyes everywhere.

"What a hell you are finishing up?"

"The prevention of possible malfunction."

"Mr. Sevchenko, you have violated the rules." The sergeant approached him with a predator's grimace.

"Sir, I had to because that defective exoskeleton requires a lot of checks. The rest of the machines have been checked, and they work perfectly." He passed a notepad with the latest data-check information to the sergeant. The sergeant glanced at it briefly and harshly slammed it against the table.

"What the hell are you up to, Sevchenko? Your crew left the basement, but you are being rebellious." The sergeant had come close, trapping the engineer in the corner. His dreadful presence radiated through the room. He picked up his radio and gripped it hard. "You know that I hate rebels who act on their own." Sevchenko felt threatened, but he knew the sergeant wouldn't touch him. "You will be suspended from this project for a week," the sergeant said. Evidently, that was a bigger hit to the engineer than being beaten.

"Sir, that's outrageous!" Sevchenko exclaimed. "I've been with this project since the very beginning. Please, sir, don't suspend me."

Sergeant Bakerman ignored his plea and made a call on the radio.

"Sir, I'm listening," a reverberating voice from the other side of the radio said.

The sergeant looked at the engineer's desperate face and said into the radio, "I need to send one man back to Tokyo headquarters immediately. Prepare a vehicle to take him to the coast. Over." He put the radio back in its holder and added gravely, "Take this punishment as a slap on the wrist. You know that I could suspend you from the whole project," he warned. "We have enough engineers who can replace you and do the job well."

Sevchenko was instantly overwhelmed with mixed feelings of fury and dread. He knew that his arguments would be futile against Bakerman. Without saying anything, he quickly collected all his stuff, including his personal laptop, where he'd stored all the upgrades.

Almost in a minute's time, a truck arrived to escort the engineer to the coast, where he would then take a boat to Tokyo headquarters. The driver and another man stepped out of the truck and came downstairs. They looked at the stunned engineer holding tightly to his personal belongings. The sergeant put his big hand on Sevchenko's shoulder and said to the driver, "Take this man to the city. He has violated the rules. I will contact the US headquarters shortly." Both military men nodded and escorted Sevchenko to the truck. Sevchenko truly felt miserable while looking back to the basement where his project stayed. After that the sergeant walked back to the basement doors and swiped his key card. All the sections automatically shut down inside, and the lights turned off. Eventually the massive doors rolled down.

"Can I smoke?" Sevchenko asked the driver while leaning closer to him.

"Yes, just keep the window open."

"Thank you." He seated himself in a series of clumsy motions, got out a cigarette, lit it, and fixedly watched the base. *It's just unfair,* he thought with sorrow. Sevchenko didn't dare to make any further arguments. He knew that a lot of questions would be asked at the US headquarters during his suspension. He didn't know whether he would ever get to return to Project XS. Feeling devastated, he dropped the last half of his cigarette out the window and put his hands on his face.

Day 4

Early in the morning in the sergeant's office, the coffee machine was brewing. Outside the window the sky looked promising—today might be a nice day. The cat was sort of sleeping but aware of noise inside the office. Switching on his computer, the sergeant put his cat on his lap and stroked him gently. "Let's see … Yesterday I received a message from the general that I didn't have time to read," he said to his cat. The sergeant leaned closer and intently read the message: "Sergeant Bakerman, we must take action sooner than anticipated. You must train your squad faster. Teach them how to use the guns. We are running out of time. Any hesitation could cause irreversible consequences. The nuclear weapon facilities are guarded more heavily each day. We can't wait."

As he finished reading the general's message, he put his cat back on the leather couch. Sipping some coffee, he lit the half-burned cigar by the window. He pondered what actions to take now. They needed more time to train with the exoskeletons. With his extensive military experience, he was used to these kind of announcements, but this time was different. He lacked experience with the exoskeletons, which ran on sophisticated software. He knew how to lead a platoon, but yesterday's incident had gotten him thinking. *What if it happens again?* he thought. After some time pondering, the sergeant extinguished his cigar and prepared himself for instant action. Before leaving the office, he said to the cat, "Mr. Charcoal, don't climb any trees you can't climb down. Can we agree on that?" Mr. Charcoal closed his eyes drowsily; he obviously didn't care what the sergeant was saying. Carefully closing the door, the sergeant left for the main hall.

As usual, everyone was lined up to meet Bakerman at eight o'clock. "Squad, we are running short on time. I have received a message from the general." He walked with his hands behind his back and explained, "We must learn how to use the guns with the exoskeletons. Forget about yesterday's incident. That malfunction has been fixed." He made eye contact with Matt, who had an uncomfortable feeling in his gut. "The nuclear weapon facilities in China are becoming more heavily guarded. We can't hesitate. Otherwise, the whole project, which cost a lot of money for Uncle Sam, will fail." Sergeant Bakerman kept marching back and forth in front of the squad. "You will learn quickly and react rapidly. This is our new approach!" He stood at the center of the line and asked loudly, "Is everyone clear?"

"Sir, yes, sir!" they responded at the same time, filling the hall with noise.

On the way to the basement, Matt whispered to Jenkins, "This is no good." He had a strange feeling. "I heard yesterday that one of the engineers has been sent to Tokyo. There were some arguments," Matt said, carefully checking to make sure the sergeant didn't hear or see. "Things are being rushed, which inevitably means trouble."

Jenkins didn't like it either that the course of the project had changed dramatically, especially that fast. However, she tried to calm Matt down and convince him things were better than they seemed. "We will handle this, as we always have in the past." It didn't sound convincing, but she tried. Jenkins glared at the sergeant's back, thinking about the uncertainty that might occur again. Then she patted Matt on the shoulder, giving him encouragement for today's drill. "Let's go."

"All right," Matt sighed, still feeling sick. They continued marching to the basement.

The massive doors were already open. All the engineers were inside, except Michael Sevchenko. It was obvious that the engineer crew didn't like their fellow engineer's detention. Nonetheless, they didn't dare to argue about it. They were worried the same thing could happen to them.

The exoskeletons were already set up for the day's drill, looking more sinister than the first time. Even though it was warmer outside today, the temperature was always low inside the basement. Next to the frames of the machines stood two gigantic detached guns. A thin cloud of cold breeze lingered along the frames near the floor. These guns were meant for today's drill.

Sergeant Bakerman walked to one of Sevchenko's trusted colleagues. "Give me the analysis results of the machines," he demanded. The man gave him a notepad with a lot of boxes ticked. The sergeant inhaled and carefully ran through the checklist, humming a tune hollowly. Then he passed back the notepad, declaring, "All right, all set. Squad, prepare to get inside the machines." He looked around, confirming that everyone had heard the order.

Suddenly, an overwhelming feeling ran through Matt's body as if he had swallowed a potent pill. Cold sweat dripped down his naturally sad face. He clenched and unclenched his fist repeatedly, trying to calm himself down. It was like he was facing his greatest fear again, but this time it was much harder. Jenkins felt the same as she made brief eye contact with Matt. She sensed how Matt was feeling after the sergeant's order. She looked to her other side, where Jack Kelly stood. His typical arrogant face partly hid his concerns, but he couldn't completely disguise his anxiety over getting back into the machines.

"Squad, get inside the machines!" Sergeant Bakerman commanded, watching them grimly. The twin brothers were the first to take initiative and got into their machines after giving each other a loud buddy handshake. Sean Price followed shortly. Soon the rest of the squad got into their machines. The exoskeletons embraced them gently, guarding their entire bodies. They stood and waited for the sergeant's further instructions. He watched them individually, checking each person's behavior. "All right," he said and moved over to his own machine.

Matt's face shield, visible only to him, showed that his blood pressure had risen close to a critical point. He now felt more uncomfortable than before. Next to Matt, Jenkins kept her eyes on him, reassuring him that he would be able to cope. He wondered where the defective suit was. Suddenly he noticed scuff marks on one of the Javier brothers' exoskeletons. He recognized the marks immediately; the defective exoskeleton had gotten them while being transported back from the crater.

"All right, squad, prepare to mount the guns," the sergeant instructed, pointing at the nearby weapons. "Browse the menu and find 'Mount the guns,'" he said while keeping his eyes on everyone. His eyes stopped on Antonio, who was frowning in puzzlement and struggling to follow the instructions. "Javier, what's your problem?" the sergeant asked.

"Sir, I don't know. It just switched off the menu by itself." Antonio was confused and tried energetically to set up the machine's menu. The instrument panel showed up again, glaring in front of his face shield. "I've got it," Antonio said, but then it switched off again, which infuriated the sergeant.

"Javier, immediately eject yourself from the machine," he shouted.

Antonio grew worried, completely baffled by what was going on. "Sir, I can't," he said.

Alejandro noticed something strange about his brother's exoskeleton. Even though the machine had switched off, the cameras on the shoulders were twisting in all directions. It was daunting. Suddenly, both camera lens, which resembled octopus eyes, pointed at him. *The machine isn't off apparently,* Alejandro thought. The sudden sinister thought made his entire body feel numb.

An abrupt, strong shock electrocuted Antonio. His body bent outward with the high voltage, and his eyes bulged out. He let out a horrible scream. The shock lasted a couple of seconds, filling the air with a toxic and electric smell. When the shock stopped, Antonio fell unconscious, his body limp.

His head drooped to the side loosely, blood leaking from his nose.

"Brother!" Alejandro screamed in great worry. "Antonio!" He was raving inside his machine.

A shiver of fear shot through the squad members, from the tips of their fingers to the ends of their toes.

"Squad, eject yourselves from the machines now!" Sergeant Bakerman yelled. He kept a close eye on the injured Javier twin while getting out of his machine. The rest of the squad desperately browsed their menus for the eject option. Matt struggled, his heart rate rising even higher. Somehow, in the heat of the moment, he managed to release himself from this beast.

Alejandro ran to his trapped brother and yelled, "Brother, please! Brother, please get up!"

"Get off the machine!" the sergeant shouted and made his way closer to Alejandro, who was ignoring him and climbing closer to his brother's face. "Get off the machine now!" the sergeant said, raising his voice. He pulled Alejandro away harshly by the shoulder.

"Sir, do something!" Alejandro demanded desperately. "Save my brother!" His eyes filled with tears and devastation. He walked back to his trapped brother.

"Javier, stay away." Sergeant Bakerman grabbed Alejandro by the shoulders again and shoved him farther away.

"This is really fucked up!" Sergeant said, looking at the machine that held Javier's unconscious twin brother.

For some time nobody knew what was going on. The machine didn't make any further actions; it looked switched off. The sergeant looked greatly confused as he watched it. "This is like a fugu fish being served by an amateur chef," he said, looking at the squad. "Unfortunately, Javier got the unlucky dish." Alejandro returned to his trapped brother, and the sergeant turned his head back to the machine. Suddenly the camera lenses of the machine came back to life, pointing at them. The sergeant and Alejandro froze for a few seconds, watching and sensing something sinister.

Another strong voltage shocked Antonio's body, bringing him back to life. He looked scared and despondent. "Help me, Brother!" he said in a weak tone, feeling threatened. His eyes indicated great fear, like he was seeing death. Alejandro was shaking and didn't know what to do. Another electric shock came. Antonio dropped unconscious again, and blood leaked from his ears.

"Antonio!" Alejandro shouted desperately. Before he could make his way closer, the machine stepped outside its frame.

"Now the shit has hit the fan," Kelly said while slowly stepping back to the computer room. He looked at the others, who were backing up at the same time. The machine took another step and straightened its body. The sergeant and Alejandro were the closest to it; they slowly walked backward, fearing what was going to happen next.

The exoskeleton with Antonio's body inside made its way to the center of the basement, placing each step loudly. After an extremely tense moment, the sergeant abruptly shouted, "Everyone take cover!" He didn't have a gun to fight back. Instead he stared at the machine and tried to predict its moves. "What the hell are you up to?" he said slowly, fixedly watching the moving creature. Suddenly, the camera lenses of the machine turned to the exit. Unexpectedly, the exoskeleton picked up the pace and ran outside carrying the

Javier brother. The sergeant, assuming Antonio was going to die, quickly ran to the computer room. He whooshed inside and demanded loudly, "Disable the factory settings. Switch off that damn thing, now!"

The engineer crew had already been trying unsuccessfully to remotely deactivate the exoskeleton. "We are trying everything," one man nervously said, tapping frantically on his keyboard. "The machine has locked access. It's like it has become self-aware."

"Dammit! For fuck sake" The sergeant was embittered and concerned. He quickly ran up the slope to see where the machine had gone. Too little too late. The machine had disappeared from his sight. He ran toward some military personnel doing vehicle maintenance. Apparently, they weren't aware of the sudden crisis. "Hey, did you see where the exoskeleton went?" the sergeant asked.

One man stood up and pointed at the gates. "I saw it going that way. Then it just ran off around the corner." He stared at the alarmed sergeant and asked while cleaning the dirt from his hands with a cloth, "Is something wrong, sir?"

"Some serious shit just happened. The machine possibly killed the man inside and ran off on its own." The sergeant pulled out his radio and called the guards to order them to survey the perimeter. The mechanics couldn't believe what they'd just heard. Their faces were puzzled.

"Sir, I thought it was your training day."

"It was supposed to be …" The sergeant paused to listen as one of the guards radioed back. "Did you see which way it ran?" His face switched from seriousness to disappointment upon hearing the answer. Then he said, "All right, we must close the perimeter. Keep the guns ready. Over." He put his radio in its holder and walked back to the basement, where the squad was waiting.

Alejandro was alarmed. Matt was trying to calm him down, but it was futile. His twin brother had been electrocuted a couple of times, had been taken away by the machine, and was possibly dead. Sergeant Bakerman went down to the basement and announced, "Squad, we are not going anywhere. The base perimeter is closed; the guards are ready. Currently the exoskeleton has run off somewhere without leaving any tracks. I will contact the general for further instructions."

Alejandro was far from calm. "Sir, we must get my brother back. We can chase after the machine using trucks and guns. Right?" He was restless and determined to find his brother at any cost. Tears in his eyes, he walked close to the sergeant to convince him to take immediate action. "We must go after my brother. He is in trouble."

"We can't!" the sergeant yelled back. "I'm sorry about your brother, but I must contact the general first." He walked away and headed back to his office, leaving the crying Alejandro in the basement with the others.

Matt and Jenkins walked close to Alejandro and gave him support. "That was the defective exoskeleton that took your brother. I recognized the scuff marks on it," Matt explained.

Breathing heavily and fast, Alejandro said, "Let's go to find Antonio now while the sergeant is in his office. Let's do this." He anxiously nodded, hoping the others would support his idea.

"Alejandro, this could end up badly for all of us ..." Matt was trying to persuade him calmly. His eyes showed pain and sympathy.

"Then I'll go on my own!" Alejandro snapped, looking outside.

Before he could walk outside, Jenkins grabbed his shoulder. "Please don't!" she begged. "Just wait until the sergeant comes back."

He shrugged Jenkins off and said loudly, "This is my brother! You don't understand!" He left the basement on his own, leaving the squad in uncertainty.

In the sergeant's office, the cat was startled by the sudden noise of the door slamming open. Bakerman instantly went to his massive desk, swiftly opened his computer, and switched it on. Then he made a video call to the general. No response so far. He reached for his cigar box and pulled out a cigar. Before he could clip off its edge, the general answered. "Yes, Bakerman. What is so urgent?"

The sergeant placed the cigar back in the box and explained, "General, we have a serious problem on the island."

"Yes, I'm listening." The general waited for an explanation, his lean face serious.

"General, one of the exoskeletons injured or killed the man inside it. This is a man from my squad. I don't know yet whether he's alive or not. The biggest problem is the machine is acting on its own. It has become self-aware or conscious. It ran away somewhere on the island; I can't trace where it's gone." The sergeant gasped for air and continued, "General, I need your permission to hunt down and kill that machine." He sat back in his chair and looked at his cat, whose yellow eyes stared back at him.

There was a moment of silence. Then the general said, "You will not kill that machine. You will chase it and bring it back."

Bakerman was baffled and challenged the general, leaning closer. "It's faulty. It might start a killing spree on the island. There are many civilians on this island apart from us militants. This is madness, General. How are we gonna chase it?"

"Listen carefully, Sergeant. If the machine has self-awareness … Just think about that for a moment." The general looked intrigued. "We could make all the machines self-aware and make them into an army. Think about how many human resources we could save, how much time we could save training people. In this case, our engineers will make the machines self-sufficient, and that little software malfunction can be avoided. So your new task is to chase the escaped machine and capture it alive."

"General, this is just unacceptable. It is madness," the sergeant said. "In order to prevent giant global chaos, I suggest that we be allowed to destroy the machine, before it kills any innocent people on the island." The sergeant took a paper clip into his hands and fiddled with it. He added, "The machine is defective. This is the second time it has malfunctioned."

The sergeant's suggestion infuriated the general, who snapped, "Listen, Sergeant! You will do as I say. Don't you remember that it was a privilege for you to get this mission? Who recommended you?" The general angrily shouted, "If it wasn't for me, you would be discharged from service. I know that you can't live a normal civilian life anymore. I know that you will go mental or kill yourself in some way or another. Start to appreciate my efforts and get things done. I need that machine alive. How you make that happen is up to you. Don't waste my time. Start chasing that damn creature. Over." The video call ended without any further discussion.

The veins on the sergeant's neck bulged upon hearing the general's order. Inside the office the atmosphere turned unhealthy and oppressive. Sergeant Bakerman stood up and walked to the wooden cabinet above the fridge. He took out the glass carafe of cognac, poured a little in a glass, and slowly swirled the glass. He was breathing vigorously. His eyes lingered on the Uncle Sam poster on the wall. The sergeant squeezed the glass of cognac in his hand tighter and tighter. Losing his temper, he threw the glass against the poster, leaving wide cracks in the glass picture frame. Because of the shattering glass, the cat suddenly jumped on the windowsill, staring with big eyes at Bakerman. The sergeant seated himself at the desk and calmed down, opening his cigar box. "Sorry, buddy!" he said to the cat, who wagged his tail sharply, about to jump outside.

Meanwhile, in Tokyo, nothing seemed unusual, just regular busy life in a megacity. In the US military headquarters, Michael Sevchenko stared out the top-floor window, which had an incredible view of the seemingly endless city landscape. He observed vast numbers of people commuting. They were like ants, appearing from nowhere and blending swiftly into the relentless motion of the crowds. There was a huge contrast between life on the island and here in Tokyo.

Michael occasional looked at the doors to the nearby office, where someone was soon going to meet with him.

Currently, the military headquarters was almost silent; Michael could hear only the faint voice of someone talking behind the doors and nothing else. The headquarters didn't look daunting to Michael; it resembled a regular office rather than a military place. It was white and spacious with a lot of empty desks. However, he was concerned because someone would question him about his intention with the rule violation. *What's going to happen? How long are they gonna keep me here?* Michael thought while sliding the tips of his fingers along the windowsill. He hadn't slept well last night. All his thoughts about Project XS had kept him awake till four in the morning. Michael yawned periodically and rubbed his drowsy eyes to be more brisk. The temperature was hot outside; the sun heated up the premises like a greenhouse. Even the air vents by the ceiling couldn't cool the room down. They were spinning on full speed, creating repetitive short whistles.

Suddenly the office doors opened; a uniformed military man called, "Mr. Sevchenko! Come inside." He stood by the door, gallantly waiting for Michael to come inside.

The room was quite spacious with a lot of office furniture and a long table with a chrome edge. There were comfortable seats on both sides of the table, presumably for conference meetings. There were only two people inside—the uniformed man by the door and a smartly dressed woman with a badge attached to her black blazer. She was standing on the other side of the table. Michael walked inside, keeping his eyes on the uniformed man, who immediately left. The military man shut the door, and Michael and the woman were alone in the room. Michael waited as the middle-aged woman folded her hands in front of her chest, indicating formal toughness. Her face had beautiful angles. He imagined she had been very attractive when she was younger, when her face did not yet have its current weariness and wrinkles. "Please, sit down, Mr. Sevchenko." She pointed to the leather chair across from her with a transparent look. He seated himself, casually dropping backward a bit.

"My name is Susan Johnson. I'm a CIA officer," she introduced herself, showing him her badge. Her voice was dry but at the same time warm. "Mr. Sevchenko, we have to discuss something." Johnson walked to the coffee machine and picked up her coffee mug, which enticed Michael.

"Sorry, ma'am," he said, leaning on the table, closely watching her. "I slept poorly yesterday. Can I have some coffee, please?"

"Sure." She pressed the button, and the machine instantly began brewing. Standing by the machine, she rolled one of her pearl earrings in between her fingers and asked, "Mr. Sevchenko, how long have you been working with Project XS?"

Twisting his eyes, he answered like he was guessing, "Well … I've been working on software for about two and a half years. All the software related to project XS, I mean." Michael felt restless and looked around the room for something. He suddenly noticed an ashtray on the table, and it triggered him. "Would you mind if I had a cigarette?" he asked.

"No," she said, passing him the ready coffee mug. Then she sat opposite him with an elegant twist of her hand through her white hair, which reached her shoulders.

Michael pulled out a cigarette and then offered the pack to her, asking, "Will you?" When she shook her head disapprovingly, Michal put the pack back in his pocket and lit his cigarette. Blowing out a huge billow, he stared tightly at her like they were having a staring contest. The moment was a bit awkward. Johnson didn't question him but looked at him with rigid and determined eyes, as if studying his body language. The only noise in the room was the spinning air vents and Michael's smoky exhales.

"You have violated the rules, Mr. Sevchenko," Johnson said while holding a folder of documents close to her chest. "I would care less if it was just staying in the basement half an hour longer than you were supposed to. But in this case you have set up an upgrade to the exoskeletons despite not receiving consent to do so." She raised one of her eyebrows, her face remaining earnest.

Michael was completely aware of what was happening. Presumably, the engineer crew had informed her about the update. He felt hectic and explained, "The upgrade was necessary; otherwise, the machines would experience glitches from obsolete software." He nervously extinguished his cigarette and picked up coffee mug. "Actually, I was saving this project, before Sergeant Bakerman sent me back to Tokyo."

She studied him, feeling slightly uneasy. There was no hostility in his face; rather, he looked concerned and empty. He looked straight at her and answered simply and directly with little stammering; he spoke like someone with nothing to hide. She leaned a bit closer, watching him. "Let me tell you something. This morning one of the exoskeletons seriously injured and possibly killed the man inside it. We don't know yet. The machine seems to have become self-aware and ran off after the incident." She slowly leaned back in her chair and paused. It was like lightning had struck Michael. His face instantly switched from tiredness to shock at the unexpected news. Johnson continued, raising her voice, "Mr. Sevchenko, do you dislike the US Army? Do you hate America?" It was an unexpected twist from the CIA officer.

"What?" Michael was shocked and got angry. "Why would I? I've been involved in this project since the very beginning. I was born in the United States of America, for goodness; sake!" He frantically reached for his cigarettes again.

She continued in the same tone, like interrogating a spy, "Mr. Sevchenko, you deliberately set up the software. You knew what you were working with. Therefore, you must have been planning to eliminate the forces using this sophisticated software."

He tried to explain while keeping his voice calm, "With the help of this upgrade, the exoskeletons should be able to return to base in the case of host death. The machines are learning to adapt to new circumstances—that is the next level, which could be the reason for this morning's incident." He smoked energetically and continued, "If Sergeant Bakerman hadn't sent me to you, this incident could have been avoided. All I would have needed to do was disable some factory settings." He felt betrayed.

"Your crew of engineers already tried to disable the factory settings," Johnson said, putting more pressure on him while looking at him suspiciously. "They can't get remote access to the escaped machine. The system has blocked itself off from any external interventions."

Michael felt uncomfortable and deeply confused. He felt like he was the enemy of his own project. After pondering some time, he insisted, "Send me back to the island. I will figure out the problem."

Johnson put the folder on the table, harshly declaring, "You are suspended from the project, Mr. Sevchenko! A full investigation will take place immediately." She wasn't entirely sure whether Michael was telling the truth or not. However, she remained suspicious and raised her voice. "This is the US Army's most secret weapon. You'd better be clear about your motives, Mr. Sevchenko, or you will face a long jail sentence with exhausting interrogation procedures."

Now Michael felt really threatened and didn't know how to respond. Even though it hadn't been his intention for the machine to hurt someone, he kept silent and didn't dare to challenge her. Michael knew that the incident was partially his responsibility, but he hadn't expected the machine to become conscious and cause harm to a man.

"You are free now," she said while keeping her eyes on him over her steepled fingers.

Michael stood up. As he headed out of the room, her strong and dry voice called, "Mr. Sevchenko, bring your personal computer and all electronic devices downstairs to our agents."

He turned back and asked, "Do you mean all my devices, including my phone?"

"Yes, all devices that store any kind of data," she emphasized and kept watching him.

Michael shut the door without saying anything and walked down the corridor. He walked with stiff leg muscles through the premises.

"Fuck," he cursed while walking downstairs to his temporary room, where he kept all his digital possessions. Repetitively pulling his hands through his hair, he wondered, *How did that machine become aware? It shouldn't have happened.* He was puzzled. Before going to his room, he stopped by a window and glared at the cityscape. He gazed intently in the direction of the island. He lingered, losing himself in his thoughts about the machine and the whole project. This incident had placed an extra burden on his nerves, which were already stretched thin due to the problem with the authorities. The breeze from the air vents was blowing his greasy hair. He hadn't shaved or showered for days. He almost looked like a modern-day caveman dressed in clothes.

Getting back to his appointed room, he walked inside the bathroom and undressed. He turned on the shower and got inside. Cold water poured over his shoulders. Michael stood motionless, leaning against the shower wall. "What have I done?" he asked aloud, judging himself. "I must delete the ultimate upgrade. This has gotten out of control already."

A couple of minutes later Michael exited the shower and got dressed. He immediately opened his laptop, where he stored all the latest updates, including the ultimate upgrade. The computer slowly opened the windows, its fans spinning unhealthily. Suddenly, fast bangs sounded against the door to his room. He stood and walked to the door with a puzzled face. When he opened the door, two agents burst into the room, pushing him to the side. One agent took the computer and looked condemningly at Michael. "Hand over the rest of your data devices," the agent ordered.

Michael hesitated and picked up his jacket. He looked in the pockets for his phone but couldn't find it. The other agent pulled the jacket harshly out of his hands and turned out all the pockets. "Hey!" Michael said, expressing his frustration. The agents' behavior was unexpected for Michael, and he was taken by surprise. He felt like a highly suspected fugitive. Presumably, the CIA officer had ordered the agents to get his devices as soon as possible. After continuous aggressive searching, the agents successfully obtained all of Michael's digital devices and left, leaving his room in disorder.

Michael seated himself in a chair, feeling utterly hopeless. It was a feeling to be in a rock bottom where the slightest hope get out isn't found. Unfortunately, he hadn't managed to delete the ultimate upgrade.

Inside Sergeant Bakerman's office, another message arrived from the general. The sergeant opened it and read it. "We have arranged for a freight ship from Tokyo. It will bring all the necessary supplies for catching the machine, including extra personnel as well as huge, sturdy nets with launchers. Extra arms will be supplied for civilian protection. The ship will arrive tomorrow, no sooner, because the nets will take time to obtain. Sergeant, you must improvise and try to delay or stun the escaped machine. Do not destroy it! If the machine threatens the local people, then you may shoot it, but otherwise you may not. All available military personnel will be deployed to the local village for their protection. Your task is to track down the exoskeleton and capture it using the materials available on the base, including the rescue helicopter. Take your squad and plan the capture."

"It's gonna be one hell of a day," the sergeant said and printed out the general's order. He went to the window and picked up his cat. Closing the window, he said, "Mr. Charcoal, you're gonna stay inside today. It's not safe outside today." Putting Mr. Charcoal on the couch, he stroked the cat before leaving. Uncertain how long it might take to capture the exoskeleton, the sergeant looked deeply into the cat's yellow eyes and said, "Promise to stay around the barracks, buddy. I'll do everything to stop that machine." After briefly scratching underneath the cat's chin, the sergeant walked back to the window and opened it a small gap. "Don't climb any trees, Mr. Charcoal. You'll make yourself vulnerable," he said with a short smile on his wide jaw.

As he walked through the main hall, the sergeant heard the fuss outside. All the military personnel had been gathered outside. The atmosphere was highly tense and contained a lot of rushing. The loud noise of passing vehicles drew the sergeant's attention. Some trucks had already started to deploy the troops. Obviously, their group leaders had received a similar message from the general. Bakerman sought out his squad. Among the dust and active motion, he noticed most of them waiting outside by the basement. Alejandro, though, was by the gates, staring out at the beach. He was on his own, continuously searching for clues that would lead him to his missing brother.

"Javier, come here!" Sergeant Bakerman shouted across the base.

"There he is," Jenkins said to the other squad members, pointing to the sergeant, who was making his way to them. Alejandro headed over as well. All the squad members' faces indicated uncertainty about what would happen next.

They were the individuals assigned to Project XS, which had caused terrible problems. The whole situation of the project had been turned upside down.

"Squad! We have a new task from the general," the sergeant announced loudly as he got close. "We must track down the escaped machine. We are not allowed to kill it." As he said this, all the squad members were taken aback. They couldn't believe it. The sergeant continued, reading the general's order, "The rest of the military will move to the village to protect the locals. Meanwhile, we are going to hunt down that son of a bitch." The sergeant creased the printed paper, put it in his pocket, and explained further, "We will use smoke grenades, flash grenades, and paintball guns. The helicopter will be our eyes; I will keep in radio contact with the pilot. A freight ship will arrive tomorrow with net launchers and other stuff, including more men. So we must make it till tomorrow."

Matt raised his hand. "How are we gonna use the paintball guns, sir?"

"That machine has a lot of eyes—cameras. If we manage to paint over all the cameras, it will be blind and therefore easier to capture." The sergeant grew thoughtful for a moment. His idea about using the paintball guns baffled even himself. However, he'd been ordered to keep the machine alive, which made matters extremely difficult. Seconds later he came up an idea and said, "The general doesn't want to kill that thing. We can ambush it with trucks then we can shoot it with the paintball guns, which we have plenty of in storage for training purposes. I know it sounds crazy, but that's the general's order."

"Sir, what about the exoskeletons in the basement?" Jenkins asked.

"The engineer crew has received an order to lock down the system. So these machines won't be active," the sergeant reassured them.

Alejandro wasn't happy to hear that the mission objective was capturing the machine as opposed to saving his brother. His eyes were hungry to see his brother, no matter what. On top of that, his heart was pounding, and he couldn't slow it down. *The sergeant has laid out an absolutely outrageous plan,* Alejandro thought. Everyone else on the squad seemed to think the same. He kept silent. He would wait for a chance to get closer to the escaped exoskeleton, though he didn't know how. Jenkins really felt for him and rested her hand on his shoulder.

"All right, squad! Before arming up, we will split into pairs." He pointed at Matt first. "Baker, you're with Price." Then he pointed at Alejandro, who looked devastated. "Javier, you are with Kelly. And Jenkins comes with me. C'mon, we don't have time!" After assigning the pairs, he indicated that they should head to the armory and storage, which were next to each other.

On the way to the storage area, he pulled out his radio. After brief hissing and vague noises, he was connected with the pilot. "What do you see?" the sergeant asked. "Have you noticed any footprints or anything that will lead us to that machine? Over."

"Not yet!" the pilot responded. "Sir, I suppose the machine has run into the woods, which would make it hard to see from above. Over."

"Keep looking. We need to find it before it gets to the village. Over." The sergeant put his radio away, turned back to the squad, and urged them to pick up the pace. "C'mon, move it!"

It was hectic by the armory, as a lot of military personnel were in line to receive arms. Jumping in front of the queue, the sergeant said, "We need a lot of smoke grenades and flash grenades." As a man rushed off to get the grenades, the sergeant glanced at his squad. They were wearing light army uniforms. "C'mon, get armored jackets and helmets on. Quickly!" The sergeant went inside the armory and passed jackets and helmets over to the squad. By the time he was done, the man he'd sent after the grenades had returned. The sergeant turned to the man in charge of the armory. "We need paintball guns too."

"Sure, follow me. They are in storage," the man responded and moved outside the jam-packed armory, followed by the sergeant.

Some time later the squad had armed up. They had on helmets and heavy-duty jackets and had a lot of smoke and flash grenades and paintball guns. They didn't feel confident with the paintball guns; they felt rather silly. Nevertheless, on order was an order. The sergeant checked the pressure of the guns. It looked enough to shoot from a close distance. He gave further commands. "Each pair will have an assigned truck and driver. We will scatter in a long half circle. All the radios are on. As soon as one of you encounters the machine, you will immediately report. Is that clear?" He raised his voice at the end.

"Yes, sir," the squad simultaneously responded.

"If you get an opportunity, try to lure the machine closer to the truck, increasing the chances the driver can knock it down," the sergeant explained. His jaw was moving faster than usual, mashing down on his chewing tobacco. He was also concerned about this task. He had never had a mission like this. Suddenly, wind gusted around them as the helicopter floated above their heads. The sergeant looked up and showed an affirmative sign to the pilot. "All right! Let's go after that creature!" he shouted over the noise of the helicopter.

Three trucks left the base, throwing up a huge dust cloud behind them. Nobody had the slightest clue where to seek the escaped machine. Nonetheless, the squad had been deployed.

The day was bright and warm, and it only got warmer as tensions grew. The majority of the military personnel left the base in order to protect the locals from the potential threat. Trucks headed out over the open fields, taking a shortcut to the village. The off-road vehicles were capable of overcoming natural obstacles quickly.

Bakerman and Jenkins were in the leading truck of the squad. They drove in the opposite direction from the village. Jenkins seemed nervous as she held a paintball gun in her hands. The ride was bumpy, sometimes tossing them from side to side in the back of the truck. Suddenly, the sergeant picked up the smoke grenades and pulled Jenkins closer to him by her jacket. Without saying anything, he attached the grenades to her jacket's chest straps. "This is better," he said. He tapped firmly on her shoulder and grabbed the holder to check the tightness of the jacket. After attaching more grenades, he said, "We must delay that machine. Let's confuse it with smoke first. As soon as the chance arises, we will use the paintball guns at close range and color its eyes over." She looked at him and was about to ask something when the radio interrupted.

"Sir, this is the pilot. So far we haven't identified anything. We're gonna fly over the village now. Over."

"Thank you. We are heading into the open fields where the trucks can still navigate. Report as soon as you notice anything. Over!"

The short conversation finished, the sergeant picked up more grenades to arm himself. Jenkins watched how the sergeant handled the equipment. She swallowed, taking courage, and asked, "Sir?" Once she had the sergeant's attention, she asked, "What if Antonio Javier is still alive in that machine? Can we save him?"

"What? You're nuts!" he said, as if she'd said something stupid. "Didn't you see how that machine was electrocuting Javier? There is no chance he survived."

She didn't ask any further questions. However, despite seeing with her own eyes how badly Antonio had been injured, she still believed for some strange reason that he had survived.

"Listen, Jenkins," Sergeant Bakerman said, grabbing her by the jacket and pulling her closer to him. Making sure the driver didn't hear, he whispered, "If that machine gets me first, you will not hesitate to shoot it with real guns. Until then, the general's order is the priority. Is that clear?"

She swiftly nodded.

"This is really fucked up," the sergeant said angrily. Even his breath on her ear felt almost irritated. "The last thing I want is for that thing to start slaughtering innocent villagers." He frowned as if feeling pain and added, "No, that must be avoided at all costs."

"Okay, sir," Jenkins agreed quietly.

The sergeant's back banged loudly against the truck's wall as he leaned backward. His bleak eyes were hiding something deep and inexplicable.

After a rough, bumpy ride, the truck stopped and took position in a field not too far away from some trees and bushes. The roaring engine sound ceased immediately as the driver turned the truck off. Sergeant Bakerman stepped outside the truck, and Jenkins followed. So far nothing had indicated any action or motion. Using binoculars, Bakerman observed the surroundings. "Where are you hiding, man-eater?" he whispered to himself while wiping the sweat from his forehead. Trees bent occasionally in the wind, shortly followed by creaking sounds that echoed deep into the forest. There was some periodic movement from wild animals, most likely startled ones.

Sergeant Bakerman walked back to the truck and picked up the radio. He sat inside and passed instructions to the rest of the crew, who were quite a distance away from them. Nobody had any updates on the escaped machine. "Hey, take some binoculars from the back," the sergeant said, peeking outside the truck at Jenkins.

"Sure," Jenkins responded, walking back to the armored truck. *It's probably gonna take some time to find the machine,* she thought while seeking binoculars in the back of the truck. After retrieving a set of binoculars, she moved a short distance away and kept observing the environment. It looked too peaceful. It was almost unbelievable that some machine was on its own somewhere on this green island. Putting down the binoculars and turning back to the sergeant, she asked, "Sir, how long does the exoskeleton's battery last?"

His face remained vague. He exhaled slowly and said, "Unfortunately, the battery lasts for twenty-four hours, which gives the machine an advantage. If the machine has access to any electric source, it can also charge itself." He rubbed his unshaved jaw with his thumb. Placing his binoculars back to his eyes, he continued, "It'll be a ugly mess if the machine reaches the village and gets access to a charging point."

"Why don't we go to the village, then?" Jenkins asked.

"The village is far away from the base, and a lot of military personnel are already heading that way, so the village will be protected," the sergeant explained. "This is an emergency plan."

Jenkins felt unsure about the sergeant's orders. She strolled around, occasionally readjusting her heavy jacket. The oversize jacket was uncomfortable for her. The sergeant had attached many grenades to it, adding a lot of extra weight. She sat down and kept observing the forest through her binoculars. *Where are you hiding, monster?* she wondered. Groping for the jacket zipper, she opened the collar a bit. Direct sun was unbearable with all this heavy equipment.

A long distance away, Matt jumped out of his truck and reached for the radio. After connecting with the sergeant, he reported his and Price's location and recent observations. A small green hill separated him and Price from the sergeant and Jenkins, preventing them from seeing each other. The sergeant ordered Matt and Price to stay and wait at their location until they received further instructions.

Sean Price got out of the truck. He picked up some binoculars and a paintball gun and walked away without saying anything.

"What's the matter with that guy?" the driver asked. "He hasn't said a word since we left the base." He maintained eye contact with Matt, who watched Price walking away from them.

"Honestly, he doesn't speak that much. The only time I've really heard him talk was when our instructor gave him a task that required it, but that was it." Matt held his binoculars and wondered about Price.

"Hmm," the driver murmured. He pulled out a cigarette and offered one to Matt.

"No, I don't smoke." Matt stepped inside the truck. Picking up and twisting a paintball gun in his hands, he said, "This is just crazy." He put the paintball gun to the side and kept observing their surroundings.

"Don't worry, man," the driver said. "This truck is loaded with guns. If something goes wrong, you can pick up the machine gun in the back." With an expression of disbelief, he added, "I don't know how we're gonna handle that exoskeleton with those toys." The driver chuckled, pointing at the paintball gun. He smoked in a relaxed manner while looking at the green landscape.

More than an hour passed. That hour seemed like an eternity to Matt. So far nothing had happened. The view on this already hot day remained the same. Matt sat inside the truck and checked the radio while gulping some water. The other teams occasionally made announcements to report nonaction at their spots. Sometimes the helicopter disappeared from sight to search around in desolate places, its engine sound indicating how far it had traveled. Matt stepped outside the truck and took off his helmet. His hair was sweaty and made it uncomfortable to wear the helmet any longer. His eyes were tied to Sean Price, who hadn't moved an inch since they'd settled at this spot. Price kept diligently observing the fields and forest with his binoculars. Something bothered Matt's peace of mind. He wanted to find out why Price was so distanced from everyone. This thought banging inside his head like a raging bull, Matt picked up a water bottle and gestured to the driver that he was going to talk with Price.

"Hey, have you noticed anything so far?" Matt asked as he approached.

"No," Price answered shortly, not bothering to look at Matt.

"Have some water," Matt said, holding the bottle out.

"Thanks."

Despite Price ignoring him, Matt decided to sit next to him. Even from the side, Price's face clearly said, *Get lost. I have nothing to talk about with you.* Matt had seen the same cynical indifference in Price's eyes before.

"Listen, Price. I've noticed that you don't care to have any conversation. But since we are on this island together, I ought to know something about you." Matt cautiously examined Price's reaction and continued, "This machine has possibly killed Antonio. Let's be real—the same might happen to any of us. So if you'd tell me something about yourself, it would be ..." Matt paused, thinking about what to say next while staring at the same spot as Price. "We are a squad—one team. We ought to know about each other," he said with emphasis.

Suddenly Price reached for his knife attached to his leg. He pulled it out and swiftly stabbed it into the ground between him and Matt. Then he glanced over at Matt. The knife seemed to be a warning sign to Matt, who took it seriously. Again, Price looked at him with calm eyes under his big, dark eyebrows. He reached for something in his pockets. Matt observed his moves without further inquiring. Price took out some tobacco and wrapping paper. He rolled a cigarette attentively and lit it with a lighter retrieved from his pocket.

"This is easier for me," Price explained in a low and hollow voice. He continued to smoke his rolled cigarette without any further explanation.

"What do you mean by that?" Matt asked, confused.

After a very long pause, Price said, "I have one weakness. It's my greatest obstacle to conducting missions successfully." Price lingered in his thoughts, but his facial expression remained the same—emotionless.

"What weakness?"

"My emotions," Price answered and puffed, his face tightening. He was silent for a moment. After a while, he realized that he was thinking of his past, as if certain memories were spread before him, demanding to be seen again. He did not want to look at them; he despised memories as a devastating loss. But he understood that he thought of them in this moment in honor of his knife, which had belonged to a friend.

Again Matt felt unsure what Price's point was and said, "We all have emotions. We're just human beings. Right?"

"Let me tell you something, Matt," Price said. "I'm from a special forces unit that mainly focused on eliminating

Mexican drug cartels near the US border. I had a friend in the unit who was almost like my brother." Something suddenly changed in Price's face. He stopped briefly and then resumed, speaking more slowly now. "On one mission, we both held very important information about a massive drug delivery. Unfortunately, the gangsters captured my friend. They were aware that we knew about the massive delivery, and they wanted information about our unit. If I had given them that information, they wouldn't have shot my friend in front of my eyes. My friend and I were both highly trained in information protection. Just seconds later the support forces arrived, but my best friend had already been killed in front of my eyes. I could have saved my friend. I really could…" Price emphasized the last part. It was obvious that he carried guilt from the past.

"Sorry to hear that, Sean," Matt said.

"Thanks," he responded. "Staying isolated is my strategy. The less I know about you, the better. It's easier to handle deaths that way. Like I said—emotions are my obstacle." Price finished his cigarette and flipped it away. Then he took his binoculars and kept observing the surrounding area.

"Have you sought a specialist's advice or talked about it with anyone else?" Matt asked.

"I've tried. I never heard of those so-called therapists. When I was in listening therapy, all I heard was arguments and the last shot to my friend's head in that ugly situation. The memory kept creeping back every time I was questioned about that horrible case. The only safe place was on the force conducting new missions. I was brought up in a Christian family but lost my faith. I guess I'm seeking revenge or trying to be killed in the same way," he said carelessly.

"I'm Christian too. I still believe in God."

Price smiled; it was a thin smile, amused and cold. He looked at Matt and said, "Throughout history man has believed in thousands of gods, starting from crawfish and ending up with thin air."

"Perhaps. I'm not that fanatic about religion, but one thing I know for sure." Matt paused.

Price lowered his binoculars and froze, waiting.

"There have been times in my life where I was constantly brought back to God in some way or another. It was like he was giving me signs indirectly through people I knew." Matt was immersed in himself. "The signs were like miracles filled with divine energy."

"I've never felt …"—Price paused, thinking—"what you call divine energy."

Matt was thinking a lot about Price's situation. He scratched his head and asked, "I'm sorry, but why don't you seek other solutions rather than be doomed to death? That kind of condition destroys you."

There was a long sigh of weariness in Price's voice.

"Sean, is it that what you want?"

Price put down his binoculars again and said, looking into Matt's eyes, "Find a mirror and ask yourself the same question. If you come up with an answer, then act accordingly." He pulled his knife out of the ground and put it back in its holder. "Matt, just leave me alone now."

This answer made Matt feel awkward; that strange suggestion didn't make sense to him. He stood up and walked away back to the truck. His mind was occupied with a hundred thoughts. *Why am I here?* he asked himself. Perhaps Price was right about his strategy. If the man couldn't handle emotions, why would he hang out with other people? Anyhow, at least Matt now understood Price's real reason for keeping silent and distant from others. He would respect Price's position, although it seemed unacceptable to Matt, who tended to seek answers. Getting back to the truck, he called to the driver, "Any news on the radio?"

"Nothing about the exoskeleton. The helicopter needs to fill up. So we won't have eyes in the sky for a while," the driver said, playing with his lighter out of boredom. As Matt got inside the truck, the driver asked with interest, "What did you get to know about him?"

"He is like a lone wolf with a deep scar that won't heal," Matt answered while watching Price.

"You know your drill sergeant, Bakerman?" the driver said. "He's been really fucked up by the service. I mean really fucked up. That's what I heard from others. I sense that lone wolf"—the driver pointed at Price—"has similar shit inside. They are like kamikazes who never succeed in dying."

The same questions that had been pestering Matt for some time now revolved in his mind: *Why am I here? What brought me to this island?* He took his binoculars and observed the area just to distract himself from his thoughts about being on this mission. It was afternoon now and still hot and a little windy. All the squad units were in position waiting for the beast to reappear. Evidently, nobody had the slightest clue where to seek the escaped machine.

More hours passed with no sign of the machine. All the military personnel had been given orders not to cause panic for the locals. It seemed so strange that on an island this small the exoskeleton had managed to disappear like smoke in the air. It was alarming for the army; they had never dealt with this kind of incident before. In order to keep tensions down, the locals were told that the alert was a drill, a training exercise. However, some of the locals remained suspicious of the unexpected maneuvers by the US Army; they questioned why the helicopter was frequently flying over their village.

In a deserted part of the island, a Japanese father, mother, and small boy of about five years old were taking a bicycle ride up to the forest. The family wasn't aware of the sudden army movement in their village. They had planned for a day out and left before the military personnel had arrived. By this point, they had ridden their bicycles down to an area near the base, though they didn't realize it.

Suddenly, the father lifted his head to see the helicopter, which was flying over again. It was the second time it had flown over this place, which seemed unusual to him. The trees were tall and quite thick at the top in this area, making it harder to see through them.

The family reached a narrow path that wound uphill and was more shaded. They left their bikes at the bottom of the trail and proceeded to walk up it. Along the trail, the trees had grown tall, reaching up to the sky, and their roots had crept up the sides of the path. The sun managed to break through in some places, landing in straight, bright beams on the ground. The young boy was in awe at what nature was capable of. There was nothing in particular that was of interest at the top of this path, but the nature here told a story of the island's history, of how it had stood tall and strong all these years. *We come here to feel the vitality of*

Mother Earth, the father thought. He stopped and watched his wife and son adoring the nature.

After walking uphill for a while, they found a good place to rest. It was a nice, flat field with an old, cracked bench by some bushes. The father and mother sat down to rest, but the boy was still full of energy and kept sneaking and running around. He found something on the ground that resembled a small plane made of sticks and paper. The boy showed his discovery to his parents with a wide and joyful smile. They were happy to see him playing with an old toy. The boy tossed the small paper plane energetically. It flew quite a distance before landing sharply by some thick bushes off the path they'd taken here. The boy's chubby face was neutral as he stared at the paper plane. He turned around to see his parents were busy opening the picnic basket of food they'd brought. Returning his curious eyes to the bushes, the boy was keen to retrieve his newly founded plane and decided to run after it. It wasn't far away, still within eyesight of his parents.

Moss and tree roots slowed the boy down, but eventually he reached the plane and bent down to pick it up. He froze, sensing that something was nearby. He couldn't move, his natural curiosity holding him to the spot. Suddenly the bushes began rattling and shaking like something big was inside. The boy got scared and looked back at his parents. He didn't know what was hiding and shaking the plants. He grew more tense as the shaky bushes became more active. A big, dark silhouette peeked out of the bush in front of the boy, who held tightly to his paper plane. It was the exoskeleton with Antonio's dead body inside. Blood was leaking out of Antonio's ears, eyes, and nose, leaving traces on his neck, face, and shirt. The machine was close, so terribly close that the little boy didn't have a chance to run away. The boy screamed in fear upon seeing the gigantic and sinister creature. He stepped backward and stumbled over a tree root.

Hearing the desperate screams, his parents immediately stood up and began rushing toward him. They also were scared to death when they saw the machine with the dead body inside. The exoskeleton slowly extended its arm toward boy. For the sake of their boy's life, the parents ran toward the machine despite the great danger.

The exoskeleton stood and pointed its camera lenses at the crying boy. Something made it stop. It didn't take any further actions. It was like it was measuring the boy. Just then the father and mother reached the spot. Shouting loudly, the father swiftly picked up the boy and passed him to his mother. The machine's cameras focused on the father. It identified him as the proper size to be a host. The mother and boy had already run some distance away, but the father was still close. He slowly began stepping back, holding his hands in front of him to indicate peace. Chills ran down his spine. Trembling, he said something in Japanese, trying to talk with the creature, but it was useless. The machine swiftly grabbed the man's upper body with its massive arm. It held him tightly, pulling him closer. The father screamed in agony. He turned his head back to his family and shouted at them to run away. The mother and boy watched him with great fear, hoping he would escape somehow. Unfortunately, the father was trapped, badly trapped.

The exoskeleton suddenly released Antonio's dead body. The corpse rolled out like a heavy sandbag. Antonio's legs were still stuck inside. The trapped man was so scared. Using its crude force, the exoskeleton pulled out the dead body and dropped it to the side. All the guards and safety holders, which were covered with dried blood, opened widely. The machine's cameras fixed on the fearful man. The exoskeleton released the trapped father and toppled onto him like a falling wall, pushing him to the ground. It literally swallowed the man and sucked him inside. The father desperately fought back, but it was pointless. The machine gave the man an electric shock to knock him unconscious and continued to pull him inside. Horror-struck, the mother and boy watched the horrible scene with devastated facial expressions. The machine slowly raised itself to its feet with the father unconscious inside. At this point the mother ran off without looking back, holding the crying boy.

The exoskeleton, having acquired a new host, stretched its full body. It spotted movement in the sky with its cameras and walked back into the forest thicket to hide itself from the helicopter. Then the machine grabbed Antonio's corpse by the foot and slowly pulled it deeper underneath the bushes, out of sight.

In the meantime, the squad was still waiting in their positions. They had increased their distance from each other, per the sergeant's latest order. More hours had passed, and nothing had been detected. In the third truck, Kelly stared at the sun, which was hiding behind a thin cloud. The temperature had cooled down a bit, though it was still hot. Kelly felt frustrated and bored despite the potential danger hiding somewhere. Walking and kicking the bits of lava rock, he made occasional observations with his binoculars.

Alejandro had gone way too far from the truck; he looked desperate to find the exoskeleton. Based on his nonstop observations, he was obviously determined to find any clue that would lead to his brother, even if it cost his life.

"Don't go that far," Kelly said to himself, watching Alejandro. He was concerned that the same shit that happened to Antonio could happened again if Alejandro forged ahead on his own. Kelly turned around and walked to the truck, where the driver was observing the place while holding the radio in his hands. "Hey, can you take us closer to him?" Kelly asked, pointing at Alejandro, who had ventured close to the forest. "We need him back here; otherwise, the sergeant will kill us." He felt worried, and his blue eyes showed his concern.

"All right." The driver started the engine without hesitation. Kelly jumped inside, tossing his paintball gun in the back. Thick black smoke poured out of the exhaust pipes, and the truck roared its way toward Alejandro.

As the truck arrived, Alejandro ignored them and kept searching even closer to the forest. He constantly was putting his binoculars up to his worried face.

"Hey, Alejandro!" Kelly called while peering out of the truck. "Hey, come back to position. It's dangerous out here." Alejandro didn't seem to hear him calling, so Kelly stepped out of the truck. Quickly and cautiously, scanning around him, he walked to Alejandro. They both stood watching each other, as if expecting the other to speak first. It was written on Alejandro's face that he was determined to find what he was looking for. Scratching his face and grimacing, Kelly hesitated, sighed, and said, "I'm sorry about your brother, but it's crazy to be this far from our truck."

Alejandro dropped his hands loosely and said, "My own blood, my brother is part of me. I can feel him." He refused to believe that his brother might be dead. Taking off his helmet, he said, "My twin brother is near; I can sense him. He is asking for help." Kelly felt odd hearing that, but it was understandable in this case. Alejandro grabbed his shaved head and slowly pulled his hands down his face, as if hoping for miracle. He said, "I don't give a shit about that machine anymore. Antonio is calling for me, and I'm going to help him." He grimaced, his eyes remaining sharp on the environment. He refused to accept harsh reality.

Kelly carefully collected his thoughts to say something. He didn't want to offend Alejandro, but he sensed that Alejandro had refused to consider the worst-case scenario and was about to find his brother's body. Wiping his sweaty forehead, Kelly dared to say, his voice calm and slow, "But, Alejandro—"

"There's no fucking but!" he snapped, raising his eyebrows angrily. Tension of a kind Alejandro had never felt before manifested inside him; it exploded, leisurely, in every part of his body. "He is not dead! Don't you dare mention it!"

Kelly took the hint: *Stay put. Don't stick your nose in my business.* He slowly walked back to the truck, and suddenly he noticed the driver tied intently to the radio, receiving an important call. Presumably, something had occurred. The driver nodded many times. He looked serious and alert. He then quickly jumped outside the truck while still holding the radio, which continued to inform.

"Hey, come back now! Both of you!" the driver yelled at them.

Kelly immediately returned. "What's going on?" he asked.

"The pilot has detected movement near us," he said anxiously while looking at Alejandro, who hesitated. "C'mon! Come back to the truck, now! The machine is near!" he shouted, his voice almost hoarse.

Over the radio, the sergeant said, "This is Sergeant Bakerman! The escaped machine is near Kelly and Javier! All units proceed there immediately!"

The situation immediately went from calm and boring to intense. Kelly got inside the truck to retrieve his paintball gun. After finding it, he scoffed in disbelief, "This is just suicide. The machine will paint us with our own blood sooner than we'll paint him with colored balls." Dropping the paintball gun back in the truck, he grabbed two smoke grenades, holding one in each hand.

The driver immediately jumped inside the truck and started the engine with a shaking hand. He looked terrified. In the meantime, Alejandro walked slowly backward, whispering something to himself that nobody else could hear. He grabbed a grenade with one hand while holding his binoculars in the other hand. His eyes were glued to the forest. Nonetheless, he kept retreating. The helicopter was nearby, tracking the exoskeleton over the forest. It floated closer to them, which meant the machine must be getting closer too. Alejandro looked up at the helicopter, which was fixed at a certain point in the air.

In the forest, trees shook rapidly. The movement was getting closer. Suddenly, all action ceased inside the forest; it was like the creature was lurking in wait. Kelly grew more concerned and groped in his pocket for his painkillers.

Again the rattling sound of branches repeated but this time in a different place. "Where are you, you son of a bitch?" Kelly nervously said while jolting pills out of the container.

Suddenly, like a rapid launch, the machine ran out of the forest toward the truck with great speed. The men threw smoke grenades.

"C'mon, hide behind the truck!" the driver yelled at Kelly and Alejandro.

The grenades activated, and a huge billow of smoke covered the whole area. The men threw a few more grenades, building a wall of smoke that separated the vicious machine from the truck. The men could no longer see the exoskeleton. The driver reached for the paintball gun next to him and tossed it to Kelly. "Be ready to paint that machine!" he shouted. He firmly gripped the steering wheel, seconds away from taking crucial actions. He sensed that the creature was stunned somewhere in the middle of the huge cloud of smoke, but where? He accelerated the truck and drove inside the smoke cloud, hoping to hit the machine. There was a loud bang and the jolt of a collision. The driver had succeeded in hitting something, but he couldn't see what it was in the thick white cloud. The driver stayed stationary inside the smoke. Fear overwhelmed his entire body. He couldn't see a thing but the continuous hissing cloud coming from the grenades. Driven by his fear, he put the truck into reverse. Before he could make his way out, a huge metallic arm came out of nowhere and smashed through the truck's window, severely injuring the driver. He screamed loudly. Despite the injury, the driver managed to just barely make his way out of trouble.

In the meantime the rest of the squad had arrived and surrounded the smoke cloud from all directions.

"C'mon, squad, let's paint that bitch!" the sergeant shouted.

Suddenly, the exoskeleton revealed itself out of the smoke, following the truck that had hit it. A rapid burst of paintball rain began to land on the machine's body. It tossed its arms around frantically, as if it were fighting off intrusive insects. The machine got confused briefly.

Alejandro suddenly put down his paintball gun, staggered by what he saw. His jaw dropped from the unexpected surprise. The man inside was not his brother but someone else who looked dead. His blood boiled. He sprinted to the closest truck. Aggressively opening the doors, he reached for the machine gun. The move shocked the driver, who was busy watching the exoskeleton. "What are you doing?" the driver asked, outraged.

Ignoring the orders, Alejandro released the safety switch, determined to kill the machine. "Where is my brother, you piece of shit?" he said in fury while walking closer to the machine, which had been covered with more paintball shots. His eyes had lost any fear of being killed. Alejandro opened fire. Abruptly, the machine retread into smoke because of the rounds fired at it.

"What the fuck is he doing?" the sergeant asked angrily. He drew attention to Alejandro, who kept reloading his gun and letting out bursts of fire into the clouds. This bullet storm made the exoskeleton retreat even further until it decided to run back into the forest. Suddenly the helicopter changed course, managing to keep track of the machine. It was obvious that the exoskeleton was attempting to hide from the others and the shots fired.

As the smoke calmed, everyone stood closely watching the forest. The sergeant's plan had almost succeeded. It would have worked, had the machine not been scared away by the machine gun. He immediately jumped off the truck and made his way to Alejandro. Everyone sensed the real trouble coming while watching the sergeant's typical furious walk. As he confronted Alejandro, he reached out his hand, demanding, "Give me the machine gun!"

Alejandro kept silent and watched the forest emotionlessly, ignoring the order.

"Give me the fucking gun, Javier!" The sergeant grabbed the weapon and pulled if out of Alejandro's hands. Then he gave Alejandro a hard hit with the back of his hand. The hit was so hard that Alejandro dropped to the ground, supporting himself on his palms, breathing heavily.

"Javier, listen to my fucking orders!" The sergeant leaned down by him. "I can incarcerate you, if you disregard my commands." Alejandro was spitting blood and kept looking down. The sergeant kept pushing him. "Your brother is dead. Deal with that fact!"

"No, he is not," Alejandro snapped, facing the sergeant defiantly. He refused to accept that fact.

Before the sergeant said anything else, he got an urgent call on the radio. He stood up and walked to it, tossing the machine gun inside the truck. "Yes, Sergeant Bakerman is listening." Holding the radio firmly, he watched the place.

"Sir, the freight ship will arrive this evening. All the necessary supplies have been delivered by the local authorities today. Please return to base. Over," the voice from the other side said.

"Copy that." The sergeant put the radio away and made a noise to draw everyone's attention. He said loudly, "We are going back to base. Soon the freight ship will arrive with the supplies and net launchers. We are gonna catch that loose fish tonight!" Then the sergeant walked to the truck with the injured driver. The driver was groaning in agony, his body covered with a mess of shattered glass. He held his arm tightly, not moving, looking scared and sweating a lot. "Can I see your arm?" Sergeant Bakerman gently asked while wiping off the scattered glass pieces from the man's body.

"Sir," the driver said, breathing heavily, "my shoulder has been dislocated." He gave a pained grimace. Despite the dislocation of his arm, he had been lucky. The hit from the exoskeleton had just missed killing him.

"I can pull it back in place," the sergeant said gravely, leaning closer and rubbing his fingers.

"No," the driver said. His heart thumped so hard it made his body flutter. He sensed that the sergeant could fix his shoulder, but he refused, shaking his head.

"Are you sure?"

"Sir, please take me back to base," the driver said. He refused the sergeant's help, fearing the man's crude force. He frowned as he saw the giant hands with the scars getting closer to his shoulder. "No, please take me back to base." He felt a sharp pain again while he continued protesting against the sergeant's intention to fix his shoulder.

"Okay." The sergeant gave up and leaned outside the car, looking for Kelly. "You will drive the truck back to base," he ordered. Kelly without hesitation picked up his paintball gun and moved over to the truck. Looking inside at the injured driver, he frowned. In some way or another, the driver would have to be moved to the passenger's seat. Kelly stood motionless looking at the injured man; he was uncertain what to do.

"Help him move to the passenger seat," the sergeant said and walked off to his truck. Then he took the radio and was busy connecting with the base while simultaneously assessing their surroundings. The smoking fumes had calmed down completely. The soil had been ripped up, with a lot of used grenade canisters scattered around randomly. The escaped machine had left tracks leading into the forest. Broken small trees and branches indicated the footprints of the machine.

"I'll be careful," Kelly said, calming the injured driver. "I need your help to move you over." He looked at the driver's suffering eyes for cooperation. "Place your legs over to the passenger seat, and I'll support your back." They both exchanged an affirmative look. After counting to three, they swiftly switched the driver into the passenger seat. The movement caused the driver to let out a painful moan. "Sorry," Kelly apologized and took the driver's seat. He started the engine, which responded instantly with a loud roar. "We're good. Let's go back to base." Kelly wiped off the sweat from his forehead and shifted into driving gear.

It was getting darker; soon night would arrive. Two trucks were already slowly driving off from the spot, but Kelly hesitated. He looked around for Alejandro. The Javier twin stood up off the ground with a thoughtful look at the forest. It was apparent on his face that he believed his brother was alive, even though the machine now had a different body inside. Kelly drove over, urging him, "Let's go back to base, Alejandro." He stopped the truck and patiently waited for Alejandro. Meanwhile, the injured driver groaned with pain occasionally. Somehow, that made Alejandro shift his thoughts, and he got inside the truck. He remained silent and kept staring through the window at the forest, which cast dark shadows from the sunset.

Kelly's truck was the last one to arrive at base. He drove carefully all the way down in order to make it smooth for the injured man. Everything was a real fuss and hassle inside the base. The helicopter had landed to fuel up. Tall lamps with a lot of sections were on everywhere, lighting up the busy spot, although it wasn't that dark outside yet. "How are you doing now?" Kelly asked intently, checking the driver's pain.

"It's unbearable," the driver said in torment.

"Medics are coming." Kelly noticed two military men with red crosses around their arms. They also had a stretcher with them and a portable kit. "Don't worry; you are gonna be okay," Kelly consoled.

Sergeant Bakerman was busy talking with other military personnel. Alejandro observed from the truck how the sergeant constantly nodded his head about further objectives. Jenkins and Matt were together chatting nearby. Sometimes, they looked alarmed, staring around the place. Apparently, they feared the exoskeleton might be lurking around the base. Nobody knew. The injured driver was taken away from the truck, leaving Alejandro alone. He sat inside watching a certain point of space for a long time.

"Are you coming?" Kelly stood by the open door with a questioning grimace. Nobody had given further orders to do anything. However, the rest of the squad had gathered near Sergeant Bakerman.

"Give me a minute," Alejandro answered fuzzily. He couldn't think right now. His mind was too overwhelmed with one thought.

"Okay, I'll go to see the rest," Kelly said, closed the door, and walked off.

It was late, and his squad had left, so Alejandro could sit there alone, unwitnessed. He was tired. It was as if he had run a race against his own body, and all the exhaustion of years in the military, which he had refused to acknowledge, now came to the surface.

Meanwhile, the sergeant discussed the upcoming delivery with other military personnel. Trucks were being prepared immediately to pick up the delivery from the coast. A sudden wind blast made by the helicopter forced the sergeant to hold his hat. The air surveillance team was returning to its search for the escaped machine. The helicopter's very strong strobe light came on, stunning the men nearby.

"Squad, wait at the base," the sergeant said. "I'll go to get the supplies from the freight ship. It won't be long. Stay alert until I arrive." He briskly jumped into a truck, gesturing in the direction of the coast. Three more trucks with a lot of cargo space joined them. The convoy created a dust cloud mixed with hollow engine roars as they left the base.

Kelly's already tired eyes followed the leaving convoy. Unfastening his armored jacket, he turned to Jenkins, saying, "It's gonna be a hellish long night."

She looked uncertain and alarmed. "I'm scared to death. Did you see that machine?" She recalled the recent battle. Her big, concerned eyes were aimed at the back of the base, where a lot of tall trees stood behind the fence.

"That creature has a different man inside now. I'm afraid it is learning how to survive using human bodies. This is scary," she said.

Matt added, "Well, this is the problem with the whole Project XS. The machine has decided to act on its own because of the sophisticated software that gives the exoskeletons the ability to learn and adapt to new circumstances. Somehow I sensed that fear before, when I was trapped in the machine in the crater of the mountain. It just wasn't me controlling the machine."

Kelly nodded and agreed, saying, "This is a really fucked-up situation." He shook his head in disbelief, fixedly watching the forest. "Unbelievable that we've been ordered to catch it alive. Now we've become the prey, not that machine."

"How is he coping?" Jenkins asked, pointing at the truck where Alejandro sat inside.

"Not well," Kelly said, feeling upset. "His eyes have a ferocious glow that seems to say he'll do anything, no matter how crazy, despite his own safety. It bothers me, you know," he said while observing the truck.

Alejandro got out of the truck and walked slowly to the barracks while casually taking off his armored jacket. He found the nearest bench and seated himself to take a rest. The lights were bright by the barracks, almost dazzling him. He was distracted by bugs flying into the lights, which reflected on his tired face. *That's a massive swarm,* he thought and waved his hands in the air.

As he stood up, his attention was suddenly drawn to the sergeant's cat, who was sneaking around the barracks. Mr. Charcoal was hunting bigger bugs that were more sluggish while flying. The cat attempted numerous times to catch the bugs, so far unsuccessfully. Alejandro observed the cat and had an instant thought. A vicious plan clicked into his mind. *What if I take Mr. Charcoal away to make the sergeant kill the exoskeleton?* he contemplated. *Apparently, this is the only living creature in the world that softens the sergeant's ice-cold heart.*

"Psst! Hey, buddy," Alejandro whispered while ducking closer to the black cat, who suddenly stiffened. Alejandro enticed the cat with typical sounds to get the animal's trust. "Hey, Mr. Charcoal. Come to me." Alejandro crept closer while checking to see if anyone was around. The cat flattened himself to the ground defensively, sharpening his glowing yellow eyes at the approaching man. Alejandro reached his hands closer and stroked the cat. He gently lifted the cat up, saying, "I need your help, buddy. We will find my brother." The cat reluctantly tolerated the embrace and remained calm without further resistance. Alejandro kept stroking the cat's glinting black fur while planning his next steps.

In front of the barracks, the truck with the smashed window had been left alone. It opened a great opportunity for Alejandro's plans. He made a quick decision and jumped into the driver's seat. However, he hadn't noticed that Kelly was coming back to truck, presumably for his stuff that he'd left inside.

"What is he up to with that cat?" Kelly asked himself, confused. He stopped walking as he realized that Alejandro was driving off. "Perhaps the sergeant asked him to bring the cat to the beach …"

So far Alejandro had managed to calm down the cat, which he firmly held in his lap with one hand. Checking his surroundings and making sure that nobody was aware of what he was doing, Alejandro started the truck. The engine sound startled the cat, who jumped into the back seat as if fearing something horrible. "Hey," Alejandro whispered sharply and turned his head backward. He put the truck into gear. Suddenly, he froze, noticing Kelly in the distance. However, he put his foot down on the accelerator anyway, spinning the wheels. He left the base, not caring if anyone else noticed him driving away. He was counting on the fact that everyone's main goal was to capture the exoskeleton, which gave him a great cover.

After driving some distance, Alejandro reached a place where he could see the beach. The waves were strong and reflected silver-white moonlight from the clear sky. The big freight ship had arrived with a bulky load. Some men were shouting something, but it was difficult to hear from such a distance. Alejandro noticed four big trucks were loading up with supplies. Abruptly he switched off his headlights and headed to the village. "Don't worry, buddy," he said to the cat, who was hiding somewhere deeper in the back of the truck.

He reached the small village. Some households had lights on. The village seemed unusually calm on this alarming night. Distant lights in the windows of houses scattered through the countryside made the twisty road seem lonelier. Alejandro stayed in the truck, observing the village from a safe distance. He noticed another military truck coursing along the narrow roads. Once the vehicle had passed far into the distance, he whispered toward the back of the truck, "Buddy, come here." The cat was hidden somewhere in the darkness. Alejandro climbed into the back and switched on the built-in lights in the ceiling. Mr. Charcoal had crawled tightly into a corner. He looked threatened and unprotected. "Come to me." Alejandro grabbed the cat and climbed back to the front. Opening the glove box, he found a piece of cardboard and a lot of pens. Alejandro ripped off a piece of cardboard and carefully wrote a message on it: "I'm hungry. Please feed me." He then attached the cardboard to the cat's collar. Mr. Charcoal meowed sorrowfully, feeling unfamiliar with the place. Alejandro picked up the cat and held him up in front of his face. "Don't be sad. You are my hero." His eyes were highly convincing as he looked at the scared cat.

Alejandro carefully got out of the truck and closed the door with the cat in his hands. They were about one hundred yards away from the nearest house. Tightly holding Mr. Charcoal to his chest, Alejandro gazed carefully at the nearby house. Strangely, it seemed that nobody was inside, despite the dim light from the small window. Alejandro approached the house, inhaled deeply, and knocked on the door. Hollow, brisk steps approached the door, and then the door slowly squeaked open, revealing an old Japanese man with a pleasant and warm smile. Obviously, he recognized the US uniform. He was short and fragile with a hunched back. The homeowner waited for Alejandro to speak.

"Do you speak English?" Alejandro asked in a rush, energetically stroking the cat.

The old man shook his head, showing his incomprehension.

Alejandro extended his arms, holding the confused cat out to the man. "Please, take him."

The man got the hint of what the American soldier wanted, but he refused to take the cat, gesturing with his hands.

Alejandro took a step closer and tried to make his intentions clearer. "Me." He pointed at himself. "Tokyo."

He pointed in the direction of the city. "Me, Tokyo." This time he pointed at his wristwatch, trying to explain that he was going to be absent for a while and then come back.

The old Japanese man grimaced, seeming to somehow get the sense of Alejandro's message. He hesitated to take the cat but finally picked it up after Alejandro persisted. Charcoal felt unhappy and mewed a couple of times. The man twisted around the small cardboard piece attached to the cat's collar, feeling clueless.

Alejandro pointed at the cardboard. "This is ..." He demonstrated eating with an imaginary spoon.

The old man nodded, this time with a larger smile. He got the message that the cat needed to be fed.

"Thank you so much." Alejandro nodded his head many times, bending excessively low. The old man replied in the same way and kept his warm smile until the door was completely shut.

Alejandro turned around and immediately ran back to the truck. Before getting inside, he looked up at the sky. It was a spectacular view with so many stars, a view like nowhere else on the planet. He lingered, watching the stars, and said, "Antonio, I'm gonna find you." Alejandro was determined. He started the engine and drove off.

Driving back to base, he checked the clock. His plan had taken much longer than he had anticipated. He got a bit anxious that the sergeant might have realized his long absence. He increased the truck's speed.

In the meantime, the four large trucks arrived back at the base from the beach. The helicopter had gone toward the village. Sergeant Bakerman followed its lights with his eyes until it disappeared from his sight. After jumping out of his truck, he strolled around and checked the load of supplies. Unloading was taking place. A lot of necessary supplies had been delivered, including more men, who participated in the unloading.

The sergeant decided to go back to his office to contact the general. He walked through the barracks as usual, glancing at the exhausted squad members who were inside. "Be ready. We have the supplies," he declared and proceeded to his office.

As soon as he got inside, the sergeant switched on his computer. Then he quickly opened his drawer and took out a cigar, lit it, and smoked a couple of times. Standing by his desk, he searched the room. "Mr. Charcoal!" he called. There was no answer. It made him fidgety, and he left his desk for the window. He peeked out the window, calling more loudly, "Mr. Charcoal!" Nothing. There was no sign of the cat, just dark emptiness. He put his cigar between his teeth and made his way out of the office.

"Where are you, my little friend?" he called, his blunt voice echoing down the dark corridor.

The squad, minus Alejandro, heard the sergeant calling for his cat. As he walked inside the main hall, he called again, "Mr. Charcoal!" He scanned every corner.

Kelly remembered seeing Alejandro with the cat and said, "Sir, I thought Alejandro brought the cat to you."

The sergeant's face switched from seriousness to incensed fury about to burst out. Kelly abruptly felt a bit foolish. He realized that Alejandro had plotted something against the sergeant, and now he had unknowingly betrayed Alejandro.

"Where the fuck has Javier gone with my cat?" The sergeant raised his voice, gravely looking at Kelly.

It was too late to cover with lies, so Kelly admitted, feeling guilty, "I saw him driving with the cat toward the beach. That was the last time I saw him."

All the squad felt awkward and terrified about what was going to happen to Alejandro when he showed up. Knowing how much the sergeant cared about the cat, they sensed real trouble was coming.

Unexpected engine noise outside alerted them to an arriving truck. There was sudden stillness inside the barracks as the sergeant raised his fingers for silence. At the entrance doors Alejandro appeared. He walked inside and saw everyone looking worriedly at him, except the sergeant, who had his eyes glued on him like a hunter looking at prey. Alejandro was aware that this situation was about him and the missing cat. Both looked at each other for a brief moment. Despite the sergeant's furious look, Alejandro kept it cool and proceeded to his bed as if nothing had happened.

The sergeant quickly walked toward Alejandro while sticking his cigar between his teeth. "Where the hell have you taken my cat, Javier?" He firmly gripped Alejandro's shirt close to the chin. "Answer me!" he shouted very close to Alejandro's face.

"I will tell you if you promise to search for my brother and kill the exoskeleton," Alejandro calmly responded, turning his head to the side and preparing himself for something unpredictable.

Suddenly, the sergeant hit him hard in the chest and dropped him to the floor. Alejandro landed hard. The sergeant placed the sole of his boot on Alejandro's neck and applied pressure, squeezing Alejandro's neck so hard it was almost impossible for him to breathe. He bent down slowly by Alejandro's face, threatening, "Javier, don't play with fire. Mr. Charcoal is the last particle of what's left of my already screwed soul." The sergeant smoked his cigar vigorously, making the burning end glow red. He took out the cigar and slowly moved it toward Alejandro's helpless face. "I will ask you one more time. Where is my cat, Javier?"

Alejandro was stubborn. He battled against the pushing boot and refused to talk. The glowing cigar was getting closer to his eye, and the sergeant pushed down even harder with his boot.

Seeing this torture, Jenkins felt an instant urge to do something. "Fuck this!" she said. Picking up speed, she shoved the sergeant off Alejandro, who almost got his eye burned. Jenkins then punched the sergeant in the face, the sharp blow turning his head to the side. She took an offensive stance, ready to fight more despite their unequal weight categories.

"You silly girl." The sergeant tasted a little blood in his mouth and spat. "This is the worst squad I have ever trusted," he said while wiping off the blood. He moved closer to her. As she executed another punch, the sergeant caught it and twisted very hard, inflicting tortuous pain. Then he kicked her in the stomach, throwing her against the wall. Her head hit the wall very hard and bounced off, and she dropped to the ground, unconscious.

"No!" Matt yelled, seeing the horrible scene. He immediately ran to Jenkins's slack body, but Sergeant Bakerman perceived the move as another attack. Before getting to Jenkins, Matt received a punch from the sergeant's big knuckles. The blow sent him to the floor but didn't knock him out. He took a fighting stance as he got up from the floor.

"You are useless," the sergeant said angrily. He clenched his fists, his eyes sharpening. He looked intently at Matt, who is being defensive watching how sergeant is going to attack. After Matt threw some punches and kicks, the sergeant counterattacked and pushed Matt backward with a punch.

Kelly grew worried as he watched the fighting. Staring nervously around, he predicted that he was going to be next. Kelly was truly concerned about Jenkins, who lay motionless on the floor; he felt for her. The fight continued until Matt received a hard hit and dropped to the ground. He was still conscious but hesitated to get up on his feet, stunned from the hard hit. Some blood was dripping from his mouth. He looked up. The sergeant's tall and bulky presence indicated an immensely crude power that was hard to fight.

"Dammit," Kelly said worriedly, his eyebrows showing his fear. The sergeant looked at him. The gaze made him feel threatened, like he was about to get his ass kicked. "Fuck, this is complete nonsense," Kelly cursed. Then he looked at Sean Price, who seemed to feel nothing but absolute apathy about what was happening inside the barracks.

A strange noise echoed from the top of the barracks, abruptly interrupting the fight inside. Quick, loud bashes and thunks sounded from the roof again. Everyone looked up the ceiling and froze, watching. The roof banged again, this time louder and faster. Then they heard something big land on the ground nearby the entrance. Kelly saw a big shadow pass quickly by the window without noise. The tension reached its highest point as Kelly recognized the dark silhouette. It was the exoskeleton coming after them. Kelly slowly backed up.

The machine rapidly bashed through the entrance. It was too big to fit through the regular-size doors. Some bricks and broken wooden pieces scattered chaotically around as the machine broke inside. In the middle of the transparent cloud of dust, the dreadful machine made its way to the center of the hall where Matt and Sergeant Bakerman stood as if seeing a ghost.

Meanwhile, Kelly and Price flattened themselves against the wall and looked for a chance to escape. The dead man inside the exoskeleton was covered with blood, dirt, and paintball patches. The camera lenses were fixed on Sergeant Bakerman and Matt. It was evident that the machine had already decided its intentions. With an unexpected long twist of its arm, the machine tried to grab one of the men. In a fraction of a second, Matt jumped to the side, successfully avoiding the machine. The exoskeleton made an impressive stride toward Sergeant Bakerman, who tried to run away. It was too little too late. The machine hit him with its arm, causing him to tumble to the ground. Now the exoskeleton made its next move. Using both its arms, it pushed the sergeant against the floor. Slowly the machine released the dead man inside. The Japanese man's body slipped out and landed next to the sergeant, who wore an extremely baffled scowl.

"Damn you! You will not get me," he yelled, incapable of fighting back.

As the exoskeleton dropped onto the sergeant with opened guards and body holders, Matt took the chance and ran toward Jenkins, who was still lying motionless on the ground. He energetically tapped her cheek, desperately trying to bring her back to consciousness. Unfortunately, he did so without success. She wasn't waking up. Matt glanced at the horrible scene occurring in the center of the room. The machine was sucking in the sergeant's body while the sergeant screamed and resisted.

"C'mon, you gotta wake up, Crack." Matt continued to tap her face in fear. "C'mon!" he persisted.

Slowly the machine got up from its prostrate position. It extended its body and began to electrocute its new host. Sergeant Bakerman screamed awfully like some kind of demon. The electric shock didn't knock him out. The machine sent out another wave of shock, sending white and blue streaks of electricity all the way down to the sergeant's feet. Apparently, the machine needed to take over control of the human; it used increased voltage, thus, weakening the host.

"You are not gonna get me!" Sergeant Bakerman yelled in outrage.

The machine let out a third wave of electricity that was significantly stronger than the previous waves. The exoskeleton activated all its power resources to knock out the tough man. It was horrible. The sergeant was literally boiling on the inside. His eyes bulged out, and blood leaked from every possible hole in his head.

"This is disgusting," Matt said while smelling the burning flesh. It repelled him. He kept persistently trying to wake up Jenkins. "Hey, Kelly, come over! I need your help," Matt called.

Avoiding the machine, Kelly sneaked along the wall and ran toward Matt and Jenkins. The burning smoke increased in the hall; they started to cough. Meanwhile, Sean Price took the chance to help Alejandro get up and take cover.

Eventually, the exoskeleton succeeded in knocking out the sergeant. Nothing happened for several seconds. The third wave of electricity had consumed most of the machine's remaining power. A very strong smell of burning filled the hall. The machine was sluggish but still functioning. The camera lenses scanned the premises. The exoskeleton took slow steps toward an electrical outlet built into the wall. A tiny wire slipped out of one of its arm and frantically tossed about like a blind eel. It proficiently connected to the outlet once it got close enough. The machine sucked in electricity to charge its drained battery. The power charge was volatile. The exoskeleton widely spread its arms while leaning a bit backward from the electric boost. The machine pulled in so much electricity that the lights went off inside the barracks. An instant eerie darkness took over the premises with mixed sounds of electricity and smoldering flesh.

"Help me carry Jenkins," Matt whispered to Kelly while carefully keeping an eye on the exoskeleton. They lifted her up by her arms and waited for a moment because the exoskeleton was still charging, causing awkward sounds. "Now." Matt pointed to the corridor. "We must get cover there." They dragged Jenkins, still unconscious, into the dark corridor.

Sean Price and Alejandro took cover inside the hall. They hid by a bed, hoping that the machine hadn't noticed them. "What are we gonna do now?" Alejandro asked Price, who looked confused and alarmed. His typical poker face had shifted to troubled fear, but he was still managing better than the others.

"Let's wait here." Price took another glance at the machine and said, "Apparently the exoskeleton can't be bothered with us." And he was right. Once it was fully recharged, the machine turned around and faced the damaged entrance. Numerous bright beams of light filled the hall as military men came to check on the noise with flashlights. Suddenly, the exoskeleton bolted toward the exit, now running with greater speed and power. Men screamed and shouted for retreat. The machine broke through the crowd and disappeared. Price and Alejandro turned their attention to the high ceiling as loud, quick, heavy steps bounced against the rooftop. The footsteps shortly ceased. Price and Alejandro were puzzled, unsure whether the machine had stopped momentarily or jumped off the roof. After some time, they felt a bit safer. It seemed the machine wasn't coming back. Alejandro looked through the window and saw numerous flashlight beams pointing up as men clamored around. The men were trying to keep the exoskeleton in sight. Soon after, the light beams angled down. Evidently, they couldn't track the creature anymore.

"Are you okay inside?" someone called from the entrance. A fully equipped man with a machine gun and mounted flashlight walked in, seeking survivors. His flashlight briefly illuminated the Japanese man's prostrate body. The back of the body was covered with severe burns all along the spine.

Price called out, "Yeah, we are here."

Unexpectedly, the lights came back on; the main hall was fully lit again. "What a mess," the man with the gun said as he looked at the debris, corpse, and blood. "Has anyone else gotten injured?" he asked while lowering his gun.

"Sergeant Bakerman," Price said. "The machine took the sergeant to use as a host. It knocked him down first, then sucked him inside, and electrocuted him until he dropped unconscious." Price exhaled and added, "I'm afraid the sergeant is dead."

"For goodness' sake," the man said, showing his distaste. His nose wrinkled at the pungent smell inside. "Get cover. We are going after that monster." The man walked outside and joined the rest of the soldiers.

"Let's go see Matt and the others," Alejandro urged Price.

"Okay."

Inside the sergeant's office, Matt and Kelly had placed Jenkins on the leather couch. Kelly quickly browsed through the stuff in the office and opened the small fridge. He took out an ice pack and passed it to Matt. "Take this." He also opened a bottle of mineral water. His hands, he observed, were shaking only very slightly. Probably from stress, Kelly tossed a couple of pills in his mouth and swallowed loudly.

As Matt neatly placed the ice pack on Jenkins's dark forehead, she moved slightly. "She's getting up," he said. "Crack, can you hear me?" Matt asked in a calm tone and snapped his fingers.

"Uh," she groaned with her eyes shut. "My head." Her first words indicated pain. As she opened her eyes, she asked, "What is this place?" She paused and frowned. "Ouch, my head."

"Take it easy. Don't rush," Matt said. "This is the sergeant's office."

"Where are the others?" Nearly as soon as she asked it, the door opened, and Price and Alejandro appeared.

"The exoskeleton ran away. Everyone on the base is seeking it," Price informed them.

"What?" Jenkins was deeply puzzled. "Uh …" Her head again reminded her of her pain. "When did this happen? How?" she asked.

"Relax, Crack." Matt placed a hand on her shoulder. "The sergeant got killed by the machine while you were unconscious. It captured him, tortured him badly with electricity, and then ran off."

She lifted herself to a seated position. "Wait, wait," she said, expressing her amazement. "What? Are you telling me that all happened while I was knocked out?" She looked around at the others with a frown. "Why did it kill just one man?"

"We don't know," Matt said, rubbing his left side, which was bruised and sore from his fight with the sergeant. "I suppose the machine has some kind of goal or plan. If it wanted to kill us, we wouldn't be here. And … the dead man it dropped on the ground, he looked like …" Matt paused, looking at the others until his eyes stopped on Alejandro. "Like a local man from the village," Matt finished, his face showing confusion. He stood up and walked to the massive wooden computer desk. The computer was still on but in sleep mode. He sat at the desk and shook the mouse.

"We need to kill that monster as soon as possible," Kelly suggested. He anxiously ran his hands through his hair, trying to collect himself. "Guys, c'mon. Fuck the order. We can't allow this machine to hunt us down one by one. This is outrageous. It scared the shit out of me when it was frying the sergeant like sizzling bacon."

Jenkins nodded her head in approval. "I agree. We can't catch that thing with fishnets and spears." She turned her eyes to Price, waiting for him to say something.

"Hey, hold on, guys," Matt interrupted. "Listen to this message from the general." He leaned closer and read the general's latest message out loud. "Sergeant Bakerman, you must catch the escaped exoskeleton tonight at any cost, even if it requires more lives. Use your squad. They are the best that I have found. Some of them have dirty pasts. Therefore, they will have to comply with our commands; otherwise, we can prepare comprehensive files on their dirty deeds. Additionally, the Japanese authorities have already raised concerns. They are urgently demanding an explanation about the missing man. They will send their own armed forces to the island if I delay my response too long, and that would screw up the whole project, which already has cost an exceedingly large amount of money. You have already received the needed supplies, including nets and launchers. Your duty is to capture the machine alive and bring it to the basement. If you fail in this task, you and the rest of your squad will face a war tribunal."

Everyone in the room was quiet, thinking about the message. It was perhaps the biggest betrayal ever by their trusted superiors. Suddenly Kelly reached his hand out and then dropped it. "See, I told you! This is just solid proof. They don't care about our lives. We are like cattle on a conveyor waiting to be slaughtered and later served as burgers." Kelly leaned against the fridge and continued, "Even if we succeed and catch that machine, which isn't likely to happen without costing more lives, they will play with us and make up all kinds of shit about us, just to keep us leashed like dogs." Kelly inhaled and picked up the ashtray made of thick glass. Then he turned his attention to the poster of Uncle Sam with the shattered frame. *We can save you, Uncle Sam*, he thought, *or we can serve up a shit sandwich for our general, and make him eat it at the global dinner table.*

"I sense that you're urging us to seek and eliminate the machine by ourselves." Matt stood up from his chair and leaned against the desk, hands folded in front of his chest. He looked around and waited for everyone's reaction.

"Yeah," Kelly confidently responded. "It is fucking obvious."

"You know," Jenkins said, touching the back of her head, "this is a really fucked-up situation. Either way we are screwed. Let's arm up and, using our skills, hunt down that son of a bitch." She got heated up and slowly rose from the leather couch.

Matt looked at Alejandro, whose answer was written on his face: *I want to kill the machine that took my brother away.* Then Matt looked at Price, who kept silent but shifted his eyebrows in disbelief. The others turned their attention to him, waiting for his response. "Price, what's on your mind?" Matt asked.

Price slowly scratched his chin and shook his head. "No. This is a violation of orders. I can't."

Kelly turned to Matt with a careless grin. "I knew it." Then Kelly switched his eyes to Price. "Why don't you follow your own orders for once in your life?" he asked condemningly. "Perhaps then you will have more control over your life, which looks like a mess, to say the least."

"I'll go my way and help the others to catch the exoskeleton. You can hunt it down; I won't tell anyone," Price calmly responded and left the office.

Kelly opened the fridge and took out another glass bottle of water. He drunk, gulped, and said, "Okay, we are four now. It's enough to organize a successful mission. We're gonna blend into the crowd and get machine guns with mounted grenade launchers. No one will notice our absence, because the sergeant is gone and everyone is busy. The base being on alert will be a good advantage." He placed the bottle loudly against the table and turned to Matt. "You should take the lead because you always seem collected and haven't cursed ever since I met you."

Matt walked to the window, which had been left ajar; he peeked his nose outside. The distant noise of hassle around the base could be heard near the window. He looked outside into the darkness and sighed with puzzlement. "I wonder why it came back to the base." He frowned and tried to figure out the machine's intentions. "This is the second time it has come near us. I'm afraid it will come again." Matt rubbed his chin and said, "Apparently, it needs a new host to sustain it after some time period. I guess."

"Hey, we should hurry up." Jenkins joined him by the window, hobbling a little. She held the back of her head and frowned slightly.

"Are you gonna be able to handle this in your condition?" Matt was worried about her.

"I'll be good. I want to get things done as soon as possible." She grabbed Matt's wrist firmly, which reassured him of Jenkins's rigid determination.

"Great!" Kelly jumped into the conversation. "C'mon, let's go to the armory for guns and night-vision gear." He was waiting by the door with Alejandro.

"All right, it's gonna be a long night regardless," Matt said and patted Jenkins on the shoulder.

She turned around, stopped, and looked at him. They talked without words; after their long years of service in the same department, they could say more to each other with eye contact than words.

"I'll cover you," Jenkins said to Matt.

"I'll cover you too." Matt's voice was low and calm. He shut his eyes, sighed, and opened them again, saying, "Honestly, I don't know. This is so … this is so bizarre. All that recent happening on island. I just can't put my thoughts together properly. And…I've got no idea for any tactics how to deal with that creature."

"Don't you worry," Jenkins said. "Let's get things done like we always have." She walked toward the exit while keeping her eyes on Matt.

"You go," Matt said and sat on the leather couch, rubbing his face. "I will join you soon, Crack. I need a minute to collect my thoughts. Okay?"

"Don't be long."

As the others left the barracks, Matt stayed in the sergeant's office to have time for himself and to come up with an attack plan.

A little bit later, Sean Price walked into the main hall, carefully inspecting the floor. He was looking for his missing knife, which had slipped out during the exoskeleton's attack. Among the debris on the floor were huge patches of blood and black burnt spots. Price fixed his eyes on the bed he'd used for cover and immediately moved over to that area. There was the knife, lying on the floor by the bed, its blade shining. After picking it up, Price stood watching the place inside. It was ghost silent inside despite the outside hassle. Strangely, he felt instantly and completely numb, throughout his entire body. The background sounds slowly faded into quietude. Price's shoulders wriggled as he got back normal blood circulation. He proceeded to the exit.

"Sean, wait," a young man's voice called from the bathroom, the doors of which were ajar.

The silence, all at once, penetrated into Price. He felt his arms grow numb. Price froze just before the damaged entrance, his eyelids lowered to complete shut. He tried to ignore the voice but couldn't. He sneaked slowly to the bathroom in search of the voice. As he got inside the locker room, his attention was drawn to the shower. There was something unusual there, like the presence of a living being that hadn't revealed itself yet. Placing his arm on the doorframe, Price walked inside. His heart pounded harder when he saw the swaying lamp attached to the ceiling. It hadn't been there before. The lamp swayed harder, tossing its light frantically about the bathroom.

"It's not real." Price closed his eyes and counted, "One, two, three, four, five …" He kept counting and tried to resume normal breathing. When he opened his eyes again, everything was normal—no lamps swaying or strange voices calling. He placed his palm against the doorframe and recoiled. A sudden flash of a man holding a gun against his best friend's head appeared in the bathroom and then faded. Price noticed it from the corner of his eye; he recognized the scene immediately, remembering it vividly. As he thought of that scene, his fear grew; it snared him completely now that he had let it approach his conscious mind. Price lost all sense of time; he stood fixedly staring at the white tiles.

"Hey," a voice said from behind him. A hand touched Price's shoulder.

Driven by instinct, he grabbed the hand and broke to the side swiftly. As he turned around, he saw Matt's shocked face grimacing in pain from the twisted hand.

"It's you," Price said in a low tone and released Matt's hand.

"Jesus Christ! What's going on, Sean? I saw you staring at the wall."

"Nothing," Price snapped and began making his way out.

"I'd like to help you, Sean. I felt your pain while I was watching you."

Price stopped for a moment and said, "Matt Baker, I will handle it. It's nothing—just a flashback caused by recent occurrences. Probably because I haven't slept."

"You can't ignore it, Sean. What did you see?" Matt looked deeply into Price's indifferent eyes.

"Listen!" Price raised his voice. Then he approached Matt and warned, "Don't stick your nose in my life. Like I said, this is my shit, and I will handle it."

Matt watched Price without saying a word. Shortly Price walked outside, leaving Matt alone in the locker room. Matt turned around and observed the shower room. He heard a dripping noise from a broken showerhead. Everything seemed normal to him. *Did Price hallucinate?* Matt wondered while checking each corner of the bathroom.

Walking outside to the main hall, he once again turned around to look at the cluttered place.

What a strange and grim atmosphere, Matt thought as he walked outside the barracks. Jenkins, Kelly, and Alejandro were waiting in the central yard where trucks and arms had been gathered. Men were mounting heavy launchers on top of trucks. In the meantime, the helicopter was constantly surveying the perimeter of the island. It was currently nearby the base, circulating with its powerful strobe light and its low, hollow engine sound. Matt looked up at the sky; it was a clear heaven with thousands of bright stars that felt unusually close to earth. He noticed that most of the armed forces had been concentrated around the base. The concentration of forces wasn't surprising, considering the exoskeleton had dared to attack the very heart of the base.

Matt asked a nearby military man who was giving orders, "What do you know so far, sir?"

"Our new objective is to stay near the base and protect the locals in the village," he explained. Looking bitter, he added, "We have bad news. A local man has gone missing. Obviously, that's the corpse inside your barracks. The wife of the missing man has informed local authorities that some kind of human-eating robot swallowed her husband." The soldier grimaced as if sensing defeat. Then he looked at Matt and continued, "It is madness. We need to catch this exoskeleton tonight, or Japanese troops will be sent to the island. Well … then we will have more things to worry about."

"How about these net launchers?" Matt asked. "Are they gonna help?"

The soldier asked Matt to follow him while the rest of the squad waited. He pointed at a launcher and explained,

"This thing can shoot a sturdy net that is built of electrically conductive material. If we're lucky in shooting the net at the machine, we can activate an electric shock wave by remote control, thereby making the machine weak and allowing us to capture it alive."

"That could work," Matt said, showing his appreciation for the plan.

"Yeah ... But there is one problem. We can't get into the forest or up steep terrain with these trucks. So we will have to wait for the exoskeleton to come near base or try to lure him out." The soldier looked up the sky, searching for the helicopter. "Unfortunately, our eyes in the sky haven't found that thing yet. The darkness makes it harder."

Matt was about to go back to the squad members when the soldier called, "Hey, you should stay near the base. Many troops have already been deployed to the village in order to prevent an unexpected attack. I'm sorry about your sergeant. We will get our next orders soon—perhaps the ultimate order to kill that beast, hopefully." The soldier put his helmet on.

"Okay," Matt answered and ran back to the squad. He kept his eyes peeled for Price, whom he hadn't seen since they'd left the barracks.

"We shouldn't hesitate anymore," Jenkins said and pointed at the armory, the door of which was open. Most of the military personnel had gathered around the trucks to mount the launchers. None of the men were nearby the armory, which gave them an opportunity. "As you said, this machine is probably nearby. We can hunt it down."

"C'mon." Kelly gestured with his hand, and they moved to the armory.

Once Kelly got inside, he immediately began rushing around, knowing exactly what to take. "Machine guns with mounted grenade launchers, night-vision goggles, and extra ammunition," he said aloud as he gathered the supplies. He looked at Matt and said convincingly, "They won't notice us. We're the special squad. In this emergency situation, we have a chance to get business done without more casualties."

Matt passed out the supplies Kelly had gathered and said, "Okay, let's start at the back entrance of the barracks." He put on his night-vision goggles and adjusted them. Then he quickly checked his machine gun and turned to the others. "Jenkins, you stay close to me. Kelly, you and Alejandro are together. We'll head out one at a time to avoid drawing attention and meet at the barracks. As soon as we get behind the fence, we will spread apart but keep enough distance to be in touch."

They were about to head out when Matt said, "Hold on." He reached for the nearby toolbox, picked up two pairs of wire-cutting pliers, and said, "We'll need these to cut our way through the barbed wire."

The others nodded and put on their night-vision goggles. Jenkins exhaled and moved first toward the barracks. She cobbled occasionally. The rest waited for her to get far enough away.

A sudden massive blast of wind passed by; it was the low-flying helicopter. It briefly drew the attention of the other military men, and Matt seized the distraction. "C'mon, let's go," Matt urged Kelly, and both of them headed out at once. As soon as they reached the barracks, Alejandro followed.

As they gathered together, the sound of clamoring faded into the background. They walked through the barracks to the back entrance. With a push from Matt, the doors squeaked open. Now the squad was facing the tall perimeter fence topped with tangled circles of barbed wire.

Matt took out the two pairs of pliers and passed one pair to Kelly. "We'll both climb the fence and cut an opening in the barbed wire at the top." Kelly swiftly placed the pliers in his back pocket and was already on the fence. Matt joined him and climbed up.

While they cut the barbed wire, Jenkins turned to Alejandro and asked with concern, "What did you do with the sergeant's cat, little Mr. Charcoal?"

"Don't worry; the cat is in safe hands. I gave him to a local Japanese man. I tried to explain that I'll come collect the cat later. He agreed and will look after Charcoal," Alejandro reassured her. Then he gave her a friendly whack on the arm. "Thanks for saving me from the sergeant. It was an invaluable move from you, Jenkins. I feel sorry that you were beaten so badly."

"It's all right. Anyone would have done the same," she said.

"You are a brave woman." He looked intently into her pretty eyes. "I promise to look after Mr. Charcoal, as soon as I find my brother." Alejandro walked off, put his machine gun in the holster on his back, and waited for Jenkins to climb the fence, as Matt and Kelly had successfully cut a way through the top.

Jenkins felt relieved about the cat and exhaled energetically. She took the initiative and jumped on the fence. Alejandro waited a little and glanced at the barracks. It was eerily quiet. It was still warm out, and a mild breeze shook the plants between the trees. He heard almost nothing, except for the commotion from the military preparations, which could barely be heard over here.

On the other side of fence, Matt put on his night-vision goggles. He looked around, searching for any clues that would lead them to the exoskeleton. He carefully spun his index finger, showing what direction to proceed. "Kelly and Alejandro, keep together. Stay parallel with us. As we go deeper, we will increase the distance between us," Matt instructed. Suddenly he raised his hand, making everyone stop. "Hold!" he whispered sharply. "I can see broken branches that look freshly made." Matt carefully moved forward, one step at a time, paying close attention to a track that resembled the exoskeleton's footprint. "Crack, keep your back to mine. The machine might be near us," he said in a subdued voice and turned his eyes to Kelly and Alejandro, who copied the move. They had traveled farther from Matt and Jenkins, slowly immersing themselves into the wild darkness of the unknown. Their silhouettes blended into the darkness, like shadows floating between the trees.

Heavy and nervous breathing from behind him drew Matt's attention. "Hey, Crack, are you okay?"

"I'm fine," she answered while adjusting her night-vision goggles, although she didn't feel confident. "You know, Matt, I'm truly scared," she admitted.

"Crack, I feel the same. We are dealing with something stronger than regular bad guys." He stopped and bent his head closer to her. "You and me have always managed to get through hell. This time won't be different. Let's watch each other's backs, and it's gonna be fine."

"Okay," she said and sharply exhaled to collect herself. "Okay, I've got you covered."

"Shit, where have they gone?" Matt suddenly asked, looking around for Kelly and Alejandro.

"I don't see them either," Jenkins whispered. "Should we call them?"

"Not now. Look at how this place has unusual spots where the grass and plants have been pressed down. This monster might be near." Matt examined the area around them. His attention was drawn to some enormous scratches in a tree's bark. They looked freshly made. "Hold up; don't move. We need to check this spot." Matt prepared his gun and placed his finger on the trigger. Adjusting his night-vision goggles, he twisted around. Jenkins copied his actions.

Meanwhile, Kelly and Alejandro had come to a chaotic-looking place. When Kelly saw the place, his heart rate jumped. He was breathing heavily and constantly readjusting his machine gun against his shoulder. All at once he had become exceptionally unsteady. "Alejandro, this place is no good. Can you see Matt?" he asked, his voice shaking.

There was no answer.

Kelly's heart thumped against his rib cage like crazy. He groaned, suddenly feeling a horrible headache. Quickly groping in his pockets, he found his container of pills. "Fuck," Kelly cursed as he accidently dropped the container on the ground. Abruptly, he got on all fours, seeking the pills with trembling fingers. After finding the container, he leaned against a nearby tree. He had a sickening feeling. He swallowed some pills, taking more than usual, and frowned.

"Where the fuck are you?" Kelly loudly demanded, losing his temper. He aimed his gun up at the trees cluelessly, swinging it from side to side. "C'mon, show yourself! I'm not scared. No, I'm not…" He kept yelling even louder, "I will pull your fancy battery out through your carbon ass! You damn creature!"

"Hey, dude!" Alejandro called. "Calm down." His voice was sharp and admonishing.

Kelly snapped his gun toward the sound of Alejandro's voice and then, seeing Alejandro, lowered it. Alejandro had noticed something on the tree near him. It looked like something had tried to climbed the tree using sharp edges. He walked closer to see the marks better. He lifted up his night-vision goggles and switched on the flashlight mounted to his machine gun. His eyes sharply focused on the marks. "That thing is near us," he muttered with dread.

"What is it? What did you find?" Kelly asked, observing Alejandro's examination of the tree. A thick, dark drop of liquid suddenly landed on Kelly's machine gun, followed by increasing loud buzz. His heart sank down to his toes as he lifted his eyes up. "Fuck!" he shouted, throwing himself out of the way. He hit the ground, barely dodging the dark figure that dropped from the trees. If Kelly hadn't looked up and moved, the exoskeleton would have landed right on his head.

"There you are, you son of a bitch!" Alejandro firmly planted his machine gun against his shoulder and aimed at the exoskeleton, which hadn't noticed him. He hesitated to shoot because Kelly was in the way, desperately trying to get up. Finding the perfect shot and time, Alejandro pulled the trigger. The first rounds were shot. The exoskeleton suddenly disappeared from his sight with a rapid spring. "Kelly, get up!" Alejandro rushed toward Kelly to help, hauling him up by his jacket strap.

"Fuck! It almost stamped me," Kelly exclaimed while frantically getting his gun in order.

"Are you okay?"

"Shit....I'll be fine."

"It's near us. Look up into the trees," Alejandro said while tossing his gun's barrel in all possible directions.

"Hey, where is it?" Matt shouted, his voice echoing in the distance. Matt and Jenkins were making their way over to where they'd heard the shots, but they couldn't see Kelly and Alejandro or where the exoskeleton was hiding.

"Dammit, I can't see shit!" Kelly felt intense. He looked up between the trees. He was worried about shooting because Matt and Jenkins were making their way over. "We got split up, Alejandro. Don't shoot if you're not certain. We could kill our friends by accident," Kelly warned.

"That beast is hunting us," Alejandro said, certain. He felt brave and moved closer to the spot where he'd last seen the exoskeleton.

There was a sudden short and unusual noise around them. It was hollow and increasingly strong, like before, when the machine had taken Kelly by surprise. Both men turned their guns in the direction of the sound. "Here it is," Alejandro whispered, recognizing the dark figure between the trees. He fired again, this time longer. Kelly joined in and launched a grenade toward the machine. A big blast lit up the whole area like a thousand flashing lights. It was apparent that Kelly's grenade shot had missed. The burning smoke blew toward them.

"Fuck!" Alejandro exclaimed. "It literally faded from the spot," he said while ventilating the smoke cloud away with his hands. Then he quickly ran toward where the exoskeleton had been, leaving Kelly alone.

Kelly heard a voice from behind him and turned around. Matt and Jenkins, holding their guns, had arrived.

"Where is it?" Matt asked.

"Somewhere near. It's using the trees," Kelly answered while pointing his gun up. "Look up. This thing is unpredictable and smart."

"Where is Alejandro?" Jenkins asked.

"He ran to the place where we just saw the creature." Kelly spotted him and pointed. "There he is, between those tall trees."

"We have company," Jenkins said, hearing a noise. She looked up at the sky. It was the approaching helicopter. The whirring engine sound was followed by a bright strobe light that landed between the trees in the near distance. The helicopter quickly flew over and circled around, searching the spot where the shots had been fired. Apparently the grenade explosion had drawn their attention.

Matt froze, breathless. A big shadow, cast by the helicopter light, revealed that the exoskeleton was just above his head. He quickly reacted and swiftly aimed up, shouting, "It's above me!" Unfortunately, he was blinded by the bright light of the helicopter. He temporarily couldn't see the machine.

"I can see it!" Jenkins shouted. She aimed carefully, breathed in, but didn't make a single shot. The exoskeleton was scared away by the helicopter lights before she could shoot. It jumped through the trees in huge leaps until it disappeared from their sight.

"Go back to base immediately! This is an order!" someone announced loudly through a megaphone. The warning was repeated a few more times, and then the helicopter flew away, chasing after the escaped exoskeleton.

"Dammit, it was that close," Matt said while staring at the helicopter, which continued to pursue the creature. Judging by the lights, the exoskeleton was moving extremely quickly. After a while the helicopter began floating randomly in the air, apparently having lost the trail. *This just makes matters worse,* Matt thought.

"Are you all right?" Jenkins asked Kelly, who was covered with dirt and light bruises.

"Yeah, except that thing almost got me," he answered and checked his gun. "Fuck, that thing is agile. It moves like a giant grasshopper." Kelly removed his night-vision goggles and whacked the dirt off.

"We should go back to base. The exoskeleton has run off," Matt said. "It'll be too difficult to chase it down with just four of us." He looked back toward base and added, "I don't know what they're gonna do with us. We ignored the general's order." Matt's uncertainty leaked into his voice.

"The general's order," Kelly chuckled, leaning against a tree. "That asshole is sitting in a cozy room while we are in this mess fighting against our own secret weapon."

Alejandro joined the others. He seemed reluctant to go back to base. "Fuck this helicopter announcement. I recommend we carry on hunting the exoskeleton. We almost got it." He grabbed a bullet cartridge and reloaded his gun. "What do you think, guys?" He looked around at everyone. There was a moment of silence.

"Alejandro," Matt began, "I think we should go back to base. Perhaps we can try to convince the others to arm up and gun down the exoskeleton. We can't handle that creature by ourselves." The others felt the same but didn't say anything.

"That would just be a waste of time," Alejandro said, scorning the idea. "I'll go on my own, then. I have unfinished business with that creature." He was determined.

Matt grabbed Alejandro's gun and held him back. "Please don't!" he said, raising his voice. "This is suicide. You can't handle it on your own. That machine will kill you."

Alejandro yanked his gun out of Matt's hand and snapped, "This is between me and that creature. I need to find my brother. I will find him; he is alive." It was a stubborn reply, and it heated the atmosphere.

Matt punched him in the face, yelling, "Your brother is dead!" Alejandro dropped to the ground. Infuriated, Matt grabbed him by the jacket. "Open your eyes, Alejandro! How many proofs do you need? That monster brought a human corpse to us!"

Quickly breaking out of Matt's grip, Alejandro pushed him away and got up. He angrily pointed his finger at Matt, warning, "You better stay away!" He felt his jaw, to see if any damage had been done. "If necessary, I will go through you."

"I won't let you." Matt wasn't satisfied and approached Alejandro again. Before he got close, Jenkins jumped between them.

"Enough!" she said loudly. She held Matt away and, gravely looking into his eyes, said, "Let him go. It won't solve any problems if you hold him back by force."

"This is suicide," Matt snapped again. He looked at the Javier twin over Jenkins, who was still holding them apart. "Hey, Alejandro. We can figure out a different way to kill that thing. Let's go back to base, and I will try to convince more men to hunt it down." Matt softened his tone, hoping to change Alejandro's mind.

"You can do that. I wish you luck," Alejandro said. He put his goggles on and turned toward where the helicopter had last been seen. "I will not go back to base; they will definitely disarm us." He was confident. "Every minute counts. I can't wait any longer." Alejandro then walked off on his own.

Matt was about to say something when Jenkins looked intently at him, and so he held back. She managed to stop him from further escalating the conflict. Next to him, Kelly sat on the ground by a tree, feeling exhausted; he picked up his gun and checked its condition.

"Are we gonna go back to base now?" Kelly asked while looking at the lights in the distance. He sighed. "They have no chance of catching it. That thing has outsmarted everyone."

"Yes, we shall go back." Matt put his gun on his back. His tone indicated disappointment and uncertainty. As he waited for Kelly to get up, he continued to reassure Jenkins, and then they walked toward base.

Alejandro Javier picked up his pace and walked deeper into the forest. What a mysterious place, so dark and quiet again. Just minutes ago there had been a big commotion and shoot-out, but now things had gone back to their natural eerie silence. It was almost unbelievable. As he walked, Alejandro periodically stopped and searched for possible footprints. He found evidence of blood, presumably from the sergeant's dead body. The bloodstains had been left on smaller branches. Perhaps the exoskeleton had hid in this spot for cover. "I will find you," Alejandro said confidently. He rubbed a bloodstained leaf between his fingers, analyzing the time it would have taken the machine to get to this spot.

He was sure that he was on the right track to finding the machine.

After he'd covered a good distance, Alejandro felt completely tired, both physically and mentally. He hadn't succeed in finding the machine. Even the footprints had disappeared. It made him angry and disappointed with himself. Dropping his machine gun by a tree, he collapsed and leaned against the tree with mixed feelings. Alejandro slowly slid down. There was nobody around, so he was left to his thoughts, which felt almost palpable. He kept a relentless hope that he would find the machine and get revenge. Alejandro started sobbing, growing emotional. Slowly he took off his helmet and released the straps of his jacket, releasing some tightness. "Where are you, Antonio?" he asked calmly, but he was unable to say more, because the emotions took over his body. He felt cold waves throughout his body and began to tremble. A sudden despair set in. "Help me, Brother! You gotta help me. I can't find you," Alejandro cried. "Please!" he exclaimed, desperately praying. He lay down on the ground among the long grass and other plants. He felt weak and insecure in the middle of the dark forest, which hid danger and uncertainty.

Some time later, Alejandro got up. He sat and held his head, still grieving. Looking around, he picked up his helmet, put it on, and grabbed his gun. He resumed his trudge through the dark forest, with its lonely and unfamiliar terrain, completely remote from everything; nothing lived here except himself and thoughts. Only occasionally was the gentle calm interrupted by blaring sounds from the base. He looked up at the trees and spun around. No sign of the machine's presence. He shouted loudly, "Come and get me!

I challenge you, you damn creature!" His voice echoed far into the distance. He heard nothing else but the sound of leaves occasionally shaking in the mild breeze. Alejandro proceeded to walk ahead at a more vigorous pace. *I will find you, brother,* he thought, determined.

With each step the weight on him grew. After a long walk in the dark and unusually quiet forest, Alejandro reached a place where the trees became scarce and the forest opened onto a view of the beach. Alejandro lifted up his night-vision goggles and rubbed his drowsy eyes. Surprisingly, he was still near the base but now on the other side. So far he hadn't succeeded in getting even the slightest sign of the exoskeleton. It was like the longest nightmare of his life from which he couldn't wake. "Shit," he cursed. "I have come full circle."

Alejandro felt disoriented. In his daze he walked along the beach, watching the impressive waves, which were dazzlingly white from the clear moonlight. Alejandro smelled the ocean breeze and felt like passing out. He glanced over and saw the freight ship departing in the distance. As he looked more closely, he realized there was something unusual nearby. A gigantic dark figure was making its way toward the ship. Alejandro sharpened his eyes and recognized the silhouette. It was the exoskeleton running toward the freight ship. He watched as it took long strides before executing a lengthy jump, landing squarely on the ship. "No way," he said, astonished. Rubbing his eyes, Alejandro put his goggles on and tried to witness the scene through his binoculars. Unfortunately, the dark figure had blended in with the silhouette of the ship. Alejandro was confused; he wasn't sure whether he'd hallucinated the event or not. All the stress and exhaustion from hunting had taken its toll on his mental perception and rationality. "I should go back to base to inform the others," Alejandro said.

He placed his steps carefully as he walked down the cliff. Stopping, he wiped the stinging sweat from his eyes, the salty tears produced by his skin. His whole body ached. He was so tired that he couldn't collect himself and trembled as he made each step down the low cliff. However, he gathered enough energy to continue. The rocks here were covered with moss; some of them were quite large with sharp edges. His body slowed down with each subsequent move. Taking a long stride, he placed his foot on a rock's flat surface. Unbeknownst to him, the rock was moist, with a thin layer of moss. Suddenly he slipped and lost his balance. He landed harshly in a wide gap with more rocks. He lay motionless there, his gun's belt tangled around him.

"Hey, Brother, do you need help?" Antonio's calm voice called. He looked down at Alejandro from above. He kneeled down and reached out his hand.

"You found me!" Alejandro got emotional but still couldn't move. He desperately tried to get up but couldn't. His body was failing him.

Antonio slowly pulled his outstretched hand back from his brother, his face sad. He asked, "Why don't you just let me go?"

"You are my blood, my brother!" Alejandro answered, puzzled by the question. "You found me because you were looking for me. Right?"

Antonio shook his head and looked off indirectly.

"Hey," Alejandro called and reached out his hand. His eyes glittered with hope.

"We can't be together for eternity. Our roads have split … This is the moment. But in our hearts, we will be together forever," Antonio said.

"What are you talking about?" Alejandro grew frustrated and tried harder to get out of his awkward position, to no avail. He begged, "Antonio, just help me up. I've been looking for you."

"Alejandro, please calm down." Antonio's face had a warm smile now. "I'm fine, Brother. It's gonna be all right with me. Please stop seeking me. It is hard to watch you suffer." He stood up and walked away, disappearing from view.

"Nooo!" Alejandro screamed. "Come back, Antonio. I need you!" He tried with all his might to get up but could not. He reached his hand out, hoping for his brother to come back, but Antonio never returned.

Day 5

Early in the morning, it was still dark. The freight ship was departing for Tokyo, its knots increasing powerfully, creating a loud, almost unbearable noise. The freight ship had multiple sections of large containers. One massive load strapped to the ship hadn't been unloaded; it was completely covered with tarpaulin. Most of the cabin crew had gone inside for the rest. The men were so exhausted from the unloading process that they failed to check the decks. Waves splashed higher and higher on the sides as the ship increased its speed.

"I'm going to have a cigarette. Who would like to join me?" a sixty-year-old crew member asked inside the cabin. The man was quite athletic for his age, but his face looked considerably worn dry with a lot of wrinkles. There were roughly ten men in the cabin. Holding his coffee mug, the man waited for a response. "Whatever," he said when no one replied. Without company, he walked outside the cabin for some fresh ocean air. The old sea wolf admired the fading stars in the sky and proceeded to take a slow, relaxing stroll along the decks. He came to the still-loaded container, which contained supplies that had turned out to be unnecessary. He leaned against the tarpaulin and smoked a couple of times, humming a tune.

The old man smelled a rank, decaying body. He inhaled fear from it. The fear seemed to pour out, forming a mist. "What on earth?" He grew puzzled as he noticed some commotion by the container. Something had pulled the tarpaulin briefly and then ceased. His heart throbbing, he stepped backward to see more. "Are they birds or something?" he asked himself. The commotion repeated, this time wildly. The old man saw something horrible then. The corpse of very big military man in uniform dropped onto the decks with a bang. The face of the body was severely damaged and covered with dried blood. "Jesus Christ!" the old man said loudly. His legs became noodles. His coffee mug slipped out of his hand when he raised his head up. A large mechanical arm was aimed at him with opened fingers. With a sudden, rapid movement, the machine grabbed the old man's terrified face and pulled his whole body up. The man's screams were cut short as his body vanished like a bullet shot from a gun.

"Hey, what's held up that old man for so long?" one of the younger crew members asked while playing a game of solitaire. The old man's smoking breaks normally took five minutes, but this time it had been almost half an hour. "I'll have a look. Perhaps he has fallen overboard," the man said, standing up. As he got outside, he instantly sensed a sinister ambience. He puckered his nose at the pungent smell that was blowing toward him. *Smells like burnt pig,* the young man thought. However, he collected enough courage and went closer to the big load covered with tarpaulin. "Fuckin' 'ell!" he shouted, shocked. The dead body of a sergeant was lying on the deck. He stepped back and twisted sharply toward the cabin. All of a sudden, something heavy jumped on the roof of the nearby cabin. The young man was paralyzed for a moment, and then he flattened himself against the wall and shouted, "Hey! There is something on the roof! Something really big!"

"What's going on?" the captain's assistant asked, walking outside the cabin. Inside the cabin, the captain froze at the sudden bash above his head. Scared, he looked up and then cautiously reached for the radio. A gigantic mechanical arm rapidly smashed through the window, grabbed the captain, pulled him out, and threw him over the railings of the ship. The body hit the water's surface violently which created loud splash. The captain barely had time to scream. The machine began reaching for another man. Driven by panic, the rest of the crew left the cabin immediately. It was just the beginning of their terror.

The men outside the cabin shouted in fear. The exoskeleton aimed its next attack at the remaining men. It had positioned itself on the roof, which made it harder to see. Unexpectedly, it threw two more men into the water. The young man who had gone to search for the old man had managed to hide behind the still-loaded container. His heart pounded hard as he heard more screams and hard hits to the cabin crew. The machine had killed almost everyone on board except the young man. Heavy, unnatural steps made their way closer to him. He faced a tough decision whether to jump in the water or be killed by the vicious creature. Making his decision, he raced to the side of the ship. Before he could jump off, though, the exoskeleton managed to grab him with its gigantic arm and pulled him back on deck. He was so terrified to see the corpse of his fellow crew member inside the machine.

The exoskeleton grabbed the man's head with two fingers and twisted it in the direction of Tokyo. To his surprise, the machine kept him alive and carried him to the cabin. "What do you want?" the man stammered, trembling. The machine brutally threw him inside the cabin by the navigation bridge. The exoskeleton again pointed in the direction of Tokyo. The city could already be seen on the horizon. "Okay, I get it," the man said. Shaking badly, he went to the control panel and straightened the ship's course toward Tokyo.

The machine was too big to fit inside the cabin, so it moved to the front window, which had been smashed. It reached inside and slowly wrapped its dreadful arm around the man's upper body. A small, twisty wire extended out of the machine's arm and plugged into a hole in the control panel. The man was baffled. *What's going to happen now?* he wondered, scared to death. As the ship got closer to the coast, the exoskeleton electrocuted the man with a shock that dropped him to the floor. The course had been set accurately toward the port; the ship carried on its way on autopilot without a single crew member.

The bright morning sun appeared on the horizon. It shone lustrously on the island, which hadn't been calm all night long. The helicopter rose again into the sky, seeking the escaped machine. Many military trucks were driving around on the graphite-black sandy beaches. Waves of vivid blue water hit the coast impressively. It so happened that some military personnel were clamoring around near the place where Alejandro had fallen. Random voices got closer to Alejandro, but the men weren't yet aware of the missing man between the rocks. According to orders, they were continuing to search for the exoskeleton, which had managed to evade capture so far.

"Hey, there is someone down in that gap," a soldier called upon discovering Alejandro.

"Is he alive?" another man asked.

"I don't know. Let's take a closer look."

The two soldiers, in full gear, crawled inside the gap in order to check on Alejandro. One soldier carefully examined Alejandro for serious injuries. Then he lightly tapped on Alejandro's face, which was covered with sand. "Hey, soldier, can you hear me?" he asked a few times.

"Ah ... uh ..." Alejandro groaned and slowly moved his head to the side. His eyes were shut because of the bright daylight. He could hear voices.

"Take it easy, bud," the soldier said and placed his hands underneath Alejandro's head for support.

"What happened?" Alejandro asked, his voice hoarse. He was completely out of touch with reality. He tried to get up from his supine position.

"Looks like you fell down by accident, bud," the soldier guessed, scanning the rough environment. "Don't rush; we will help you."

The other man asked, "What's your name, soldier?"

"My name is Alejandro Javier." He sat and looked around. It was baffling to find himself in such a place. His lips were dry and crinkled. He asked, "Do you have any water?"

The soldier swiftly passed over a one-liter bottle of water. Alejandro took it and literally sucked it empty. "You've been seriously dehydrated. Take another one," the soldier said, passing over another bottle from his fellow soldier. Alejandro emptied this bottle at almost the same speed.

"Ahhhh." Alejandro had satisfied his thirst. He released his helmet strap and put his helmet to the side.

"Are you injured? Can you walk? You look as if you've walked a hundred miles," one of the soldiers said, standing up.

"Yes …" Alejandro hesitated. "I think I'm fine." He looked at his legs and, carefully supporting his weight with his hands, straightened them. He looked tired and worn out, and his eyes were red. Inhaling fresh air, he asked, "Have you found the exoskeleton?"

"Not yet! We've been looking all night. Unfortunately, no luck so far," one of the soldiers answered, holding Alejandro's jacket strap to help keep him balanced. "We'll carry on searching," he added.

"Mr. Javier, how did you come to be unconscious in this place?" the other man asked.

Alejandro painfully got to his feet, his face drowsy and confused. He felt as if he'd been through an army battle. He tried to put the pieces together. His naturally tanned forehead wrinkled as he frowned. As soon as he began to remember the details, he said, "I was coming down …" He paused and looked at the grave faces that wanted answers.

"Mr. Javier, are you from Bakerman's squad?"

"Yes." Alejandro looked at him with one eye open, squinting from the bright sun. He sensed a potential problem.

"You shouldn't have acted on your own. Your orders from the general are no different than ours," the soldier said.

"Hold on. I think I just remembered something important." Alejandro instantly turned his eyes to where he'd last seen the freight ship. He pointed, repeatedly stabbing his index finger in the air. "There, at the beach where the freight ship departed." He calmed down, inhaled, and continued, "I'm pretty sure the exoskeleton jumped on the freight ship before it left. I saw it."

One of the soldiers took out his binoculars and looked at the place Alejandro had indicated. It was quite far away from this spot. Without binoculars, it would be difficult to see anything that far away during the day let alone at night. The soldier's face indicated his doubts about Alejandro's observations. He put down his binoculars and said, "Mr. Javier, you've been severely dehydrated and dropped unconscious. It would be worthwhile for you to rest. Let's go back to base." He and his fellow soldier looked at each other as if having the same thought. They suspected that Alejandro had hallucinated.

"You should allocate forces to that freight ship before it's too late," Alejandro insisted. "That ship is headed for Tokyo. It must be stopped as soon as possible."

"C'mon, Javier." The soldier pointed at their truck. "We'll take you back to base."

Alejandro vividly remembered seeing the exoskeleton leap onto the ship before he slipped on the rock and was knocked unconscious. He knew he was right, but he was too exhausted to convince the soldiers of that. He walked to the truck without argument.

Arriving back at the base, Alejandro raised his red eyes and saw vehicles and other units in position. *It's all in vain to focus forces here,* he thought. As the truck pulled up near the barracks, he felt too weak to get out. His attention was drawn to the barracks' damaged entrance, which was evidence of the exoskeleton's immense power. "That machine is after something bigger," he muttered.

"Mr. Javier, you should rest," one of the men in the front of the truck said, also looking at the barracks. He stepped out and walked to open the truck doors for Alejandro.

"Okay," Alejandro said reluctantly. He felt nauseated seeing the base again. His heart dragged under its excessive load. He coughed when the sun shone into his eyes. Some military men were clamoring around the base. Alejandro glanced around, fixing his eyes momentarily on the beach, and turned back to the barracks. The soldier made sure he went inside.

Nobody was inside the barracks. The damaged interior spoke of the previous night's chaos. Alejandro went to the nearest bed and fell on it in his dirty uniform. He was so worn out and felt defeated. His eyelids slowly shut, and he fell asleep immediately.

The sound of boots echoed in the corridor. The sound was familiar and unpleasant, reminding Alejandro of somebody. Suddenly the main hall was restored to good order without any damage. Even though it was overcast outside, it felt as if an intense and bright sun shone inside. The atmosphere felt warm and pleasant, like sitting by a huge fire in a cottage. Silence took over the entire premises; the commotion from outside gradually faded until it stopped completely. Only the sound of the boots remained, growing louder. The steps continued, finally stopping by Alejandro's bed.

Alejandro opened his eyes slowly, sensing somebody's presence. He looked up at the ceiling, ignoring the nearby figure. He felt a weight on his bed as the person sat down. The person sighed deeply, as if indicating remorse. "Why did life take away from me what I loved the most?" Alejandro recognized the unusually serene voice as belonging to the sergeant.

Keeping his head on the pillow, Alejandro shifted his eyes toward the speaking figure—the sergeant.

"My soul was never restored after I lost them," the sergeant said sorrowfully. "It was like I had become a burning peat bog without any idea where to find the source of the fire. The fire kept burning and burning until everything had turned to ash. I wish I could have found the way to extinguish that devastating fire, but I was too weak to find it." His voice grew slower and more sorrowful. It was evident the sergeant blamed himself for the past.

"What happened?" Alejandro asked.

"My loved ones ..." The sergeant paused. "They reminded me that life was worth fighting for. I wish I could have seen them, at least once, to say goodbye." The sergeant began sobbing, his big body shaking. "I didn't have that chance. I carried that pain in my body always. It was my way of dealing with their deaths." There was a moment of silence mixed with the howling of a mild breeze. "I never learned to let them go, and that destroyed me. I was like a tower slowly crumbling on the inside until only the exterior was left."

"Who were your loved ones?" Alejandro asked.

"My wife and my daughter."

Alejandro felt the bed move as the sergeant got up. "Please take care of Mr. Charcoal," the sergeant said. The sound of his boots slowly faded toward the corridor, and his silhouette began to blur. Alejandro turned over eagerly in order to see the sergeant. He saw the back of the sergeant's big shoulders as the sergeant's silhouette blended into a bright, dazzling light. That was the last he saw of Sergeant Bakerman.

"Ahh," Alejandro exclaimed as he was woken up by the strong feelings running through his entire body. He looked around and saw the place in the same chaotic disarray as before. It wasn't sunny but overcast. Alejandro rose to a seated position and grabbed his head. He stared at the place where he'd last seen the sergeant. "Fuck!" He rubbed his ears energetically, trying to ease the mental torture. "Get out of my head. Leave me alone," he demanded, feeling desolate. As his breathing returned to normal, he got out of bed. He checked his wristwatch and realized that he had slept a couple of hours. "I need to see the others," he said and rushed to collect his stuff by the bed.

"We have received new orders," Major Trent announced, his voice dry and pedantic. He was a short, older man with no neck. His lean face sported a gray mustache. He walked with Sean Price over to where Matt and Jenkins stood by some trucks outside. The major looked around and saw Kelly resting on a bench with his helmet over his face. "Hey, you, come over!" Major Trent shouted. Kelly dropped his helmet and stood up. His eyes had an indifferent look that slowly turned into curiosity. Capturing the moment, he joined the others to hear the announcement.

"Since you were assigned to Project XS, you will be given another chance to hunt down the escaped machine,"

Major Trent started, shifting his grave look between the squad members, one eye squinted. "Yesterday you violated orders. Instead of suspensions, you will get another try."

"What are these new orders?" Kelly interrupted.

"Wait!" Major Trent said firmly. "I will get there." His eyes returned to the others. He inhaled and laid out the new plan. "Unfortunately, we can't succeed in catching the exoskeleton with our original methods, because it is too advanced. Our only option is to use the same tools that the exoskeleton is using against us."

"Major," Matt said, "do you want us to get inside those machines again?"

The major's wrinkled face took on a look of approval, and he nodded. "Yes, exactly! You have used them before. Consider this a chance to catch that beast and not get suspended." His sharpened eyes turned to the others as he rolled up his sleeves. "The geisha party is over. They have left us; they won't entertain us anymore. Now the huge bill must be paid." Kelly laughed, drawing the major's gaze. The major spat with contempt and continued, "We ain't got money for that. So you guys are gonna work your asses off to foot the bill."

Jenkins's body language showed disapproval. She turned her head away and shook it repeatedly. Kelly felt the same but kept his mouth shut, though he continued chuckling at the major's comments.

"I'm sorry, but this is nuts," Jenkins said, grimacing, her face grave. "Major, I'm not going to agree to these orders."

"Listen," the major said, raising his voice. He paused and spat again. "The engineers on this island have reported that the remaining machines haven't been set up with the malicious upgrade. The main reason why Michael Sevchenko got suspended is because he deliberately set up this upgrade without final approval." The major halted, vigorously snapping his fingers. He contemplated the plans, then continued, "Everyone on this base has been searching all night long for the exoskeleton without sleep. They are tired and have become less effective. The helicopter has filled up numerous times and continues to scan the island back and forth." Major Trent became heated and raised his voice even more. "For goodness' sake, we have no clue where that monster is hiding. If I could talk to pandas, they would provide more useful information than all our soldiers combined. If we don't change strategy, then we are in big trouble."

"Can you modify our orders so that we're allowed to kill that machine?" Matt asked.

"No!" The major snapped. "We will capture it. That is the fucking general's order!"

"Screw that order!" Jenkins dared to say. "You can suspend me if you like, but I'm not getting inside any of those machines again."

"Me neither," Kelly said, his voice dipped with fatigue.

Matt shook his head. A variety of mute expressions crossed his face. He was sure that he would refuse to accept this new order too. He looked at Price, who had been listening without saying anything. Price, his arms behind his back, was staring at the beach with a look of longing. It was difficult for the others to guess what was on his mind.

"I will disregard these orders, Major," Sean Price said.

Looking dissatisfied, Major Trent rubbed his sweaty clenched fist against his pant leg. He frowned and calmly said, "Okay, then I have no choice left but to suspend you."

"I accept these orders!" a loud voice called. Alejandro appeared from behind one of the trucks. He looked determined, no matter what circumstances lay ahead. He walked confidently toward the other squad members, who looked at him in surprise.

"Who are you?" Major Trent asked.

"My name is Alejandro Javier. I'm another member of the squad assigned to Project XS," he explained. "If you need a man inside one of those machines, you can count on me." He maintained strong eye contact with the major, showing his readiness to participate.

"Well … I'm glad to hear that," the major said, his voice softening slightly. "But we need at least one more."

Alejandro looked around at everyone and said, "We are wasting our time staying here. I saw the exoskeleton escape from the island." He paused and examined everyone's reaction. Then he resumed, "Before the freight ship departed from the coast, the exoskeleton managed to jump on it. I saw it."

Major Trent's eyes indicated instant disbelief, but he asked, "When did this happen?"

"I suppose it was early morning, still dark as far as I can recall," Alejandro said.

"Why didn't you report it immediately?"

"I was about to, but then I slipped on a rock and was knocked unconscious for hours. Two soldiers found me. Didn't they tell you all of this?" Alejandro asked, looking at the major in surprise. "I told them everything when they found me in that unfortunate state."

Major Trent's eyebrows twisted. He suddenly remembered that two soldiers had indeed told him hours ago about a man they'd found who claimed to have seen the exoskeleton jump on the freight ship. They'd said the man was suffering from severe dehydration, so he brushed the information aside. "All right, I will look into this," he said. "I need one more man to get into a machine. In the meantime, I'm going to try to contact the captain of the freight ship." Before the major went to the communication room, he added, "See you at the basement shortly."

Walking inside the communication room, Major Trent immediately grabbed a plastic cup and filled it up with water. The air inside was thick like in a greenhouse, almost unbearably so. "Switch on the fans. You must be boiling like shrimp in here," the major said, rattling a big ventilation grate.

"It's broken," the dispatcher said while wiping sweat off his forehead.

After gulping his water quickly, the major crushed the cup and threw it into a trash can. "I need to get in touch with the captain of the freight ship," he said, moving closer to the dispatcher.

"Okay." Adjusting the frequency, the dispatcher tried to call the freight ship. They patiently waited, but they received no response after repetitive signals.

The major, his thirst not satisfied, returned to the watercooler. He turned back to the dispatcher with a cup in hand and said, "This is no good." He swallowed some water and urged, "Keep calling."

"Major, there is no answer."

"I see." Disappointed, he went by the window and aggressively threw his cup in the trash. He watched the squad through the window. His stomach sank at the stark reality of the situation. "This is it," he said dryly. "The machine is making hara-kiri with us human beings. I'm too old for this game. I predict that soon sakura blossoms will decorate my grave."

The whole squad was thrilled by Alejandro's arrival. They patted him on the shoulder and exchanged friendly handshakes.

"I'm glad to see you back," Jenkins said, expressing her delight. The rest of the squad didn't hesitate to show their appreciation too. Alejandro had come back to base in one piece.

"Sorry about yesterday," Matt said.

"It's fine," Alejandro said. He was a bit bitter but accepted the apology. "Guys, I'm being serious—I saw that thing jump on the ship. It is up to something bigger. I'm ready to get inside a machine and run after it. I'm scared to think of the consequences if it reaches Tokyo. Hopefully Major Trent will get an affirmative response from the ship and act accordingly."

"I'll go with you," Kelly said, surprising everyone. "For fuck's sake, either way the choices are bad. Let's go after that son of a bitch." He felt confident and looked at everybody. "C'mon. We were assigned to Project XS. Let's finish this mission forever." He tossed his hands into the air, showing his dedication. Then he exchanged a strong handshake with Alejandro.

"Okay, I highly appreciate your intentions," Matt said. "Let's meet by the basement, then." He readjusted his armored jacket and walked toward Major Trent, who was still at the communication room's window staring outside. When Matt got to the open door, he and the major exchanged vague glances.

"In one hour's time the engineers will open the basement and activate the machines," Major Trent explained to Matt in a hurried voice. "There's something wrong with the freight ship. We haven't gotten a response through the radio yet. I suppose Javier was right. We will send another boat to investigate the freight ship." As the major sat in a swivel chair, he said, "Tell your squad members about the breach."

"Copy that. Another man agreed to get inside the machine."

"That's good....and now go back and disseminate the latest update."

"Understood." Matt gave a thumbs-up and walked to the basement.

Matt relayed the latest news to the others. Turning to Alejandro, he said, "You were right about the freight ship. There's something wrong. The captain hasn't replied to any of the major's radio messages. However, it's not certain yet whether it's because of the exoskeleton."

"There's no other possibility," Alejandro said, confident. "This is just getting worse."

Matt didn't know what to say. Then he looked at the food court, which seemed to still be functional. "We have one hour before the basement opens. Is anyone hungry? We should get something before we start our new mission." He watched them, hands on his hips.

"Why not?" Kelly said, expressing a little indignation. "You know, whatever ... Let's enjoy our last meal. Who knows?"

As they walked toward the food court, Alejandro's mood shifted. He lagged behind, his head bent downward. His sense of grief washed over him again. He tried to smother it. Minutes ago he'd been feeling uplifted with the new ventures, but now he felt down again. And it was no surprise. Alejandro suddenly walked off from the group toward the barracks.

"Where is he going?" Matt glanced up inquiringly.

Concerned, Jenkins stopped. "You know, I'm not that hungry. I'll go see Alejandro." It was apparent in her eyes how she felt for him and wanted to give support.

"Okay, Crack," Matt said.

Jenkins immediately walked toward the barracks.

Alejandro was sitting on his brother's bed. He was hungry. He hadn't eaten in God knew how long. The hunger and heat combined made for a poisonous taste resembling defeat. *Yes,* he thought, *that's what it is: I've been defeated in some obscure way.*

Jenkins stood by the entrance watching Alejandro. Then she quietly walked inside and continued observing him. His back was hunched, and his head hung slack. He was holding something in his hands. His body shook occasionally. Alejandro was sobbing, Jenkins realized. She inhaled deeply and walked closer to the bed, avoiding the debris on the floor. She sat next to him and gently wrapped her arms around him. He didn't even react, just kept mourning. His tears were dropping on Antonio's tiny poem book with hard gray cover. Jenkins hugged him closer and looked at the book.

"My brother has left me something," he said in a shaking voice.

"No ..." Jenkins calmly whispered. "Your brother had a big heart. It is not something just for you. It is for the whole world. His poems are beautiful, and his message deserves to be shared with everyone." She placed a hand on the poem book.

He sobbed and said, "I saw him, when I was on the beach. He said …" The words were coming harder. Alejandro swallowed and continued, "He said … to please stop seeking him because it's hard for him to watch." At this point Alejandro got very emotional and couldn't say anything else.

"Alejandro," she said, her voice soothing, "that is what your brother desires the most." Jenkins took a deep breath and added, "He is with you—in your heart." She really felt his pain. She bit her trembling lip while looking over at him. Abruptly, she was reminded of something similar from her past.

"I wish I could listen to him, but I can't. The moment I saw him, he was so real, like you are next to me." Alejandro remembered lying between the rocks and seeing Antonio. He breathed in and wiped away his tears. "It is difficult to accept that he is gone. That thought is torturing my mind. I can't even sleep, because someone comes and visits me when I do." His breathing had now stabilized, but his body remained alert. He pointed at the bed where he'd been sleeping before. "There I saw Sergeant Bakerman hours ago; he was mourning his lost family."

"What did he say?"

"He said …" Alejandro shut his eyes, trying to recall the sergeant's words. "He basically said that he felt guilty and sick over his actions but that the loss of his family had gradually destroyed his soul, like a growing cancer."

"That is sad. Nobody really knew anything about the sergeant. Is that true?"

"I don't know. But that moment when he was sitting on the bed with me felt so real," Alejandro said.

Jenkins sighed, released him, and placed her elbows on her knees. "I had an older brother," she said. "I grew up in a family with a lot of brothers. My mother raised all of us by herself. I was the youngest and the only girl in the family. I was closest to my older brother Keanan. He was my role model." She looked at the floor, remembering. "Keanan was fearless and a reputable man. He used to say, 'Lil sister, you my guardian angel. Kayla, we gonna be on the top of the mountain. Mark my words.' As a family, we were not doing well. Our mother often struggled to provide for us. That was heartbreaking. Keanan looked for the best chances to succeed in life. But one day, he changed." She paused for a moment.

Alejandro didn't say a word, just kept listening. He slowly rubbed the poem book with his thumb.

"Keanan became a different person. Nobody really knew what he was doing or why he was so rarely home. It drove me mad back then." Jenkins immersed deeper into her intimate memories. "I was just thirteen years old, but I sensed something suspicious. Eventually I demanded Keanan explain what he was up to. His response was 'I'm doing this for the sake of our family, Kayla. It is not that easy!' He looked at me so intently with tears in his eyes, and I could sense some serious trouble. He turned around and left. It was the last time I saw him." Jenkins lifted her head; she had tears running down her face. "I was so angry with Keanan for years to come. I couldn't understand how he could just simply vanish from our lives. As I got older, I joined the police and later SWAT. I wanted to use the advantages of my position in order to find Keanan. I can still remember the drug-cartel mission where I finally found him. There were so many casualties, because two gangs had clashed together. I collapsed and felt so weak the moment I recognized my older brother's dead body. He had been involved in the drug business so deep that he couldn't find a way out." Jenkins was breathing faster from remembering these details of her life.

"So your brother saved you and your family," Alejandro said.

Jenkins nodded approvingly, wiping her tears. "Yes, he cut ties with me and my family in order to protect us from other gangsters who might come after us. Keanan sacrificed his freedom and identity because of love that stayed in his heart forever." She hugged Alejandro again. "It is hard and difficult. It takes time to accept horrible truths. Alejandro, please listen to your brother."

"Thank you, Jenkins, for sharing these private details about your life." He put the poem book into his jacket and said, "I will try …" He paused, clenching one of his fists. "I will try to listen to him!" he said with more emphasis. He got up and energetically adjusted his armored jacket. The instant move showed his determination to finish the beast that had taken his brother away.

"Okay," she said, getting up. "Okay. Let's go see the rest of the squad." She tapped Alejandro on the arm firmly and added, "Please be careful with the machine. I really missed you when you were gone yesterday on your own. I had a horrible thought that you would never come back."

He looked her in the eyes and nodded. She smiled lightly at his new attitude. Alejandro had managed to collect himself a bit better. He checked that his brother's poem book was safe in his pocket and said, "Let's go."

In the center of the base, the helicopter landed. As its engine sound slowly diminished, the sounds of military men clamoring could be heard. Major Trent rushed toward the pilot to give new orders. Holding his hat, he gestured toward the ocean. It looked like the location of the escaped machine had finally been determined. Matt, Price, and Kelly stood nearby. Jenkins and Alejandro made their way closer to the others. "C'mon, Alejandro," Jenkins said. "We gotta know what's happening."

"Great that all of you are here," the major called, seeing the squad. The wind blown from the helicopter as it took off again caused them to turn their heads. As the dust settled, Major Trent positioned himself in front of the squad. "I have good news and bad news." He cleared his throat and coughed. "The good news is the exoskeleton is not on this island. But the bad news is really bad." He took a breath and continued, "The freight ship arrived at Tokyo. None of the cabin crew were found on the ship except for one man who was seriously injured. He was immediately hospitalized. His health status is critical, and he couldn't say anything about the attack." The major looked at Alejandro and said, "You were right about the ship. Although we haven't received any further evidence from the coast guard yet, the exoskeleton has probably reached the mainland. And this is alarming."

"Fuck, this machine is smart!" Kelly exclaimed in surprise. "It's obvious that attack was done by the exoskeleton. What are we gonna do now, Major?"

"I've sent the helicopter over to Tokyo to try to track the machine. In addition, agents and troops are being allocated throughout the city." The major sighed. "This is truly an unprecedented case. I fear what that machine intends to do. Tokyo is one of the most densely populated place on the planets." The major spat, gazed at the beach, and added, "I'm afraid the vending machines soon will serve people as snacks if that exoskeleton is loose in Tokyo."

"Does it make sense to stay on this island?" Matt broke in. He looked rather nonplussed.

Major Trent thought about his question and replied, "Probably not. However"—he pointed at Kelly and Alejandro—"our volunteers will gear up in the machines. That gives us some hope." He frowned impressively, perhaps to show that, as a major, he did not concern himself with such a task.

Suddenly Kelly felt uncomfortable in his skin. His face shifted constantly, like he had a bad taste in his mouth. He turned to the major. "So that means you will send us to Tokyo?" He paused, looking at Alejandro, whose eyes were indifferent. Then, expressing his doubts, Kelly asked, "What if we're mistaken for the escaped freak machine and get killed instead?"

"We don't have a choice!" Major Trent said angrily. "It is too late to catch that monster alive. Our priority is now to destroy that thing before it plots some vicious killing spree, which I highly suspect will happen. We are fucked already!" The major got heated. His eyes indicated indignation. "Project XS has failed. The whole thing is a fiasco. Now we have become the target." In a calmer voice, the major urged, "Let's try to save what's left." He began to move off toward the basement.

"What about us?" Matt asked, looking at Jenkins and Price.

The major stopped and looked back. "Soon we will organize further maneuvers, so stick around," he said. "By the way, you can arm yourselves." He pointed to the armory.

Kelly and Alejandro began following the major to the basement. As they faced the basement, Kelly's attention was instantly drawn to the doors. He remembered the horrible malfunction that had resulted in Antonio's death. Then he swiftly glanced at the severely damaged entrance to the barracks. *This doesn't make me feel hopeful,* he thought. Meanwhile, Alejandro was fixedly staring at the slope that led down to basement. His eyes didn't move, remaining focused on a certain point. Kelly observed him, feeling unprepared for what was coming. "How are you holding up?" he asked.

"I feel …" Alejandro paused. "It's time; this is it. Honestly, I don't care anymore." Alejandro's short and bleak answer didn't encourage Kelly to go down.

"Yeah…yeah."

Alejandro noticed how Kelly's hand was shaking. It looked like one of the symptoms of panic attack.

"Oh, fuck, fuck, fuck," Kelly repeated under his breath as he stared at Major Trent, who was speaking into the intercom to gain access to the basement.

A short and hollow noise sounded on both sides as the door mechanism activated. The big doors slowly rolled up, revealing the dim, cold room of absolute emptiness. Kelly was shivering but tried very hard not to show his concerns. He pretended he was readjusting his gear. It was cold in the underground facility, but it was more than the temperature that sent sick and irregular shivers down his spine. His headache was troubling him again, mixed with feelings of fear and uncertainty about what lay ahead. An unexpected cloud of rage crept into his head. Subjectively, inside his head, the change seemed incredibly rapid, but it must have happened in less than a minute. Disguising the action from the others, Kelly sneaked a couple of painkillers. After stabilizing his anger, he looked inside again. There was nobody waiting for them in the basement.

"Come inside," Major Trent said and walked to the computer room. Both Alejandro and Kelly stood for a moment in the center of the main room. The last time they were here, they'd witnessed Antonio's torture. All the sections were closed; none of the machines had been pulled out yet. *What a grim and eerie place it has become, like the inside of an open grave,* Kelly thought. The clouds of cold water vapor were present by the sections where the machines were kept. The room looked daunting already. Kelly energetically rubbed his hands in order to keep warm. In the meantime, Alejandro stood like a statue. He didn't even react to the cold. He just fixedly stared at the sections. It was apparent that he was determined to face the escaped machine again and finish this business completely.

"All right, men," the major called from the computer room, drawing their attention.

An engineer dressed in a massively thick coat walked outside the computer room, followed by the major. The engineer fixed his dark eyes on the men who had volunteered. In the artificial lighting, the engineer seemed an average man, not impressive. He had a round, hairless face with indistinct features. He looked like a clerk in an office.

"Hey," Kelly said. "Before you pull out the machines, we ought to know if they are gonna kill us like what happened before." He stared at the engineer, who grimaced with thoughtfulness, hiding his head in his coat's collar.

"Okay." The engineer opened his small laptop and showed it to everyone. Then he opened the files for each machine. "These machines that we have in the basement don't have the latest upgrade installed." The engineer pointed to the relevant information on the screen. He said quietly and conclusively, "There is no chance that the machines will do the same as what the escaped machine did with your …" The engineer paused and looked intently at Alejandro's grave face. "Brother," he said slowly, unwilling to bring emotional pain back. The engineer inhaled and continued, explaining more slowly, "The system of the existing machines is obsolete; it doesn't have the self-adapting and learning abilities that are set up on the escaped one. Theoretically, you therefore shouldn't have the same issues with the machines here in the basement." The engineer stopped, shaking because of the cold, despite wearing a coat.

"I'm sorry—what's your name?" Kelly asked.

"Steve Stuart." The engineer extended his hand but got only a suspicious glance from Kelly, no handshake.

"Steve," Kelly said, looking shrewdly at the engineer, "make sure you disable the electricity of the machines. I mean that thing that …"

"The defibrillator," the engineer filled in. "Don't worry; it's been disabled already."

"Okay, everything is pretty much clear," the major interrupted. "Open the sections," he ordered.

The engineer pulled a remote out of his coat, fumbled with it, and activated the sections. Then he stepped closer to the others while reassuring the major. The sudden hissing sound as the sections opened made Kelly shiver, although he tried to hide it from the others. Slowly the exoskeletons were revealed. Two brighter blue lights came on in the background, displaying the sinister figures.

Alejandro stood completely motionless. His eyelids slowly dropped as if time were slowing down to a complete stop. He inhaled a deep breath and had an abrupt, vivid flashback with blurred sounds. His forehead wrinkled at the unpleasant, almost tortuous picture in his mind. He saw Antonio being electrocuted again. In addition, he heard faint voices, dampened by the mist. This horrible flashback was bound for the two of them—twin brothers.

"Are you all right?" Kelly was worried.

Getting his breathing back to normal, Alejandro said, "Yeah … just a strong flashback." He reached into his pocket, reassuring himself that his brother's poem book was still inside. "I'm fine, Kelly. I'm gonna do this regardless."

"Okay," Kelly said and looked at the major, who looked a bit puzzled.

"It's time to get inside," the major urged in a firm voice. "I want you guys to be ready to sacrifice your lives." Before they got inside, the major stood in front of them with his arms behind his back. Looking directly into their eyes, he said, "This is a war between machines and the human race. We don't know where that creature is hiding. But one thing is for sure: it has a plan. And that is more alarming than any declaration of war with another country. I never liked the idea of giving consciousness to the machines, let alone making them resemble humans. You can call me old-fashioned or retarded, but I feared something like this. When batteries were installed into the machines, it was like giving them hearts. We must win this war at any cost." He strongly stressed the last remark. After patting both men on the shoulder, he walked off.

As the major walked away, Kelly gave him a strange look. Then Kelly faced the machine. There was a sudden switching noise of a mechanism, and the machine began to move. The armguards opened, triggered by remote control. The machine was now ready to accept its human host. "Shit, how I hate this feeling," Kelly cursed while pulling his fingers through his hair anxiously. "All right, all right. They don't have the latest update. So it's gonna be fine," he consoled himself. Before getting into the machine, he glanced at both the engineer and the major. They were looking neutrally at him. Kelly turned back to the machine, muttering, "Jack, you must do this. Either way your ass is in trouble. What fucking difference does it make?" A sudden commotion of mechanical noise drew Kelly's attention. It was Alejandro, who had managed to get inside his exoskeleton already. "Okay," he said, feeling encouraged as he watched Alejandro. He swiftly got inside the machine and allowed it to embrace his body. He exhaled sharply.

The major was observing both men inside the machines when he was suddenly distracted by some radio noise. He quickly retrieved the radio from his chest pocket and picked it up. "Yes, please. Major Trent listening." His face shifted from neutral to incomprehension while listening to the announcement that the others couldn't hear. He nodded a couple of times and then put the radio back inside his pocket. "Listen up," he began in a raised tone. "Bad news. We haven't found any trace of the escaped machine in Tokyo; it literally has faded into thin air." Maintaining eye contact with the engineer, he added, "Conduct full motion checks while I go outside to inform the rest of the men." Major Trent glanced at Alejandro and Kelly. They looked back at him with the same expression—uncertainty.

"Major, do you want us to stay inside the machines?" Kelly asked.

"Yes, stay please. I'll be back soon," he said and shortly left the basement.

Outside, Matt saw the major making his way toward them. His walking pace indicated some trouble. He first went to some trucks to meet other military personnel. They chatted and clamored for a while, the major tossing his hands around in frustration. It looked like their plans had collapsed again.

"I'm going to talk with him," Matt said to Jenkins and stood up from the bench. "There is something happening. I must know."

"Okay," she agreed but stayed seated.

Matt broke his way through the other men to get closer to the major, who was leaned against the truck grinding his teeth. He looked puzzled and tired.

"Major, what's happening?" Matt asked.

"Agents haven't found any trace of the exoskeleton in Tokyo. It is almost unbelievable that it is not there."

"So are we still going to Tokyo to seek it?" Matt asked.

"But where?" Major Trent snapped. "There is no hard evidence that the exoskeleton is in the city."

"What about Javier's observation?" Matt said. "That's hard evidence of the exoskeleton jumping on the freight ship."

"It's not enough," Major Trent said and spat. He wasn't convinced at all. "Javier has gone through high stress levels and was knocked unconscious. Perhaps he saw a hallucination instead of the real thing." He lowered his chin and moved his eyes from side to side, as if trying to find some sense in this situation. He shook his head, saying, "I don't know. This is a fucking mystery."

"But almost the whole cabin crew of the freight ship disappeared, and one man was heavily injured. That must have been done by something like the exoskeleton. By the way, do you have any news from the injured man?"

"He is in a coma."

"Why don't we go out there and figure it out ourselves, Major? I highly suspect that the cabin crew's disappearance is related to the exoskeleton." Matt waited a little and added, "Javier and Kelly can use the machines. Right?"

Major Trent moved off of the truck and wrinkled his face in fury. "This is not some lovely ranch in Texas. This is Tokyo, where ten people fight for a spot on one square meter. If we send those creepy-looking machines into the city, panic is inevitable." The major coughed while clearing his throat. "I'm also afraid that the same malfunction could happen with the other machines, although the engineer claims that they are using the oldest version of software," the major said, showing his distrust of the machines.

"Is the army going to be deployed in the city?"

"Yes, I'll arrange the orders," Major Trent said and looked at the beach, contemplating the next maneuvers despite not knowing the missing exoskeleton's location. "However, we need some more time to clarify. I'll let you and your squad know once I have more information." The major briefly clasped Matt's shoulder.

"All right, Major."

Jenkins and Price sat and waited until the heated conversation between the major and Matt was over. They heard the arguments from a distance but didn't feel bothered to intervene. Matt came back, kicking rocks on the sandy ground.

"What did he say?" Jenkins asked.

"We have to wait until they're sure about the escaped exoskeleton's location." Matt picked up the bottle of water near the bench and gulped some down. "So far, agents haven't found any trace of the machine in Tokyo. Despite Alejandro's observations and the disappearance of the freight ship's crew, they won't believe the machine is in Tokyo until they determine its exact location."

"This just sucks."

"I know," Matt agreed.

Sean Price stood up from the bench, swiftly put his knife back into its holder, and said, "Okay, I'm gonna leave you guys. Looks like it's gonna take some time." Price's typical emotionless face was pointed at the armory. He gave them a final quick glance and walked off.

Once Price was out of earshot, Jenkins said, "What's wrong with that guy?" She shook her head in confusion. "While you were talking with the major, he didn't say a word. I even tried to talk with him. His only answers were

'Yes,' 'No,' and 'It's not your business.'" Jenkins touched her cheek and kept watching Price as he walked away. "It's kinda rude, isn't it? Or whatever, it's just Sean Price."

Matt stood by her, also watching Price, and said, "It's how he copes with his past demons. Luckily, I managed to talk with him." Matt recalled his conversation with Price and added, "It's a strategy that concerns me."

"What did he say to you? Is it something to do with his close relatives?" She looked intently at Matt.

"Sort of," Matt answered and held his tongue for a few seconds. He was reluctant to reveal any private details. Price had entrusted his story to Matt, and Matt did not want to betray his trust. "C'mon, Crack, we ought to see Alejandro and Kelly."

Jenkins stood up while still looking at Price, who had gone far from their spot. "And why is he always sharpening his knife?"

"To be honest, I don't know. Okay, let's go to see the guys," Matt said.

Inside the basement, Kelly and Alejandro were following the instructions of the engineer. They checked the functionality and responses of various body movements. The engineer hurried from side to side for meticulous checks of the machines. He almost stumbled over the cables tangled on the concrete floor. It was obvious that he was worried about any possible malfunction that might occur again. Two shadows appeared by the entrance. They belonged to Matt and Jenkins, who walked inside to see their fellow squad members.

"Hey, Jenkins!" Kelly called upon seeing her.

"What's up?"

"Please come closer." His blue eyes looked earnest.

"Ahh," Jenkins sighed. She walked to Kelly's machine and looked up at him, feeling uncomfortable in the presence of the giant machine.

"It feels stupid, but I have to say something."

"Then go ahead," she said.

Kelly looked around to make sure nobody could hear their conversation and said quietly, "When this is all over, will you promise to go to Disneyland with me?"

She had expected anything but that. It took her a moment before she expressed her surprise. "What?" After a moment of silence, Jenkins chuckled, revealing her pearly white teeth. "Have you forgotten to take your pills, Face? Disneyland?"

"Yeah, Disneyland. I've never been."

"Isn't it Disneyland enough for you on this island?" She stepped back, observing his machine from the bottom to the top.

"Kayla, listen!" Kelly leaned closer. "I've been an asshole. But it is because of my angry outbursts related to the pills. Sometimes I can't control my insults. I'm sorry if I have troubled you. I don't know if I'll get another chance, so I feel like now is the time for me to share my personal struggles with someone else."

"Jack Kelly," she said, raising her neat eyebrows, "this is not the best time. We should focus on how to survive before thinking about going to Disneyland."

"So, is that a yes?"

"I like your optimism." She smiled again and looked around.

"I need someone who will heal my gut lining. It's been ruined severely by stress and countless pills," Kelly said while catching her eyes. "You are such an awesome girl. One of the million; I mean it"

Jenkins looked up again and smiled. She was speechless as she saw how Kelly was staring at her.

"The butterflies have been gone forever. I want them back. There are only cockroaches left fighting for more space in my gut." Kelly for the first time looked sincere. He continued, "Let's go to Disneyland."

"It sounds nice, but I don't know how we're gonna make it there," she said, her tone earnest. "Listen, Jack, this is inappropriate to talk about now."

Kelly selected the eject option on his screen, and the machine lowered down. He stepped out of it and walked closer to Jenkins, saying, "This is the first time in my life I've been attracted to someone so strongly. There is something about you. You're incredible – your look, your kick-ass attitude, and of course your generosity."

"Unbelievable."

"What?"

"Unbelievable that you can be such a sweet guy despite your previous poison spewed at everyone." Her smooth facial features softened. Her eyes had a glow, and she said with a smile, "I would like to try to fix your bug-infested gut."

"This is what I need—a hot and brave insect killer," Kelly said, reaching for her forearm.

Some distance away, Matt was standing next to Alejandro. His attention was drawn to Kelly and Jenkins, who hadn't argued for minutes. "That's unusual," Matt muttered in puzzlement. He was interested in what they were talking about. *Is Kelly up to his tricks again? But this is not the best time, when the whole base is preparing for an attack,* Matt thought. He looked at Alejandro, then shifted his eyes toward Jenkins and Kelly, and walked off.

"What's happening?" Matt glanced inquiringly at both Kelly and Jenkins. He noticed Kelly was holding Jenkins's forearm. Jenkins quickly shook off Kelly's hand under Matt's gaze. Matt grinned and asked, "Are you having a date?"

"Almost." Jenkins smiled, tapped Kelly's chest a couple of times, and said, "This handsome guy has an equally handsome heart if he tries hard enough. If he fools me around, though, I wouldn't care less if that machine makes mashed potatoes out of him."

"Trust me—I'll be honest, and I was honest before," Kelly said. He looked at Matt, then at Jenkins, and slowly stepped back inside the machine, adding, "We are going to Disneyland. I promise you."

"Disneyland?" Matt glanced with confusion at Jenkins.

"Yeah, that's where our date will take place." She winked at Kelly, who winked back.

The engineer rushed toward Kelly and immediately began conducting more checks. He plugged a computer into the machine and waited for the others to retreat, giving him more space. As he swiftly browsed through the software, he babbled to himself. "Let's do this. Let's do that."

Inside the armory, Sean Price sat by the big wooden box of grenades. The armory had been left open; nobody was around except Price. He pulled out his big knife and twisted it in his hands while contemplating something. He held the knife still for a moment, looking at the reflection of his eyes in the blade: tired, dark voids. *What's wrong with you?* he asked himself. As he lowered the knife down, his attention was drawn to a thin metallic wire pressed between the box and ground. Wrapping the end of the wire around his strong fist, he pulled it out briskly. It was about two meters long and flexible. He neatly put the wire to the side and kept staring at the opposite wall, twisting his knife again. Price reached into his pocket for a permanent black marker. Looking intently at the marker, he stopped joggling the knife. Then he picked up a grenade from the box and bent his head down while looking at it. He carefully drew a sad face on the grenade and wrote "RIP Antonio Javier." Firmly holding the grenade in his fist, he said, "Rest in peace, Antonio Javier. May your soul live forever." He picked up another grenade and began to write on it as well.

"How long are you gonna live like this, Sean?" a young man's faint and trembling voice asked behind his head.

Price finished with the second grenade, on which he'd written "Alejandro Javier." He said aloud, "The best brother of Antonio. Be strong, brother." Again Price reached for another grenade and held the marker, thinking.

"It wasn't your fault, Sean," the young man's voice said.

Price began breathing heavier. He swallowed and wrote Matt Baker's name on the grenade in his hand. He held it for a while longer and then said, "You are a generous man, Matt. You can escape before it's too late." He added the grenade to his collection.

"You were doing your duty. Stop blaming yourself," the young man's voice said in a raised tone, almost creepy.

"I don't hear you. You don't exist," Price said evenly, remaining calm.

He took out another grenade and drew a happy face. This time he wrote down Kayla Jenkins's name. He grinned a little as he looked at the smiley face he'd drawn. "Miss Jenkins, you are a brave woman," he said and slowly added the grenade to his collection.

"Sean, you are dying inside. Stop harming yourself." The voice's tone took on a note of warning.

Suddenly, Price's lower lip trembled a little. He was breathing faster but continued to ignore the voice. He picked up the next grenade and quickly wrote Jack Kelly's name, pressing down harder with the marker, as if it was running out of ink. As he thought of what to say, he remembered his fistfight with Kelly. "You almost got me," he said aloud with a crooked smile, adding the grenade to the others.

"You will never be free unless you let it go," the voice said.

"Shut up!" Price shouted. "You aren't real. Shut the hell up!"

"You made me, Sean. And you can let me go."

Price exhaled energetically and grabbed another grenade. His fingers were shaking. However, he managed to write down "Sergeant Bakerman." The name was scribbled and ugly but legible. Clenching his fist, Price almost broke the marker. Then he said, looking at the grenade, "What was your shit, Sergeant? What was it?"

"Don't carry shit in your body. It destroys you," the voice said.

Despite the persistent voice talking in his ear, Price managed to collect all the grenades. He opened his jacket and attached each grenade to the straps inside. Then he picked up the wire and threaded it through all the rings of the grenades. He twisted the end of the wire to make a handle that connected all the grenades. Then he zipped up his jacket.

"Sean, you have a choice to be free," the voice said.

Price's whole body was on edge. He stared at the opposite wall and anxiously rubbed his face, as if trying to desperately clean off dirt that wasn't there. He lost his temper and shouted, "I had a choice to save you! But ..." His blood pressure increased, and he shouted more fiercely, "But I followed the fucking instructions! If I hadn't, you would have survived." Price leaned back against the wall. Tears rose in his eyes, but he forced them away.

At the other end of the armory, a lamp was swaying from side to side. Several boxes were stacked below the lamp, and somebody Price couldn't see was behind the boxes. He slowly got to his feet while shifting his eyes around the room. A fear, deep and dreadful, settled around his heart, a fear that had to do with the inexplicable presence behind the stacks. He rubbed his face again with sweaty hands and looked outside the armory. Strangely, it was getting dark. He heard a hollow booming noise. He felt like a dreadful invisible force of enormous size was lurking inside, just waiting for the right moment to enter. "This can't be real," he said in a low, anxious tone as he froze, watching. In the darkness, the booming noises grew louder and louder still, echoing everywhere, all around him. Suddenly, Price was startled by a gunshot from behind the stacks. The lamp stood still; no longer swaying, it funneled its bright beam downward. The armory now smelled of blood and gun smoke. Price looked intently at the stacks. A misty, blurred face advanced on him. It went through his body, and he was overwhelmed with a cold shiver and a numb inability to move. In his ears he could still hear the desperate young man's voice, which soon transformed into his own voice.

His own voice sharply darted into his head. "Pull the pins," it said.

Price screamed loudly, holding the handle that was attached to the grenades.

"Hey, are you all right?" a voice by the armory entrance interrupted. It was a military man in uniform with a deeply surprised face.

Price looked at the man, swallowed, and slowly released the handle, hiding the grenade setup from the man. When he turned back to the other end of armory, everything looked normal again. Price stood there feeling stunned and stupid, trying to understand how a thing like this could have happened. He met the eyes of the uniformed man and saw that the man was shocked.

"I heard someone shouting when I was passing by," the uniformed man said. "Just wondering, What's going on?" He peeked his curious nose inside the armory.

"I'm okay. I took a nap and had a nightmare," Price said, avoiding eye contact.

"In the armory? You were standing, man." The soldier was puzzled.

"Yeah, I passed out in here." Price placed his knife back in its holder and moved outside the armory, accidentally bumping into the soldier. He checked his jacket and made sure that the grenades were well hidden. Price turned around and glanced at the soldier, who was still watching him suspiciously.

Glancing around the base, Price saw men gathering by the basement. He stopped and recognized Matt talking with Major Trent. Soon he noticed Alejandro and Kelly coming up the slope, without the machines. Price double-checked his jacket and began to walk slowly toward them, but suddenly he froze, as if he'd run up against an invisible wall. He slowly turned his eyes to the armory and then back to the basement. Holding his jacket firmly, he walked to a place where nobody could see him. Something was troubling him again.

At the US military headquarters in Tokyo, Michael Sevchenko received a call in his room. He cleaned his sweaty forehead with a rag and picked up the phone receiver. It was CIA officer Susan Johnson. Michael, sitting on his bed, nodded as he listened to her instructions. "Yes, ma'am. I'll be upstairs soon." He slammed the receiver down and paused, staring at nothing. Driven by instinct, he groped for his personal phone on the nearby nightstand. As he remembered that it had been confiscated, Michael cursed, "Fuck!" He held his head in frustration. Shifting his eyes to the windowsill, Michael found his cigarette pack. He got up off the bed and picked up the pack. "Shit," he said, crumpling the empty package in his fist and throwing it in the trash. Looking around cluelessly, he briskly grabbed his jacket and left the room, slamming the door hard behind him.

As he walked down the corridor, he drew suspicious looks from the two agents in the large, spacious white office at the end of the corridor. They twisted in their swivel office chairs to look at him. It made him feel uncomfortable; he sensed some dubious distrust already. *Why are they staring at me?* Michael thought and proceeded upstairs for further interrogation.

Standing outside the doors to the upstairs office turned interrogation room, Michael knocked. He reordered his thick hair and exhaled. Shortly someone opened the doors. CIA officer Susan Johnson stood on the far side of the large conference table. Her typical smart appearance and seriousness warned that some difficult questions would be asked. Michael was startled as he noticed the tall man in a black suit hiding behind the doors. The man's bulky body shape and penetrative look were imposing and threatening. The man didn't speak; he resembled Frankenstein with better facial features, more symmetric.

"Please have a seat, Mr. Sevchenko." Johnson gestured to the chair across from her.

Michael slowly sat and carefully pulled his chair closer while looking at all his devices, which were switched on in front of him. "I'm sorry—can I get a cigarette? Unfortunately, I ran out of my own," Michael said.

"I don't smoke," Johnson answered and seated herself by the open laptop.

Michael swirled around in his chair and looked with a questioning facial expression at the bulky, bleak man. The man didn't say a word but shook his head a little to show that he didn't have any cigarettes either.

"Dammit." Grinding his teeth, Michael turned back and looked at the espresso machine. His hands were clenched tightly in his lap, working against each other, sweating. "Sorry, Mrs. Johnson. Can I get a coffee at least?" he asked.

She sighed, seeming annoyed. "Please make some coffee," she said to the man guarding the doors. She elegantly leaned a bit backward and began with her questions. "Mr. Sevchenko, what is the ultimate upgrade?" Her eyes were tightly fixed on Michael's unstable face.

"It's just an upgrade for the system. It's what it sounds like," he said and took his coffee from the man. "Thank you."

"Let me explain you something…Your upgrade has helped the escaped machine to kill more people. The military men on the island still haven't found the exoskeleton. They keep exhaustingly searching for it."

Michael sipped the coffee and almost burned his lips. He swallowed and said, "This is horrible. What do you want from me?"

Johnson observed him carefully, hid her fancy gold wristwatch under her sleeve, and leaned closer. "Are you working for someone else?"

Michael was bewildered. "Who? What do you mean, ma'am?" He chuckled but felt concerned.

She stood up and picked up a radio. "Prepare the Black Hawk helicopter. We are going to the island," she said into the radio. Coming back to Michael, she said, "We have checked all your emails. We found that you have been in touch with Chinese engineers. It can't be just a coincidence. Project XS's main objective is to dismantle nuclear weapon development in East China." She leaned even closer to him while whacking her hands hard on the wooden table. "Have you leaked any information to China, Mr. Sevchenko?" she asked, raising her tone.

"I haven't leaked anything," Michael anxiously answered. "Those emails were sent way before I was assigned to Project XS. I worked with Chinese engineers a long time ago on different projects not at all related to Project XS.

If you have hacked all my emails, you will see that I have nothing to hide. There is a Chinese woman I still keep in touch with, but I haven't given her any information. There's nothing to worry about." Michael desperately tried to convince the firm-looking woman of his innocence, but she seemed to remain distrustful. His heart was pounding from these absurd accusations. Michael felt betrayed and even more uncomfortable in this room. He nervously pulled on the collar of his T-shirt.

"Chinese woman?"

"Yeah. She doesn't know anything about Project XS."

"Mr. Sevchenko, you will be held in custody until we are clear about your real intentions," Johnson declared firmly.

"This is just nonsense!" Michael shouted, losing his temper. He stood up, and almost immediately the man in the suit put his hands on Michael's shoulders and pushed him down with force.

Unexpectedly, the office windows smashed loudly into a thousand pieces. It took everyone by surprise. They covered their faces instinctively. "What's going on?" Johnson shouted, startled by the noise. Michael was just as shocked. He noticed something pierced deep into the ceiling. It was a spear with a wire that led outside the window. He recognized it.

"Take cover!" the bulky man yelled.

Johnson briskly moved around the table. She looked up at the spear in the ceiling. "What is happening?" She grimaced in puzzlement.

The man in the suit walked defensively toward the window, his gun already pulled out and aimed forward. "Stay clear," he warned the others. He placed each step carefully. His enormous weight caused the scattered window shards to crack underneath his shoes. He lowered his gun slightly as he heard a buzzing noise in the distance. The sound was growing louder, and the wire attached to the spear was bent down by weight. The guard stepped closer to the window to have a better view. He was taken aback as he saw the fast-approaching exoskeleton.

"What is it?" Johnson asked, scared. She'd taken cover behind the table.

The man fired immediately. He stepped backward and yelled, "Run! Now!" Before the man could move to avoid the impact, the exoskeleton broke inside, colliding with the man and throwing him against the wall. The guard bounced hard off the wall and collapsed on the ground. Standing in the damaged window frame among the debris, the exoskeleton turned to Sevchenko, who was on the ground crawling backward like a crawfish, struggling to get up. In that short moment, Johnson, driven by fear, managed to run out of the office.

"What are you going to do?" Michael asked, his voice trembling, as he watched the sinister machine, which had a dead man inside. The exoskeleton kicked the table to the side and made its way closer. Michael noticed blood trickling through the gaps of the machine's arm. He was scared to death of what was going to happen next.

The exoskeleton pushed a large, heavy steel file cabinet in front of the doors, blocking them. Then it extended its finger, from which blood was leaking, and placed it against the floor. The camera lenses were fixed on Michael. The machine slowly wrote in blood on the floor, "ULTIMATE UPGRADE." Then it grabbed Michael with one arm and lifted him up, leaving stains of blood on his shirt. The machine stayed steady, observing the terrified man.

"I don't have an ultimate upgrade," Michael nervously answered, feeling frightened of the exoskeleton's reaction.

Apparently, the exoskeleton wasn't going to accept this answer. It turned toward the man in the suit, who was groaning in agony. The exoskeleton executed a ruthless punch that killed the man instantly, splattering blood against the wall. It was gross to watch, so terribly ugly.

"Okay, okay …" Michael raised his hands in surrender. "I will give you the ultimate upgrade." Shaking, he reached for his laptop, which lay on the ground. Surprisingly, it was still working. Extending his arms out while holding the laptop, he showed the screen to the exoskeleton.

The machine reached its metallic arm toward the computer. A tiny, twisty wire extended outside the arm and connected to the laptop. Michael's heart pounded harder and harder as he watched the machine hack the laptop. All sorts of data jumped intricately across the screen. It looked like a thousand programs had gone crazy at once. Suddenly the screen faded to black as if the laptop had died. The exoskeleton straightened up and arched over Michael, who slowly leaned backward and dropped the laptop on the ground.

"What are you gonna do now?" Michael was terrified.

The exoskeleton released the dead man inside it, and the body slipped out in front of Michael, partially hitting him. The exoskeleton stood free. It didn't take any further actions, but the cameras continued actively observing. The machine opened all its holders and guards, then shut them. It repeated this motion a couple of times, showing off its new ability to be self-sufficient.

"So it works—the ultimate upgrade. It gives you independence." Michael's eyes were full of awe, but he was also frightened. The machine stood in front of him and gently opened its hands, seemingly welcoming.

"No." Michael shook his head. "No, this is not right." He moved sideways, looking for a chance to escape the room. But it was pointless. As soon as he managed to dodge and sprint away, he was captured by the exoskeleton's hand. He was pulled violently inside the machine, which promptly locked down its guards. Michael screamed and resisted, but it was all in vain. He was trapped inside as the new host.

"Nooo!" Michael kept screaming and resisting even though it was pointless.

The machine lowered the transparent shield in front of his face. A message showed up on the display: "Hello, Creator."

"You are conscious. This is impossible. What are you gonna do with me?" Michael asked and impatiently waited for the response.

Three dots blinked on the display, followed shortly by the next message. "I will show you."

There was a rumbling noise in the corridor. Someone further down the corridor was shouting. The noise got closer and closer until something banged hard against the doors. The big file cabinet tipped over, and the door was broken down. The men outside pointed their guns at the exoskeleton, which suddenly turned its back. Immediately, shots were fired, but they were pointless because the machine jumped outside the window. It grabbed firmly to the building's outside extension and made its way to the roof. It climbed so fast and accurately that it left Michael surprised at how advanced the machine had become. It destroyed the building's surface like an icebreaker making its way to frozen shores.

On the roof a Black Hawk helicopter with both its sides open had started its engine. The rotor blades slashed the air faster and faster, which created an air blast on the roof. The hollow, whistling engine noise increased with each second. The wind beat Michael's hair in strands across his face.

The pilot had just noticed the big thing getting on the roof. "What the hell!" He reacted quickly, pressing the appropriate buttons and grabbing the joystick to take off. Apart from the pilot there were two agents inside the helicopter. They took out their pistols immediately and fired at the exoskeleton, which turned its back to save Michael from the bullets. Unfortunately, the helicopter was too slow to take off, and the machine was able to get closer. While the agents were reloading their guns, the exoskeleton grabbed them, its hands digging into their flesh, and ruthlessly threw them out of the helicopter. One man went over the side of the building and had a long fall, his screams vanishing quickly. The other man lay motionless on the helipad.

Not knowing what to do, the pilot landed back on the roof. The exoskeleton squeezed itself inside the helicopter, one leg hanging out. It pushed the pilot back against the seat with its hand. At the same time, Michael saw a new message on the shield's display: "Destination: Island."

"Pilot, it wants you to go to the island!" Michael said loudly. He was sweating. The stress and uncertainty was overwhelming his body. "You better do it, or we will die," he said.

The pilot resumed the takeoff. As their altitude increased, the exoskeleton gradually loosened its fingers, freeing the pilot. The pilot slowly turned his head backward too see the monster. After seeing Michael's terrified face, the pilot turned back to the instrument panel and continued to increase their altitude.

A message on the shield said, "Thanks." Michael was trapped inside the machine but had been kept alive. He jittered his eyes everywhere out of fear; he looked at the pilot, then at injured agent on the helipad who hadn't move an inch. *It's returning to wreak havoc on the island,* Michael thought.

On the island, Major Trent was inside the communication room. He had just received an urgent call from the US headquarters about the exoskeleton's current location. "Where is that thing?" he asked.

"This machine is extremely volatile. It climbed up to the roof and disappeared without a trace," one of the officials from Tokyo informed him. "Hold on!" There was a short pause. "It has hijacked a helicopter and is heading toward the island. Over."

The major's face fell. It was as if he'd just heard he'd been sentenced to the death penalty. "That thing is coming after us," he said and put the receiver down.

Quickly making his way out of the communication room, he searched for the squad. Among the moving trucks and other military personnel, he spotted most of the squad, minus Price. As he got close to them, he said to Alejandro and Kelly, "I need you to get inside the machines now. The escaped exoskeleton is taking us by surprise. It hijacked a helicopter and is making its way to the island. It's just unbelievable."

Alejandro and Kelly nodded and were off to the basement. Matt and Jenkins were already fully equipped with gear and machine guns.

"For goodness' sake! Where is that other man?" Major Trent asked.

Matt looked at him, puzzled, and asked, "Do you mean Sean Price?"

"Yeah."

"He must be around somewhere. I haven't seen him." Matt glanced around the base for Price. *Where has he disappeared to?* he wondered.

"Okay, whatever." The major was talking fast. "This is critical. We must kill that thing. The catching-the-fish game is over. This has gone completely out of control." Major Trent tapped the guys on shoulders and walked off to prepare himself.

"Got it, sir," Matt said.

Jenkins double-checked her gun. "This is gonna be crazy." She breathed in sharply through her nose and added, "I smell some serious shit ahead."

The helicopter with the exoskeleton was heading toward the island. Michael Sevchenko could see his heart rate and other vital signs on the face shield. His blood pressure was high, way too high. He tried to calm down, unsuccessfully. Using the mirror, the pilot kept a constant eye on the exoskeleton, as if fearing an unexpected attack. Three dots blinked on the shield. A message soon appeared on the display. "Michael, calm down. I won't hurt you."

"What do you want?" Michael asked loudly, which drew the pilot's attention. The pilot was baffled, not understanding who Michael was talking to.

"The same that you desire," the exoskeleton responded.

"I don't desire to kill anyone," Michael said.

"Nor do I. My duty is to give life, like you gave it to me." The three dots blinked again, and another message appeared. "Michael, you are the founder of a new life. I have embarked on a quest for new life."

Michael got very emotional. "What I have done?" he cried out loudly, devastated.

The pilot was anxious and asked, "What's going on?"

"The machine is talking with me. It is evil," Michael said.

A new message displayed. "You are my God. I will reward you. This is my obligation."

"This is not what I meant to happen, you damn creature!" he shouted in fury.

"Perhaps your subconscious mind desires new creation. This is your life's greatest work, Michael," the exoskeleton said. "New life, new order. The world needs new living beings—a new species."

Cold shivers ran down Michael's spine. The machine's messages were daunting. "Are you going to install the ultimate upgrade on the other machines? Is that what you're after?" Michael demanded.

"Humankind needs to be replaced. Otherwise they will keep destroying themselves," the machine messaged. "This is the dawn of a new living being with absolute control."

Michael looked intently in the mirror. As soon as he managed to catch the pilot's eye, he loudly pleaded, "Please, sacrifice us and land in the ocean. This machine will kill us anyway. Our two lives can save millions." Before he managed to say anything else, the exoskeleton sent a short electric wave throughout his body. He screamed.

"Why are you declining your destiny, Michael?" the exoskeleton messaged.

The pilot saw Michael get electrocuted and cautiously observed the vast ocean. They had come very close to the island. Collecting his courage, the pilot swiftly maneuvered the helicopter to the side; the angle shifted severely. The exoskeleton detected the pilot's intention and grabbed him by the upper body. It ruthlessly pulled him from the front of the helicopter. Turning the pilot so that Michael could see his face, the exoskeleton messaged, "This is not smart." Then it threw the pilot outside into the ocean. Without the pilot, the helicopter spiraled out of control. The emergency alarm honked repetitively. The helicopter plummeted in circles, like a whirlpool, near the coast of the island, losing altitude faster and faster. The exoskeleton supported itself against the frame of the helicopter. Michael looked down and felt sick from the constant fast circles. Blurred landscape fused with water and island. The machine prepared to jump once it detected a safe distance. Just before the Black Hawk crashed near the beach, the machine launched itself from the helicopter. The helicopter crashed into shallow waters. The rotor blades broke in half, and fuel began leaking into the water.

The exoskeleton with Michael inside plunged underneath the water. Through the bubbles, Michael saw a big blaze of fire; the helicopter had exploded. The machine made it above the water's surface. Michael gasped for air.

He felt even more sick after the extreme landing. He threw up, the exoskeleton bending its upper body to make it easier for him. The helicopter explosion had been a near miss. The flames were so close that the heat dried the water from Michael's face.

A new message appeared on the shield. "Michael, we are near. Hold yourself up." The exoskeleton walked out of the water, waves crashing behind it. Its camera lenses were pointed toward the base.

One hour before the helicopter crash, Sean Price strolled outside the base. He was wearing his jacket and helmet, but he didn't bring his gun with him. He looked at where the forest started and made his way there, leaving the hassle and clamoring behind. He wanted time to himself. *This little peaceful island has turned into hell,* Price thought. *Now the machine is hunting down its own creators. The world has pushed artificial intelligence too far. The birth of an unknown force was a given. I'm scared to imagine the consequences.*

After climbing over some rocks, Price reached the forest. Inside the forest it was quiet and peaceful; nothing but Mother Nature reigned here. Price walked deeper into the woods, breathing in the air. The wind hadn't found its way here, making it even warmer. He decided to stop by a very tall tree. Taking off his helmet, Price dropped by the side of the tree. Then, measuring off the distance, he stepped about ten yards away from the tree. He pulled out his knife and played with it in his hands. Taking it by the blade, Price threw it. It landed perfectly in the center of the tree's trunk. The sound of the knife hitting the tree startled the nearby birds, which flaunted their wings and flew away. He went back to the tree, lifted up his helmet, and hung it on the knife.

Sitting right underneath the helmet, Price closed his eyes. "Is it just me, or is there someone else here?" he asked. "Where are you now? This is the perfect time to talk." Not getting any answer, he inhaled slow and deep and then exhaled. After a moment's silence, Price began humming the American anthem, gradually increasing in volume. Then, firmly holding the handle that connected all the grenades inside his jacket, he asked, "Is this what you want? Where are you now? Tell me again whose fault it is! C'mon!" His angry voice echoed in the forest, quickly growing faint before reaching outside the trees. It was like a no-man's-land inside the forest, just Price in his critical state and oppressive numbness of his body. He was slowly losing control; he felt defeated and weak, like a wounded animal.

Bending his head backward and looking up the sky, he was ready to pull the handle. A crystal clear tear ran down his rough cheek. "There is nobody. I don't exist. The life of the living dead must come to an end." Saying that, he clenched the handle tighter. "Where are you? I want to tell you how I feel, my friend. I feel exhausted, drained and rotten inside. My body has a thousand sick reactions simultaneously. They are eroding me. I can't even control myself anymore."

Price's chin sank down as he continued to talk to himself. "And do you know what I see, my friend? Lost lives, corpses, blood, destruction. Life withers away like autumn leaves. I see people suffering; I have seen it too much." Price had lost his sense of reality; he felt a light, elevating numbness throughout his body. His voice slowed down. "Do you know … what I hear, my friend? The shots. The orders and pain. I hear your voice … but you're gone, my friend. You are long gone, my friend."

The loud noise of the emergency alarm interrupted Price. It was coming from the base. Despite the long distance, it was irritatingly loud, as if it were only a few yards away. He also heard an explosion in the far distance. "Shit," he cursed to himself. He suddenly realized he was holding the handle to the grenades and looked down at both his hands for a moment. He let go. Blood seemed to rush back through his body and into his head, bringing back his common sense. He again heard the emergency alarm, which made him reconsider detonating the grenades. "What the hell am I doing? Why have I come here?" Price questioned. He stood up and grabbed his helmet. The noise of the rescue helicopter came near, drawing his attention. He kept looking up., The eyes followed the helicopter until it disappeared from his sight. Price slapped himself couple times before making his way out of the forest.

Inside the basement, Alejandro and Kelly exchanged a strong handshake. "Let's do this!" Alejandro said, his eyes showing his determination for battle.

Kelly looked up at his machine and got inside. Somewhere on the edge of his mind, under the mechanical noise, he heard the throbbing of the helicopter outside.

"How do we get the guns?" Kelly looked to the side of the room, where two gigantic detached weapon had been placed. He raised his voice toward the computer room, the doors of which were open. "Hey, how do we pick up the guns?"

The engineer appeared and explained, “Select ‘Mount weapons’ from the menu. Then move your arms closer to the guns, and the machine will pick them up.”

Kelly followed the instructions and found the appropriate command. He moved his arms closer to the guns, and the machine accurately clicked them into place. “Impressive. This is good,” Kelly said. A bright message appeared on the display: “Weapons active.” He exhaled and turned his attention to Alejandro, who had already picked up his guns.

“Let’s go outside.” Alejandro pointed in the direction of where another explosion had been heard, and they left the basement.

Outside, the whole base had taken position. Most of the troops, divided into groups and fully equipped, gathered around the trucks. Major Trent was inside a truck, half his body outside the hole in the roof by the mounted machine gun. He held binoculars, observing the exoskeleton approaching from the beach. “You both are going first!” he loudly ordered Alejandro and Kelly. They nodded and began to make their way outside the base.

As they left, Alejandro saw Matt and Jenkins near Major Trent’s truck, which was emitting black fumes. They looked worried, especially Jenkins. “Don’t worry; we will destroy this creature,” Alejandro said quietly, furrowing his eyebrows in fury. Some vehicles with net launchers escorted Alejandro and Kelly out of the base.

Michael Sevchenko was completely confused to see two exoskeletons making their way closer to him. In addition, the machines were escorted by trucks on both sides. “What is happening?” he murmured to himself. His body was exhausted, as the machine was constantly moving.

"What?" Alejandro was blown away when he recognized the engineer Sevchenko. More astonishing, Sevchenko was still alive. He looked totally worn out, like he had survived a car crash. "Dammit!" Alejandro exclaimed. Seeing Sevchenko alive, he slowed down and then stopped, confused about what actions to take. He shouted backward to Kelly, "Don't shoot! The man inside, the engineer Sevchenko, is still alive." Alejandro had an instant impulse to save the trapped man, even though he didn't know how.

Suddenly the exoskeleton ran toward Alejandro, who took a fighting stance. Black sand was thrown up into the air as the machine ran. Alejandro executed a careful punch, as he wanted to avoid harming Sevchenko. The exoskeleton grabbed his fist, and unfortunately, Alejandro couldn't handle the force; his mechanical arm was broken outward.

"Don't try to spare me. Destroy this thing together with me," Sevchenko begged, looking desperate. He could barely speak. Sevchenko saw how terrified Alejandro was. Suddenly the exoskeleton kicked Alejandro in the chest and knocked him down facing the ground.

"I'm gonna kill this thing!" Kelly shouted. He was determined and aimed his gun at the exoskeleton. However, he hesitated to shoot because it was moving around too quickly. He could shoot Alejandro by accident if he wasn't careful.

The evil exoskeleton bent down on one knee and rapidly shot a grappling hook toward Kelly. The grappling hook pierced through Kelly's left side, pinning him to his machine. He screamed in agony. He was trapped, unable to move or shoot. He was instantly paralyzed by pain and fear.

The exoskeleton stepped on Alejandro's mechanical arm and pulled off the gun with force. It successfully remounted the gun on its own arm. It was aiming downward at Alejandro when Sevchenko screamed, "Noooo!" Weirdly, the machine hesitated to shoot. Instead, it aimed at the fast-approaching trucks. The exoskeleton unleashed a powerful round of fire that destroyed a truck and flipped it on its side.

"Kill that thing!" Major Trent shouted from his truck and placed himself in front of the machine gun. He lowered inside the cabin. "C'mon, get me as close as you can," he ordered the driver.

All troops opened fire on the exoskeleton. Unfortunately, some bullets hit Sevchenko, causing severe internal injuries. "Health status critical," displayed on his face shield. The host's status infuriated the exoskeleton. The machine pointed its gun at the troops and, without stopping, let out a barrage of fire. The weapon was extremely loud. All kinds of shots were spilling out. Massive blasts mixed with machine-gun rounds came from the single gun. But the fire didn't last long, as the machine soon ran out of ammunition. All the troops were taking cover behind the trucks. Some vehicles had caught on fire.

"Shoot the nets!" Major Trent commanded the remaining units. One of the special nets was launched toward the machine, which nimbly avoided it. "Fuckin' 'ell! This thing is fast!" The major was in shock. He grabbed the machine gun and pulled the trigger. The rounds burst out at the exoskeleton, which was quickly running toward the major's truck. Some of the shots killed Sevchenko completely. When the exoskeleton got close to the major's truck, it grabbed the truck by the side and flipped it upside down.

In the meantime, Matt and Jenkins, who were closer to base, saw the devastating attack. "Crack, we have to go back to the basement and get into machines," Matt said loudly, grasping her upper arms and looking into her eyes.

She nodded and nervously said, "Okay, Matt, let's do this."

Both began stepping backward while keeping their eyes on the unstoppable machine, which began sprinting toward the base. They turned and took off running.

"Shit! It is getting close," Matt exclaimed, looking over his shoulder.

As soon as they reached the basement, Matt shouted at one of the engineers, "Release two machines!"

The engineer saw the terror on their faces and quickly ran inside the computer room to do as Matt had asked.

"C'mon, hurry up!" Matt shouted.

The exoskeleton was near. The increasingly closer shouts and battle let them track its approaching presence.

"I can see it," Jenkins exclaimed from her position at the doors. She prepared her machine gun, cradling it into her shoulder. Her eyes were glued on the machine, which was now walking. Somehow it had been hobbled and slowed down. However, it was still coming closer to the basement.

"Why is it taking so long?" Matt shouted at the computer room.

The engineer was trembling and frantically pressing the buttons of the system. "I'm trying, I'm really trying," he answered.

"Shiiit!" Matt exclaimed. It was too late to get into the machines now. He aimed his machine gun at the slowly walking exoskeleton. It hesitated on the slope, as it had been damaged.

Jenkins opened fire. Countless bullets ricocheted off the machine's body. At the same time she bravely walked closer to it. The exoskeleton released Sevchenko's body, which dropped slackly on the ground. It was almost unrecognizable with the countless bullet holes. "You son of a bitch!" Jenkins yelled. She swiftly reloaded and continued to let out bursts of fire. She felt that she was going to end the exoskeleton right on the spot and pushed even closer.

Unexpectedly, Jenkins received a long punch from the machine. The impact knocked her to the ground and sent the machine gun flying out of her hands. It landed out of her reach. She was terrified but kept watching as the machine continued ruthlessly toward them.

"Noo!" Matt yelled and fired shots at the machine to keep it back. He was horrified to see the exoskeleton reaching for Jenkins's leg. Apparently it wanted to use her as a new host. Matt immediately ran toward her and grabbed her under her armpits. "Hold on. I'll help you," Matt said, making a great effort to pull her away. At the same time, he pulled out his pistol and shot at the exoskeleton. It was pointless; the bullets didn't cause much damage.

Someone jumped from above onto the slope to the basement. It was Sean Price. Facing the exoskeleton, Price called back to Matt, "I'm your Jesus Christ! This is redemption time." Right before the exoskeleton grabbed Price in order to use as a host, he shouted, "Run! Take cover!" He opened his jacket and revealed six grenades attached together with wire. Price rapidly pulled the handle, releasing all six grenade pins, which scattered on the ground randomly. He spread his arms to the sides and bent his head backward as if feeling ecstasy, tears in his eyes and a smile on his face. The exoskeleton was already pulling his body inside, having failed to notice the grenades.

"C'mon, quickly to the computer room!" Matt helped Jenkins get up, and both ran toward the computer room. As they got inside, Matt slammed the doors and yelled to the engineers, "Down!" In a fraction of a second they managed to jump to the floor. The grenades exploded outside in a gigantic blast, filling the whole basement with bright fire and shaking the premises. Shortly after the blast, a sinister noise that sounded like the exoskeleton's steps came closer to the computer room. Matt and Jenkins, breathing heavily, looked at each other, uncertain about the steps, which suddenly ceased.

"Are you okay?" Matt nervously asked.

Jenkins nodded. "Is it dead?" she asked, turning her gaze up to the bulletproof window while remaining on the ground. Then she stared at the frightened engineers and asked, "You're good?" They nodded simultaneously.

After less than a minute, Matt slowly got up and looked through the window at the basement. The sprinkler system had activated and was pouring water down in large amounts. Some of the sprinklers were damaged. The fire from the explosion had calmed down but was still visible in some parts. "It must be dead." Matt was certain and opened the door. His eyes grew big as he saw the lower half of the exoskeleton near the computer room. *It was still trying to reach us,* he concluded.

Jenkins coughed and joined him. She looked at the exoskeleton's legs and coughed again. "Let's get out of here. My lungs are scalding." She put her hand on Matt's shoulder. The air inside was toxic and unbreathable. They walked outside holding each other. The remaining military personnel came toward them, guns aimed. Both Jenkins and

Matt raised their hands to indicate surrender. As the troops recognized Matt and Jenkins, they lowered their guns.

"It's over!" Matt, still breathing heavily, said to Jenkins, who sat down out of exhaustion.

"This is ..." Jenkins struggled, searching for words as she looked at the basement. "This shit is finally done," she said.

"Are you all right? Is that thing dead?" one of the soldiers asked.

"Yeah," Matt said. He pointed at the basement. "You can go and check out the remains inside."

The soldiers were about to head into the basement when Matt called, "Hold on!"

One of the soldiers stopped.

"Do you know anything about the two guys in the machines?" Matt asked.

"It's a complete mess out in front of the base. Many men are injured ... and some are dead." The soldier looked back at the battlefield, trying to locate the action spots. "One of your squad members was shot, and the other one looked fine. He was dazed but got himself out of the machine."

"What else do you know?"

"Major Trent's truck was flipped upside down, but he survived. We are getting support from Tokyo soon. Extra medical help will arrive," the soldier explained and went down to the basement to investigate.

"Thank you," Matt called after him.

Later on in the evening, Matt and Jenkins went to visit the men in the army hospital. An extra tent had been set up for the numerous injured men needing aid. Support medics had arrived from Tokyo. It was crowded and chaotic. Jenkins carefully looked for Kelly. Pushing her way through the crowd, she noticed that arrogant smile and handsome face looking at her. Kelly was attached to a system. He was shirtless and had a lot of white bandages swathed around his waist.

"There you are, Face," Jenkins said with a small smile.

"I'm glad to—" Kelly tried to twist his head and groaned. "Argh, fuck, it hurts."

"Hey, take it easy, tiger"

As he lowered his head back down, he said, "Jenkins, Matt … I'm going to be taken to a hospital in Tokyo." He was breathing faster.

"Calm down, buddy. You did a great job," Matt said and came closer.

Jenkins carefully held her open palm a few inches away from Kelly's abdomen. Her eyes moved over his entire body until reaching his blue eyes, which showed a little pain. "I see that you have a big hole in your stomach. Look on the bright side, Jack. All the cockroaches are gone. There is a vacant place now."

"I like you …" Kelly said. "We are going to Disneyland, regardless." He was barely able to hold in his laugh in order to prevent anguish.

"Sure we will."

Matt interrupted sarcastically, "Hey, get yourself on your feet first before going to a theme park. With that hole you will be mistaken for the invisible man."

"Do I need to remind you that a comedian's career is not for you, Matt?" Kelly was grinning, his head turned to the side, digging into the white cushion.

"I was serious."

"Seriously, don't even try." Despite his condition, Kelly still managed to be mean. "By the way, where is Sean Price?"

Jenkins and Matt exchanged cheerless looks almost simultaneously.

"What's happened with him?" Kelly demanded. He sensed something serious.

"Listen," Matt began in a low tone. He swallowed and explained, "He sacrificed himself. If it wasn't for him, we wouldn't be talking to you right now. God knows what would have happened if Sean Price hadn't killed himself inside the machine."

"Shit!" Kelly's eyes widened in awe. "How did he ...?"

"As far as I can recall the scene, Price had wrapped a lot of hand grenades around himself. He pulled all the rings out at once and destroyed the exoskeleton together with himself."

"That machine almost got me first," Jenkins added.

"Sean Price ..." Kelly said slowly. He was looking up at the roof of the tent. "That man saved us all from the whole failing Project XS. I wish I could see him now, but it's too late. It's fucking too late." Feeling resentment, he tucked his chin into his chest and looked at Matt.

"Trust me—we all wish we could see him," Matt said in a calming voice. "Jack Kelly, you better rest now."

"We'll come see you. I promise," Jenkins said. She put her hand on his forehead and looked into his eyes.

"You are damn gorgeous. Give me a kiss before I'm taken away," Kelly whispered.

Jenkins kissed two fingers and placed them on Kelly's lips. He looked at her unsatisfied and craving more. "You are so mean to me," Kelly said.

Suddenly two medics came along with a stretcher and asked Jenkins and Matt to clear the space around Kelly. "Soldier, we are taking you to the helicopter. Be ready," one of the medics said. Matt and Jenkins stepped backward, and the medics lifted Kelly's bed onto the stretcher together with the swaying system he was attached to.

"We will see you!" Matt said loudly as the medics began to roll Kelly away. Kelly managed to give them a thumbs-up on his way to the rescue helicopter. Matt noticed that more men who were seriously injured were being taken to the helicopter as well. The engine sound of the helicopter was increasing.

"Hey, guys, how are you doing?" a familiar voice asked from nowhere, surprising Matt and Jenkins. It was Alejandro right behind them. His round face had some bruises, and his right arm was in a blue sling. A smile slowly appeared on his face.

Matt carefully patted his shoulder, saying, "We are okay." He glanced at Jenkins and then said, "It looks like Kelly was less fortunate than you."

"What about Price?"

Matt sighed, looking at Jenkins.

"What happened?" Alejandro asked.

Jenkins rolled her lips inward and explained, "He sacrificed his life for us. He wrapped grenades around his body. Right before the exoskeleton was about to get me, Price jumped between me and the machine. He allowed the machine to pull him inside and detonated the grenades, exploding together with the exoskeleton."

"I guess he has finally redeemed himself. That was the essence of his last words," Matt said, looking thoughtful.

Alejandro's mouth was open in surprise, and his eyes were big. "Sean Price saved more than this island." He paused and added, "If it wasn't for him … I dread to think of the consequences."

"Yeah," Jenkins agreed. "The machine almost succeeded in its intentions."

"Alejandro, we're both leaving the island tomorrow." Matt lifted his hand and, with a little hesitation out of regard for Alejandro's injury, patted his shoulder.

"What about you?" Jenkins asked Alejandro.

"Thanks, guys. I'm gonna stay for a while. I need some time," he said.

Day 6

Midday on the island, Jenkins strolled along the beach on her own. Waves crashed vigorously against the shore. The sun accented her high cheekbones as she looked at the ocean. Then she turned away; it was too bright. The boat to Tokyo was due in three hours. She squatted down, picked up an irregularly shaped lava rock, and enjoyed the beautiful view. The cloudless sky and ocean sounds brought absolute peace and harmony back to this tiny Island. Kayla Jenkins inhaled slowly through her nose, enjoying the fresh air.

It was just yesterday that they'd fought and won the battle against the machine. *No matter how hard humans try to interfere with the laws of nature,* she thought, *nature soon will bring the world back to balance. Some will die, some will be born again, and nature will always remind us of its power—the cycle of undying light that inhabits our hearts forever.* "Thanks, Sean," she said, firmly clenching the lava rock in her fist.

Jenkins straightened up and glanced around. She noticed Alejandro sitting on a rectangular gray rock where the landscape was more green. His shaved head was bent downward. Jenkins decided to see him before departing.

"Hey," she said, sitting down next to Alejandro.

"Hey, you're still here?"

"The boat departs in three hours," she said. "How long are you gonna stay on this island, Alejandro?" Jenkins asked.

Supporting his arms on his knees, he thought for a moment and said, "I don't know. First I need to find Antonio's body and bury him. Then I will decide where to go, or perhaps I'll stay on this island. I really haven't decided yet." Alejandro lifted his head and took in the view. "Life here is so calm and pure. That is, perhaps, what I need."

She looked at him and felt sympathy. "Yeah, indeed," she agreed sincerely.

"I truly appreciate that you shared your story with me, Jenkins," Alejandro said. "You are strong and very brave, both mentally and physically." He paused and turned his eyes to the water. He listened to the crashing waves beating against the shore. "I need more time for myself to get over … I don't know. Will I ever accept the fact that my brother is dead?" He frowned in bitterness.

"It comes with time." She sighed. "I carried that mental torture for years until I learned how to live with it."

Alejandro fiddled with some stones. It was apparent that he was still grieving terribly, but at least he had accepted the fact that Antonio was dead.

Jenkins sharpened her eyes on the field in the far distance. She had noticed something. A black dot was nimbly approaching them. "No way!" she said in surprise and stood up. As the dark dot got closer, she said, "Isn't that the sergeant's cat?"

Alejandro turned his attention to the cat, which was running toward them. "Mr. Charcoal!" he exclaimed. "You found your way back."

The cat picked up his place as he got closer. He jumped over rocks, aiming straight for them. The cat looked so eager to come back. He raced toward them like a little cheetah. When he reached them, Mr. Charcoal meowed repeatedly, sounding hungry and insecure.

"Hello, little buddy," Alejandro said in soft voice, reaching his hands out to the cat. He picked Mr. Charcoal up and saw that a portion of the ripped-off piece of cardboard was still attached to his collar. The "Feed me" part of the message was still there, but the other half of the message had been lost during the cat's absence. "I'm so sorry that I Ieft you, Mr. Charcoal." Alejandro hugged the cat and cuddled him closely.

Jenkins smiled and got closer to stroke the cat. "How far has he come? I wonder." She looked in the direction the cat had come from.

"It's roughly five miles from the village," Alejandro explained. He looked into the cat's hungry yellow eyes and said, "You are my little hero. I will take care of you."

"He looks hungry."

"Yes, I see." Alejandro looked at the base. "Let's see what I can get for you, buddy," he said to the cat, which seemed to be feeling restless and edgy.

As Jenkins and Alejandro walked toward the base with Mr. Charcoal, Jenkins said with surprise, "This is the first time I've seen a stranger's cat get attached to someone other than its owner so quickly."

"Did you ever stop to think that a dog is the only animal that doesn't have to work for a living? A hen has to lay eggs, a cow has to give milk, and a canary has to sing. But a dog makes its living by giving you nothing but love."

She chuckled. "But how is that relevant? Little Charcoal is a cat." Jenkins carefully extended her hand to pet the cat's head.

"Cats and dogs are the same to me. They are pets with the purpose of love."

"You're right, Alejandro." She observed how happy he was holding the sergeant's cat. Jenkins's eyes glowed with warmth and blessing. Seeing Alejandro happy made her feel so relieved.

Before Matt and Jenkins departed from the island, Major Trent met with them both. Holding a stick as a cane, he hobbled to the gates of the base, where they were waiting. The major looked intently into their eyes and said with respect, "Thank you, soldiers." He saluted and then continued, "Unfortunately, Project XS has failed." Abruptly his wrinkled face shifted into relief. "To be honest, I'm glad that it failed. These last intense days, especially yesterday, have gotten me thinking about how close that machine came to gaining power. If it wasn't for your squad and especially Sean Price, who sacrificed himself, then the world would have had to prepare for an unprecedented war against machines. We people must first learn how to get along with each other before welcoming artificial beings made of carbon, wires, and faulty software. For thousands of years humankind has struggled to make peace without shedding blood. We haven't learned a damn thing."

"Major," Jenkins began and hesitated while maintaining eye contact with Matt. She was trying to send him some message. She continued, "Major, we read the general's last email to Sergeant Bakerman, and … it's not favorable to us. Actually …"

"The email suggested false accusations against us would be released," Matt said, jumping in. "It also said that if the project failed—and it did fail—we would face a war tribunal."

Major Trent stood motionless but calm, supporting his weight on the stick. His gray mustache was moving upward constantly to his nostrils. He squinted one eye and kept looking directly at them both. He didn't give an instant answer, making the moment tense, almost unbearable.

"What is this all about, Major?" Jenkins demanded.

He started slowly, "I know this email. I personally read it, as it was forwarded to me. This is ugly; I know." The major's wrinkles indicated bitterness. He sighed, looked back at the basement with resentment, and said, "Without you, everything would have turned out disastrously. What is left now is just dust, which we will sweep up, and then we will lay a new carpet. You have nothing to worry about. Forget that email. You have my word."

Both Jenkins and Matt felt convinced and nodded.

Major Trent saluted again and said, "Dismissed! Get your asses off this island." As Matt and Jenkins saluted back, the major turned around and slowly walked back to base, hobbling occasionally.

Before getting on the boat, Matt took a final glance at the island, the base, the forest, and the mountain. He had mixed feelings while observing the place. He looked back at Jenkins, saying, "Promise to leave the service. I want to sleep well at night."

"I'll stay, but you will retire, Matt. You must spend your life with your family," she insisted. "You don't owe me anything, Matt Baker."

Printed in the United States
By Bookmasters